THE KIMBERLEY FILE

MICHAEL GERARD

Copyright © 2021 Michael Gerard

All rights reserved. No part of this publication may be reproduced, stored in a retrieval system, or transmitted in any form or by any means, mechanical, photocopying, recording or otherwise, without prior permission in writing of the author.

ISBN: 9798743798681 (paperback)

To the two women
who have meant everything
in my life.
Rita, my mother who passed away
before seeing this book in print.
Diane, my dearest
who guides me daily.
All my Love.

                                                M.G.

For Eoin and Adam.

CONTENTS

Glossary ix
Preface xi

One: A Box of Wine 1
Two: City of Gold 15
Three: Diamonds Galore 22
Four: Jeppe 33
Five: The Friendly Plumber 44
Six: Dutch Courage 59
Seven: The Aftermath 71
Eight: The Auld Sad 86
Nine: Visitors from Across the Pond 105
Ten: A Winner at Galway Races 117
Eleven: A Girl With a Plan 126
Twelve: Reluctant Houseguest 140
Thirteen: A Shot in the Dark 153
Fourteen: The Spider and the Fly 159
Fifteen: A Favor from "Honest Frank" 172

Sixteen: Partners of Convenience	185
Seventeen: Showtime	194
Eighteen: The Exchange	213
Nineteen: To Pretoria without Invitation	228
Twenty: Learning the 'Trade'	245
Twenty-one: A Ride in the Park	253
Twenty-two: Kill or Be Killed	266
Twenty-three: A Present for the Captain	282
About the Author	287

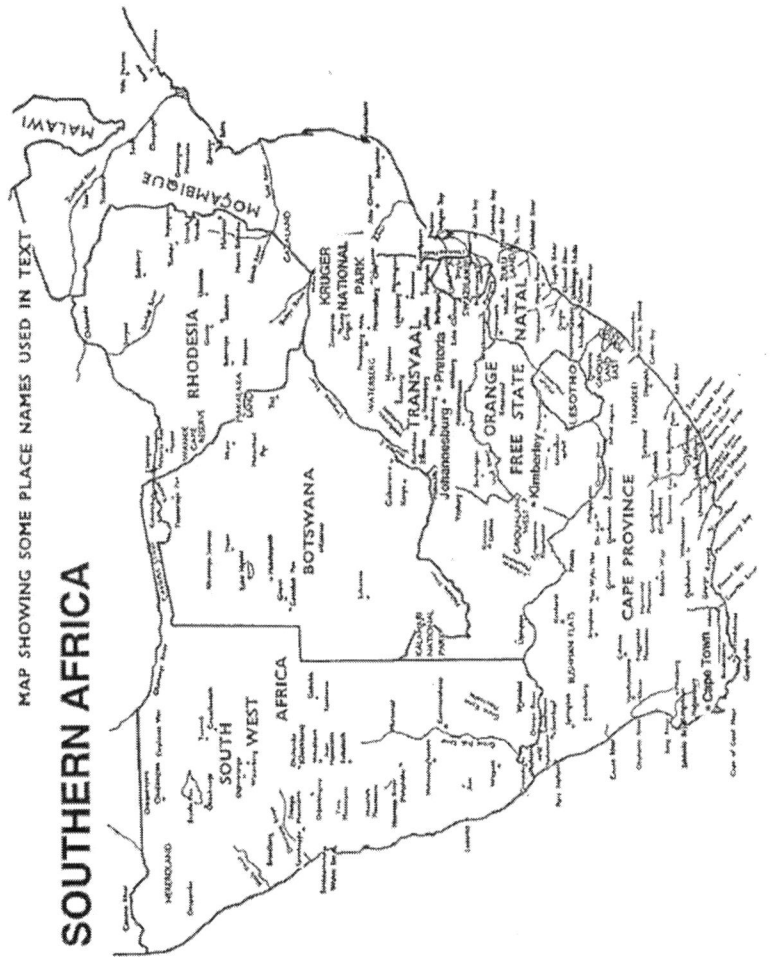

IRELAND

GLOSSARY

Baakie – Afrikaans word for pickup truck

Meneer – Afrikaans word for mister. The Afrikaaners are very formal in their greetings.

Diggings – Alluvial mining area.

Baas – Boss. Used primarily by blacks to their white bosses during the days of the apartheid system. It had a fear-respect usage.

Tot siens – Afrikaans for goodbye.

Dorp – Village, e.g. Krugersdorp.

Kaffir – A black person, usually a man, e.g. a kaffir or a kaffir girl. An unflattering term taken into Afrikaans from the Arabic word Qafir meaning infidel.

Seisiun – Gaelic Irish word for session. Usually refers to a traditional Irish music get together.

Craic – Gaelic word to describe a fun time or evening.

Hurling – Very fast Gaelic field game, close to hockey.

Boervoss – A spicy beef sausage,

Braai – Barbeque.

Rand – South African unit of currency.

Robot – Traffic light.

Sheebeen – Illegal bar used by blacks. A term also used in Ireland for late night drinking clubs.

Obrigado – Thank you, in Portuguese. S. Africa has many Portuguese because of neighboring former Portuguese colonies – Mozambique, Angola.

Biltong – Jerky, dried meat.

Fanagalo – A pidgin language, mixing various black dialects, English and Afrikaans. Used by blacks and whites in the mines for basic communication.

PREFACE

I first published The Kimberley File in 1997, when independent publishing was a more arduous task than it is today. The novel grew out of my first and only creative writing course, taught by Brewster Robertson in Beaufort SC. On the first evening he challenged every participant to make a start on some creative piece – a short story, novel, memoir, or whatever. Over the following days I brainstormed and was amazed how difficult it was to come up with a suitable subject for such a work. By the second class I had a vague idea that I wanted to try my hand at a novel, and I reasoned that it had to be about a subject that I possessed a lot of knowledge about. Having worked for years in the mineral processing machinery business, it had to be the background for my story. Having lived in South Africa for several years prior to emigrating to America and having grown up in Ireland, I knew these two places had to figure in the plot. By simple trial and error and much guidance from Brewster the skeletal outline of a story began to take shape. When the six-week class ended I had learned the basic elements of a viable novel and I had acquired enough confidence to proceed on my own.

This turned out to be more difficult than I had expected. Many times, I found myself at dead ends and I lit up Brewster's telephone asking for help. I was fortunate to have travelled all over South Africa and many of the surrounding countries and knew the places I wanted to set the story. I had been to all kinds of mines, had knowledge of the separating techniques they used, and met an array of people from across the spectrum of race, ethnic and tribal affiliations. Being Irish was a tremendous help – I had none of the baggage of the colonial or apartheid eras and everybody regarded the Irish as a friend. The African wildlife was awesome – I never tired of visits to game reserves like Kruger Park and very often came face to face with wild animals as I roamed the dirt roads searching for business. These great beasts had to feature in my story, and writing the book brought back happy memories of special people and special places. Through a combination of Brewster's ongoing encouragement and my own determination, I completed a story in about one year. Next came several re-writes and a search for a suitable title. After all of that was complete, I spent a year sending out letters to prospective agents and publishers – all to no avail. I was not about to let all this hard work go to waste, so I set about the process of self-publishing. That was a journey in itself – correcting, editing, formatting, getting ISBN number, designing a cover and so forth. Cost quotations for printing and binding the book almost doomed the entire project. I stuck with it, swallowed hard and decided on an optimistic number of printed copies to reduce the per copy cost. The Kimberley File was a reality and ready for sale by late 1997.

Despite my life in equipment sales, I was not prepared for the challenge of selling books. I garnered some token publicity locally in South Carolina and in the West of Ireland. South Africa was still in governmental transition, and other than sending some copies to friends there I decided to forego that market. Books were hand distributed to SC book shops for sale on consignment, and boxes were shipped to Ireland for similar distribution there by my family and friends. Numerous copies were sold on both sides of the Atlantic and I received many nice compliments from readers which I appreciated very much. However, I was unable to gain any real traction in the marketplace and the book was not a commercial success.

Fast forward to 2021 – I recently published 'Ireland's Final Rebellion and An American Dream'. This years-in-the-making two-part book is written as historic fiction but is very much biographical and autobiographical, being that part one is based on my father's direct participation in The Irish War of Independence (1919-1921), and part two is based on my own life journey in search of The American Dream.

Modern publishing methods have changed completely since 'the old days of 1997'. This time I published via KDP Amazon which greatly reduced my workload in getting the manuscript from a word file to a finished book ready for sale.

The difficulties for an independent author / publisher to get meaningful exposure for a new book are still formidable. Newspaper circulation and readership has greatly decreased, and obtaining reviews is nigh on impossible, but Amazon have at least removed some of the heavy lifting. Now that I have an ongoing established presence on Amazon.com/books I can free up more time to get on with the important process – writing.

The Kimberley File has now been re-published on KDP Amazon, both as an e-book and paperback. I hope this new edition gives more people the opportunity to read and enjoy it.

I welcome emails from readers and politely ask you to post reviews on my books on the relevant Amazon listing page.

Michael Gerard

Website – www.MichaelGerardAuthor.com
E-mail – michaelgerardcmi@gmail.com

ONE

A Box of Wine

1981 in rural South Africa. It was a beautiful morning in South Africa. Geordie McKay received his wake-up call on time at six o'clock, accompanied by the traditional cup of tea. Hot and freshly made, just like he used to get from his mother in Ireland when he lived there. Some things in Africa were not very civilized but a cup of tea first thing in the morning made up for a lot.

Sitting up in the bed he slurped the tea with pleasure and thought about Ireland. It would be starting to get real cold there at this stage of mid November. His mother hated the long wet winters when it got dark at three o'clock in the afternoon. Meanwhile summer was just beginning for Geordie in the southern hemisphere. He wished he could afford to bring mother over for a visit to this strange and wonderful world of his at the other side of the globe.

The tea was finished and with it went his daydream. Geordie showered, dressed and went to breakfast. Unlike most of the small hotels that travelling salesmen like Geordie were confined to, this one had a nice breakfast buffet; with lots of fruit, juices, and even boiled eggs. He was in great spirits. A signed sales contract for a crusher the previous evening sat in his briefcase and he hoped to sell a front end loader by ten o'clock. After a strange start this week was beginning to look good.

Eight o'clock found Geordie searching for his next victim, as he called his good sales prospects. He was in Kimberley, *thee* diamond capital of the South African Cape Province. Diamond mines were not plentiful any more in the local area, but Kimberley was still the center for the industry in the region. It had its history of the great diamond finds and it had "The Big Hole", a vast chasm where men had followed a diamond "pipe" down into the earth so deep that it was now one of the biggest tourist attractions in Africa.

Geordie wasn't thinking diamonds, he was calculating his commission from the loader sale that he was about to make to Boer Transport. Despite his abysmal Afrikaans he was able to follow the scribbled notes Van Rensburg had given him at the mine and presently drove into the customer's large yard. He was halfway to the truck repair shop when the police car cut in front of him, forcing him to stop. A burly uniformed policeman jumped out and rushed to Geordie's car door, pulling it open.

"Where do you think you're going *Meneer?*" the man shouted, in Afrikaans.

"To visit David at the truck repair shop, Officer," answered Geordie in English. His annoyance was soon evident to the policeman when Geordie stepped out of the car to tower over the Afrikaaner. He pushed his business card in front of the man's face.

"Here's my card. What's your problem, man?"

This time the response was in English.

"This business had been impounded by police, Mr. McKay. You cannot make any business calls here."

"But I have—"

"No buts, *Meneer*. Here is your card. You must leave these premises immediately, please, *Meneer*."

Geordie was looking towards the buildings as the policeman finished his pleading. Police and military personnel could be seen moving about there. He took his business card back from the officer and left without another word. Exiting the gate Geordie took two right turns to bring his car along the side road that circled the back of the transport company yard. From there he had a better view of the search in progress. Something big was going on, and Boer Transport would not be needing the spare parts Geordie had promised to deliver from their sister company, the Olantsfontein Mine in Taung.

Yes, he distinctly remembered Van Rensburg at the mine telling him that the companies were related. Geordie's dormant ulcer now began to act up, a certain indicator to him that his anxiety levels were rising rapidly. He felt an urge to check the cargo in his trunk and began to slow the car till he realized that he was still visible from the Boer Transport yard.

"What the hell is going on, McKay?" he shouted aloud to himself, banging the steering wheel with his fist. He took the first turn leading away form the search area, his gut tightening by the second and his brow and palms sweating.

A Checkers supermarket came into view ahead. Geordie pulled into the entrance late, almost knocking over the boy at the newspaper stall. As he swerved, the headline caught his eye. He parked and hurried back to buy the morning paper. It was in Afrikaans but still obvious – "Boer Transport Seized By Police." With a little help from the newspaper boy, Geordie soon had a fuller picture. They were caught with illegal diamonds, and even suspected of involvement in a recent huge gem robbery in Southwest Africa.

Returning feebly to his car, Geordie sat in numbed silence, staring at the front page headline! Then he opened the car trunk and peered at the wine box full of parts he had carried from the mine at Taung. The box was sealed. He took out his penknife and began to cut the tape, thought better of it and instead, moved the heavy box to the rear passenger seat of the Ford Cortina. Sitting beside the box he cut the tape away furiously and pulled open the lid. Under a layer of crumpled newspaper packing he lifted up some metal parts, brake pads, he figured. Discarding these on the car floor Geordie dug deeper into the box and fished out a green canvas bag.

It was quite heavy and sealed at the top with a wax material. Another dip into the box produced an envelope addressed to a Mr. Botha, Houghton, Johannesburg. It was a suburb of Johannesburg which Geordie knew quite well. Lots of big houses with security gates and high privacy fences. Many of the older homes were now communes, or shared houses where five to eight boys or girls lived. Geordie and his pals went to parties there all the time.

Putting the paper and brake parts back in the box, he found a note attached to one of the parts. It was addressed to David, the mechanic that Geordie was to see and hand the box to. Cursing his lack of Afrikaans, Geordie tried to decipher it, recognizing only his own name and that of a brand or front end loader, presumably the one they were keen to buy. Everything was now back in the box except the green canvas bag and the letter to Mr. Botha. Geordie rolled the bag around on his lap, feeling the stone contents through the canvas. He opened the barely sealed envelope with his knife, so that it could be easily glued later. Seeing Afrikaans again he didn't even try to read it, turning his knife and his attention to the canvas bag. This wax seal was a different story. Despite his best efforts, the red wax could not be cut clean so Geordie hacked it open in frustration and reached inside.

The stones in his open palm were clean with bright shiny sides. They had to be precious stones, Geordie knew, probably uncut diamonds. The headline on the newspaper glared back from the front seat, the connection now painfully obvious. Visions flashed through his head. He was rich. He was scared. He was in big trouble. He felt weak. He felt sick. Geordie's stomach began to churn again. He became claustrophobic in the car and the hot sweat was back. Fumbling for the door handle he scrambled out and sucked in some rapid breaths of fresh air in a vain attempt to calm himself. He managed to reach some shrubs, then with a loud heave, vomited up his buffet breakfast.

◆

Two hours later Geordie's red Cortina pulled into a petrol station in Warrenton. It was decision time for Geordie McKay. The nausea following the Checkers carpark find had been slow to pass. Geordie had drank a large bottle of tonic water and sat for a long time on a bench in Kimberley's Queen Park. He had quickly dismissed any thought of going back to Boer Transport or visiting the police station. Nobody answered his telephone call to the mine at Taung. The road home to Johannesburg took him near the mine, so he had settled on that plan, comforting himself with the knowledge that he had an hour's drive to Warrenton before deciding whether to return to the mine.

On the open road, Geordie's thoughts wandered back over his sales trip since leaving Johannesburg the previous week. He had breezed though Botswana to reach the rich mining areas of the Atlantic coast of Southwest Africa, where he wrote up two sales orders. Then he worked his way down the sparsely populated northern coast of the Cape Province, so that he could spend the weekend in Cape Town, beautiful Cape Town. As usual he had stayed with his pal, Joe McCool, an Irish born South African with a heart of gold and the thirst of an elephant. After three nights of boozing and partying, Geordie stumbled into a quarry customer on Monday in Beaufort West and made a sale. His happy call to the Johannesburg office with the sale details was spoiled when he was instructed to divert to the Olantsfontein Diamond Mine in Taung.

Just over a year earlier Geordie had a nasty run-in with the mine manager there, an ignorant gobshite named Vermullen, and had never gone near the place since. Vermullen had beaten a black truck driver one day in front of Geordie, calling the man a Kaffir and worse, all because the driver had given a lift to some family members in the company truck. Geordie had been riding with Vermullen in a pickup truck to survey a new gravel deposit being cleared for mining. When they overtook the slow haul truck Vermullen had seen the occupants, flew into a rage, and forced the driver to stop. He then proceeded to beat the man with his heavy stick. The passengers had escaped out the side window but the driver was cornered and taking some nasty blows.

As a kid, Geordie had been the victim of many beatings by a cruel schoolmaster and could not condone this vicious attack.

His first attempts to persuade Vermullen to stop, were met with angry insults, so Geordie intervened. He pulled Vermullen off the hapless driver and when the stick was then wielded towards his own head, Geordie lost his cool. Grabbing Vermullen by the scruff of the neck with one hand, Geordie forcibly removed the stick from the man's grasp with the other, then dropped him, so that Vermullen sprawled on the dirt on his backside. The man cursed under his breath, looked up at Geordie in fear, scrambled over to his *baakie* and drove away at high speed. The truck driver had hidden in bushes during this confrontation between the two white men. He came out now and literally threw himself at Geordie's feet in gratitude. Richard was his name, a Zulu with quite good English. They rode back to the mine in the haul truck, to where Geordie's car was parked. A clerk emerged from the office as Geordie looked around for Vermullen's *baakie*. The manager had left strict instructions that Geordie was to leave the property immediately, and was not welcome to return.

The mining company had continued to purchase spare parts on a regular basis, but had not requested any machinery quotes or service, and Geordie had not attempted to visit them, till now. A hydraulic flexible coupling failure had their plant down and asking for service help. Geordie carried those in his spares kit in his trunk, and his boss was eager that he use the opportunity to improve relations with the customer. On the drive to the mine Geordie rehearsed his lines for Vermullen, only to be told at the security gate, to his great relief, that a new mine manager was in place, a Mr. Koos Van Rensburg. Geordie was directed to his office.

Van Rensburg was a quiet spoken, chubby man in his early fifties. His excess stomach rolled out over the belt of his polyester safari shorts, the standard Afrikaaner attire.

"Welcome, Mr. McKay" he said, extending his handshake and smiling broadly. "Thank you for such prompt service."

"No problem. Please call me Geordie. Let me get your plant up and running immediately, then I'd like to visit with you, *Meneer* Koos."

"Excellent, *Meneer* Geordie. I'll call Stiempie to meet you here and take you out to the diggings in his *baakie*. We have new owners, you see, *Meneer*, and security is very tight. You must leave your car here. Could you meet Stiempie out front with the spare parts, please?"

"Sure, and I'll see you later Koos."

Stiempie arrived almost immediately in his Datsun *baakie*. He was a younger leaner version of Van Rensburg, dressed also in the trademark shorts, with tanned muscular legs. Quite tall, but inches shy of Geordie's six foot two, Stiempie introduced himself very formally to the Irishman, in Afrikaans. On the drive to the diggings, conversation was scarce between the two men. Stiempie had no English, and Geordie's few Afrikaans phrases didn't make for much discussion, so Geordie passed the time sizing up the changes made to the mining operation during his long absence. Security was indeed much more evident. He had seen a few armed men near the office area and Stiempie had a holstered revolver on his hip.

The diggings had expanded too, and they were now hauling gravel from many different sites on this ancient river flood plain, where diamonds had been deposited amongst the rocks millions of years ago. Geordie's bright orange Finlay separation screening plant was still at the heart of things. All the raw gravel was fed into it by front end loader, where the machine first rejected the large rocks at the feed grate. The finer material was then screened such that the marble-sized fraction was separated from the fine sand and bigger stones. This marble fraction was the diamond bearing one and it was carried on a conveyor to a barrel washing screen where it tumbled with water, to clean it even more. The rinsed stones were collected by another conveyor which deposited them on a stockpile under an open-sided shed. A screw auger protruded from this pile, carrying a small but steady feed of clean stones onto a long wide table. This was the only part of the operation still running. Four middle-aged white men worked the stones over the table, two each side. They each had what looked like a ruler in their hand, with which they divided up portions of the stones into halves, quarters and so on. Some pebbles were worked out to the edge and flicked into metal drums standing beside the table.

Stiempie's *baakie* had stopped in front of the pickers, giving Geordie a full view of their work. As he watched admiringly, Stiempie interrupted and directed him over to the processing plant where a white mechanic and four black laborers stood beside the disabled machine. Richard, the driver that Geordie had rescued, was among them and greeted *"Baas* Geordie" with a huge smile. A tarpaulin had been erected over the work area, and in the welcome shade Geordie and Piet, the mechanic, began to replace the broken coupling and to re-align the drive motor. Within an hour everything was back to running again. While Stiempie was in high spirits Geordie asked for a tour of the diamond picking area. He was introduced to the four pickers. They shook his hand very firmly, speaking in joyful sounding Afrikaans, words Geordie assumed were praise for his mechanical genius. One of the men reached into a metal drum and produced a handful of dull whitish stones. He picked out one of the stones and held it in the palm of his hand.

"Good, very good," the man said, in probably his only English.

Geordie had only ever seen the type of diamond one finds in engagement rings and this stone didn't look like any fancy gem to him, no real shine or sparkle to it.

"Is that a diamond, for real?" Geordie asked.

"Good, very good diamond," the four Afrikaaners chorused.

Noticing that all four had pistols at their hips too, Geordie thought it best to resist his urge to handle the adored stone. He lingered a while, watching the picking when it resumed, till Stiempie's radio cracked into life. It was Koos, speaking excitedly and mentioning Geordie by name. They drove back immediately to the office where Koos stood waiting. Stiempie was sent away and Koos addressed Geordie.

"*Meneer* Geordie, please follow me to my office."

Once seated, Geordie offered some equipment ideas that he felt would improve the plant. Koos nodded politely, then asked.

"Where are you heading from here, *Meneer*?"

"Kimberley, Bloemfontein, Welkom and then working my way back to Johannesburg," Geordie answered happily.

"We need to send some small truck parts to our sister company in Kimberley, Boer transport. By the way, they are in the market for a new front end loader. If you could drop these parts in for me, you could speak to David about it and on my recommendation, get yourself a sale."

"Great!" replied Geordie. "That would be no trouble at all. Just give me some directions, and thanks for the lead."

Koos then called Stiempie on the radio. The man appeared in moments, while Koos was sketching out a map and directions for Geordie. The phone rang as they were getting ready to leave, delaying Koos. He directed them to the car, saying he would follow immediately. Stiempie carried the cargo outside, a wine box securely taped at the top. A spot was cleared in the trunk of Geordie's car and the box was fitted in snugly. They attempted some basic conversation until Stiempie was called inside again by his boss.

Minutes passed. Geordie took the time to catch up on his notes. Both men then appeared. Stiempie bid Geordie a quick "Tot Siens" and hurried away in his *baakie* towards the diggings. Koos looked uneasy, prompting Geordie to comment on it.

"Is everything okay, Koos?"

"Yes, yes. Just. . . Just another crisis. That's the mining business for you."

"Can I do anything to help?" Geordie asked.

"Leave now *Meneer*. . . Oh, you need to change your route. I just found out that the army has one of those security roadblocks at Warrenton. Turn right at our gate and you will come out on the Christiana road. Go right again and that road will take you through Christiana to Boshof, then go into Kimberley that way. It will save you a holdup *Meneer*, and it's a good road."

"No problem, and thanks again for the lead, Koos," replied Geordie.

Koos grasped Geordie's hand and shook it warmly. "You have saved my bacon on this one, *Meneer* Geordie. Thank you very much. Goodbye."

With that, Geordie set off. He noticed that the security man at the main gate had the engine of his *baakie* running and didn't want to chat. The man locked the gates behind Geordie and set off back toward the mine. On the Boshof road Geordie passed a quarry that was high on his prospect list. What was to be a short call turned into a long one when the customer pronounced his readiness to buy. After lengthy negotiations Geordie signed a sales contract for a crusher. It was dark when he left the quarry and in the euphoria of the sale he completely forgot about Boer Transport until he was settled in his hotel room. A telephone call went unanswered so Geordie resolved to visit them the following morning.

◆

So, it was decision time for Geordie in Warrenton now. He telephoned the mine again. A man answered who demanded to know his business with Van Rensburg. Playing the travelling salesman routine, Geordie asked for an appointment with the manager. More questions followed which Geordie answered as Mr. Black, a welding rod salesman. Eventually the man at the mine told him he was a police officer and that the mine was closed temporarily for investigations.

Geordie ended the call quickly now, and got back in his car. He turned onto route twenty-nine for Johannesburg. Johannesburg 438 km – the sign read.

TWO

City of Gold

Johannesburg is the great sprawling metropolis of South Africa. It stretches from the huge ghetto townships like Soweto through suburban featureless mining industrial towns like Germiston, Brakpan and Benoni. The downtown is a bustling grid system of traffic, trams, buses, taxis, markets, office buildings and people, people everywhere. On the northside of the city are the fashionable and wealthy suburbs with expensive homes, up-market shops, parks, malls and bars. Flying over the city, the enormous gold-mine waste slurry ponds attract the eye more than anything else. They seem to be everywhere with huge rectangular fort-like retaining walls and milky yellow syrupy interiors. But there's gold in them there ponds when technology further improves the efficiency of recovering it. The first mines had gold-bearing waste rock piles, later it changed to sand piles and now it was at the slurry pond stage.

Gold rules this city and it is talked about constantly, by people in all strata of life. Its rise and fall affects all of its inhabitants on a daily basis. Jo'burg is fast, it is rich, it is sensual, it is cool. Literally cool too, situated on a five thousand foot escarpment. The heat would be unbearable without the altitude. One could say it was closer to heaven.

Jo'burg was heaven for Anna Terblanche, at least for now. She smiled admiringly as she dressed in front of her mirror. Was it too vain to enjoy looking at herself, her long bronze legs and firm buttocks? Blonds have more fun they say and she was doing just that. Anna was really enjoying Jo'burg now, but the people who said it would take a year to settle in were right on the mark.

Mama had wanted her to stay in Bloemfontein in the Orange Free State, nearer home, but Anna would have none of it. She wanted to put some distance between her and the sleepy dorp she grew up in. Her brother would get the farm anyway, so what was she to do, marry another Boer farm boy and go to Durban once a year, if she was lucky? The farm crowd went to the same beach at the same time. Even in swimsuits, they were recognizable by their "Dutchman's Disease" tans, which ended at the line of their everyday wear; khaki shorts, short sleeved shirts and long socks. On the beach they looked like a team of striped rugby players, and Anna did not want to be their cheerleader.

The mother and daughter had quarrelled over the issue. Anna was three months shy of her twenty-first birthday when she finished the business and secretarial course. As a compromise she took a job with a firm of attorneys used by her father in Bloemfontein. Mama was happy with that and helped her plan a big twenty-first birthday party. It was a great party except for the obvious positioning by her parents and Joseph Van Der Walt's to try and make the affair into an engagement. They had dated many times and liked each other, had even done it together a few times at the club parties down at the dam. But this was the nineteen-eighties and Anna was going to discover Jo'burg on her own without Joseph and without any ties. He was smart enough to know that their affair was over. Neither of them wanted a show-down, so they had a last fling and parted good friends.

Anna liked the legal secretary work but not Bloemfontein, finally confiding to her boss where she wanted to be. With his help, she had a few promising interviews lined up in Johannesburg and in August she packed her little Beetle and headed for the smoke.

Now, a little over a year later she was happy in Jo'burg. She had a good job with attorneys in Hyde Park and lived with five others in a big commune house, off Jan Smuts Avenue. It was close to the park where she like to jog and cycle, close to work, close to the "single" scene and close to the multiracial melting pot of Hillbrow. They had a full-time maid and garden boy at the house. Everything from laundry to meals to the pool and garden was taken care of, leaving Anna to live life to the fullest.

◆

It was eight o'clock that Wednesday evening when Anna got in, after drinks with friends at Rosebank Steak Bar. Wednesday was the mid-week drink specials night with free boervoss sausage, hot of the charcoal braai. Anna and her friends were finalizing plans for the Long summer holidays over Christmas. Two adjoining apartments in Cape Town's Seapoint area had already been rented for three weeks, with views of the Atlantic and Table Mountain.

A note with her name on it was pinned to the notice board in the hallway of her commune house. Geordie McKay had called at six o'clock and again at seven, it was urgent. He left word that he would be arriving at about eight o'clock. Before Anna finished checking her mail in the hallway, the doorbell rang and she answered it.

"Geordie! What are you doing in Jo'burg this early in the week. Are you trying to catch me with one of my weekday boyfriends?" she asked, with feigned anger.

"I don't care if you have the President in there with you, girl. He'll just have to hold his whist until I talk to you. For God's sake give me a hug."

Anna readily obliged with a full kiss and took his hand to lead him into the house.

"No, come over to the car first, it's more private there."

"Okay. Is there anything the matter?" she asked.

"Plenty, girl, plenty."

Once in the car Geordie launched into the whole story. She listened in stunned silence, eyes ever wider and her mouth held steady by her pressed fingers.

"Oh my God," she gasped in Afrikaans, and began another sentence before she realized she had lapsed away from English.

"Sorry, I was saying that possession of illegal or stolen diamonds is very serious."

"Hell, I know that much myself. What I need from you is your help in figuring out what to do. Here, translate these notes to David and Botha that were in the box."

Anna took the notes and scanned them quickly.

"This first note is to David. It says... Smith has not shown up here to collect this package for Botha. I have just got word that we are to be raided. This salesman, Geordie McKay was here so I have sent you a box with the urgent truck parts you needed. He thinks you want to buy a Cat loader so play it along to keep him happy. Get this package to Botha as soon as possible, note enclosed. Koos."

"Go straight on to the second note Anna, the one to Botha," Geordie urged.

"Okay. . . Dear Piet. . . No courier. We are expecting a raid. I've sent these (568) in a sealed bag to David at Boer. He will pass to you. Will call you later when I can leave the mine. Koos."

"What next, Geordie?" Anna asked.

"Those bastards were just using me. But does Botha know that I have their stones or will he think the police have them?"

"You must lie low here till we figure something out. Have you spoken to anyone at work, won't they be wondering where you are?" Anna asked, anxiously.

"I'm not expected back this week, I'll worry about work later. I've got plenty of clothes with me and I've hidden the bag of diamonds in a safe place."

"Good. Does anyone else know of this?"

"Of course not. Anna, let's just go to Brazil or somewhere, turn them into money and live the life of Reilly, what do you think, eh?"

"Brazil isn't ready for the likes of us. Park your car at the back of the house and bring your clothes up to my room. I need coffee to settle my nerves, I'll make a pot and take it up. My housemates know you pretty well by now and I don't see anyone objecting to you staying for a few days while we sort this out."

They were on their second cups when Anna had the idea of enlisting Mr. Goldstein's help. Geordie liked the idea and they talked it over in bed as they lay naked in each others arms, soothing their fears.

"I must be worried 'cause I haven't even thought of sex tonight," Geordie joked, after a long silence. "Have you?"

Obviously not, Anna was already asleep. He felt better now also and followed her quickly to the land of nod.

Geordie was still sleeping soundly when Anna got up quietly in the morning for work. Her note greeted him two hours later when he awoke with a start.

"Stay put and rest, will call you at twelve-thirty with a plan. Love Anna."

THREE

Diamonds Galore

Harold Goldstein got to work at seven o'clock as usual. He liked to have an hour to work alone before the office staff and other attorneys came in. A few minutes later he heard the front door open and went to the foyer to investigate.

"Anna, good morning. You are early, or is my watch wrong?"

"Morning Mr. Goldstein. I'm early, on purpose. I need to talk to you in private before the others come in, if I may?"

"Yes, yes, of course. I was just dictating some letters for you concerning the upcoming Krugersdorp murder trial. Is there something wrong, Anna? You look a bit tense this morning, please sit down and tell me about it."

Anna proceeded to outline the details of Geordie's predicament to her boss. She was not up to the usual efficiency that he always praised her for, but she managed to articulate the story into a concise summary.

Mr. Goldstein was an experienced defense attorney and she knew that if anyone could help, he could. He listened intently without interrupting her, then asked a few pointed questions which Anna answered as best she could.

"Let me check on a few points of relevant law. The coffee machine is on, meet me in the library with two cups."

Anna fixed their usual coffee and followed him to their law library. He was reading from three open large volumes. She put his coffee in front of him quietly and waited for him to finish, then seated herself across the table drinking her coffee. Her stomach felt much better now that she had been able to tell someone. It was lucky for Geordie she worked here. What they would have done without Mr. Goldstein didn't bear thinking about.

Mr. Goldstein closed his books.

"Okay, Anna, the law is much as I had thought. You know me, I like to double-check before giving an opinion. Based on the facts you have told me, Geordie should be able to exonerate himself completely. However, this must be handled delicately and by the right people. We must not underestimate the danger he is in from these criminals, who no doubt have realized their mistake by now and will want their booty back. I happen to know that the police are under pressure to bring in some big fish on this diamond case. DeBeer's have succeeded in making illegal diamond dealing a top priority issue."

The old man paused, drank some coffee and continued.

"Let me see. We are in court tomorrow in Krugersdorp, as you know, and you and I must get a lot done in preparation. I have an appointment at Jeppe this morning at eleven. While I'm there I'll talk discreetly with my contacts about Geordie's situation. Have him sit tight, but he needs to be ready to meet with the police at short notice. Now, don't worry. He has done nothing wrong and we'll sort it all out. We might even manage to get him a reward out of this. Can I leave it at that for now, Anna? If we rush, we can get our court prep work done early."

"That's great Mr. Goldstein. I'll be happy to work through lunch to get the typing finished early. Geordie will be so relieved, I can't wait to tell him. Thank you, thank you."

◆

By twelve-thirty Anna had heard nothing from Mr. Goldstein. She called Geordie as scheduled and told him what she knew and to stay near the phone. Mr. Goldstein phoned in at five minutes to one. He was on his way back, offering no details on the car phone, except that he had met with important officials and would recount the situation at one-thirty when he returned. Anna typed furiously to finish off the court work. Something told her she would need a free afternoon to deal with Geordie's problem.

When Mr. Goldstein walked in Anna was tidying up the

Krugersdorp files and adding the thick wad of typed sheets she had just completed.

"Excellent, Anna, I'll go through the file this afternoon in preparation for court. Let me just wash my hands and I'll be right with you."

She was seated in her chair by her boss's desk when he returned, eagerly waiting with her notepad for news of the police meeting.

He closed the door behind him.

"Now, about your friend Geordie," Mr. Goldstein began in his stoic methodical manner. "I met with a Captain De Klerk at Jeppe and explained the circumstances of Geordie's acquisition of the diamonds. The Captain is in charge of this police operation against illicit diamond trading, which they are connecting to recent robberies like the big South West Africa one. Everything can be worked out, as far as he and I can see. The police want to take a statement from Geordie and want a little help with their ongoing investigations. They want to meet him as soon as possible. I took the liberty of setting up a meeting for him at four o'clock this afternoon. Oh yes, they want the diamonds, of course. Once everything is cleared up Geordie can expect a sizeable reward, but that will take a while."

"Wonderful, Mr. Goldstein, that's wonderful news. I've been so worried. Four o'clock you said. That's about two-and-a-half hours from now. I must call Geordie with the news right away. I have all the typing finished, can I take some time off this afternoon to be with him?"

"Sure you can, Anna," Mr. Goldstein said and smiled. "He is special to you, I can see. Just spend a few minutes with me on this file after you call your Geordie and the rest of the day is yours."

Anna ran to her office and called Geordie. When he answered, she babbled the news excitedly until she came to the "d" word, which stopped her suddenly.

"You must take the, the, green bag with you, you know what I mean," Anna stumbled. "You must go and get it."

"I've already done that since we last talked. It's right here. Don't worry, the maid is finished and gone. Nobody here but me, I. . ."

"Mr. Goldstein is letting me have the afternoon off," Anna interrupted. "I'll be there in fifteen minutes. Bye."

After the telephone call Geordie took a cooling swim. The trip out to Randfontein for his cache had raised his anxiety levels again and made him hot and sweaty. He was still in the pool when he heard the car on the gravel driveway. As Anna got out, he rounded the corner of the house, dripping water everywhere.

"How goes it, how goes it?" Geordie spoke in his pidgin Afrikaans, "the water is great, come on in."

"Oh, what they hell, okay. Just don't get that water on my nice dress," Anna answered.

Geordie reached for her hand, lifted it to his wet face in Shakespearian manner and kissed it.

"Your pool awaits thee, madam. Hurry, pray tell. Get your togs on pronto," he said, with a smile.

"You are a fool!" she said, shaking her now wet hand at him. "Just give me a minute to change."

Geordie waddled back to the pool while Anna went through the front door and upstairs to her room. She took off her dress and hung it up carefully. Reaching for her bathing suit she saw the green canvas bag, lifted it up unwittingly and dropped it again as the enormity of its contents struck her. She was very tempted to open the string and look inside, but resisted the urge.

Geordie was lying on the bottom at the deep end when Anna got to the pool. It gave her a fright until she saw the tell-tale bubbles rising. Diving in, she poked his back as she surged passed him. Both hit the surface at the same time.

"Stop doing that, Geordie. You know it frightens me, especially now."

He swam across and embraced her, kissed her on the lips, wet and deep, while they both treaded water. Then, he stopped treading and though Anna continued, they both began to sink. Geordie held the kiss and they touched the bottom. Finally, Anna broke away and kicked for the surface where she gasped for air again as Geordie surfaced just after her.

"Sometimes I don't know if you are man or fish, Geordie McKay," Anna blurted, still catching her breath.

"I'm just an auld blackguard, ma'am," he blarneyed in his put-on Stage-Irish voice. "Sure I can't swim at all. I just drink water very fast."

"Be serious Geordie. Let's get out now, okay? You've got to be downtown by four and we have to go through some stuff."

They swam, side by side, to the shallow end, climbed out and towelled off. Anna led the way through the side door and up the stairs after locking the side and front doors.

Her bedroom was cool, making their wet bathing suits uncomfortable. Like most rooms in these older homes it was big, allowing plenty of space for one's personal effects and thus making it imminently suitable for commune living. The bed was an adequate double and there was plenty of walk around space, closets and drawers. Anna began to peel off her bathing suit, standing in front of her dressing table. At almost five-foot-nine she was tall for a girl, not skinny or fat, just solid and muscular. Her generous breasts were firm. Now, after the cool swim, her nipples stood large and pointed. With her hair slicked back and her almost all-over tan she looked great. In the mirror, she could see Geordie's bare white backside at the back of the room. When he turned around he had a tray in hand with an open bottle of champagne and two glasses sitting on it.

"I think this deal calls for a celebration," Geordie said. "Jasus, Anna, you look amazing. Marilyn Monroe had nothing on you, girl. I could hang my hat on those doodies."

Stopping a few feet in front of her, he handed Anna a glass, then poured her champagne and his own.

"To Anna, my shining star. Oops, I've got a rising star of my own right now."

Anna had the champagne glass to her lips. She sipped,

looked down and giggled, blushed a little and turned back to face the mirror.

"You're definitely a man all tight, Geordie McKay."

He had put the bottle down and was leaning over her shoulder as they both faced the mirror. She could see him looking admiringly at her body and could feel his flesh pressed against her buttocks, sending a surge of electricity through her. They both sipped the bubbly and laughed.

"Missus, could I borrow your body for ten minutes please?"

She took both glasses, set them down on the dressing table and turned to face him.

"Oh Geordie, you are a beast. What am I going to do with you?"

On her tiptoes she was almost as tall as he. She kissed him hard, pressing her tongue deep into his mouth and her thighs against his. They held the kiss, shuffled the few feet to the bed and fell onto the covers.

There was no denying their relationship was rooted in physical attraction. They enjoyed making love, often, but it didn't end there. A certain chemistry existed between them. They had met at the Saturday scene at the Tavern, an in-pub in the affluent north Jo'burg suburbs, with nice gardens. It was always crowded on Saturdays from noon onwards. There were darts, skittles and horse shoes, usually a live band and the ever present charcoal braaifleis with the wonderful smokey aroma of South African boervoss sausage that was cooked in long pieces coiled up like a snake. People walked around with a drink in one hand and a piece of boervoss in the other. The English influence was clear in the Tavern layout with many draft beers on tap, but the Afrikaaner-Dutch side was well represented too, with the flower gardens and food. The place drew the English and Irish ex-pat's, the English-speaking South Africans, the Afrikaaners and various other mixed white nationals. People wore everything from Ascot racingstyle clothes, to beach wear, to jeans, to the khaki shorts and shirts of the Afrikaaners. It was a veritable melting pot of languages, accents and mannerisms.

Both Anna and Geordie had been regulars there before they met. Because of their backgrounds they were inevitably drawn to their own kind first, but once familiar with their surroundings, hungrily explored others. Her English was good and his Southern Irish accent was quite easily understood, if he didn't talk too quick, unlike the Northern Irish and Scots, which she couldn't understand at all.

Because Anna was tall, most of the ex-pat's were out of the picture, being rather short. Geordie was six foot two, big enough to carry his many surplus pounds. He explained it as "having a weakness for Guinness Stout." She liked his sense of humor and boldness, he made her laugh. So many of the Afrikaaner types and English were too serious. Anna revelled in the devil-may-care attitude of the Irish lads. They had no interest in marriage, just having a good time. She laughed at their stories of aged uncles who had been courting the same girls for twenty-five years or more without any thought of marriage. The parties at Geordie's and his friends commune houses were wild. Anyone arriving before ten was early and anyone leaving earlier than four in the morning was booed out of the place. The sing-songs were raucous, especially after one of the Gaelic football or soccer matches. Geordie's team didn't win much on the field, but they always won the sing-songs. Before long Anna was smitten with Geordie and "his gang" as she referred to his pals.

"Let me see the diamonds, Geordie," Anna asked softly as they lay on the bed.

"Sure."

He went over to the drawer, took out the green canvas bag and poured its contents carefully out beside her on the bed.

"It's hard to visualize them as sparkling gems mounted in rings and such," she mused, "they look so ordinary now."

"That's what I think too. I suppose its the cutting and the polishing that does it all."

"How many stones are there?"

"Five hundred and sixty-eight. I've counted them three times."

For a few minutes Anna sat with all the diamonds laid out on the bed cover between her spread naked legs. She fiddled with them with her hand.

Geordie laughed. "You'd make one hell of a picture right now, girl. You could get a part in the next James Bond film."

The clock chimed downstairs bringing them both back to reality.

"Gosh, it's three-thirty," Anna exclaimed. "We'd better get dressed and down to Jeppe."

She carefully got off the bed and began getting ready at her dressing table while Geordie gathered up the diamonds, put them back into the bag and checked around for any stray ones. He dressed then, this time in shirt and pants, rather than shorts. Anna suggested they use her car and a few minutes later she drove out onto Jan Smuts Avenue and headed into town, to the central police headquarters.

"Jeppe" as it was called, was a huge four story imposing building off Jeppe Street.

FOUR

Jeppe

Captain De Klerk had only been in Johannesburg for three months. In his native Kimberley he was a twenty-five year veteran of the police force. He was pleasantly surprised to be chosen to head the high priority investigation into the illicit diamond trade, but it was a great opportunity for him and he readily accepted the challenge. When he was encouraged to move to Jo'burg with the job he was tempted to refuse, although he knew it made sense, That is where the kingpins were, where all the strings were pulled, where the case had to be cracked, and it was the Jo'burg end that had been letting the investigations down from the start.

The decision had to be a family democratic one. Both his son and daughter were in universities in Jo'burg and voted to go. His wife eventually voted yes too, making it conveniently unnecessary for him to vote. There would be further promotion on the cards if he could wrap up this investigation with some major convictions.

So, move he did and he had to admit that on a personal and family basis it had gone great to date. He had mixed feelings about whether the investigation itself had improved or suffered. Most of his own chosen men had to stay behind in Kimberley and were doing a good job at that end. In the Jo'burg move he had lost some of his authority, having to work under the guidance of the Chief of Police, Chief Ferreira. It was only a formality he had been told, there was to be no interference. That had not turned out to be the case. The Chief had assigned him too few men and their quality was questionable, as was their loyalty to the Captain. Despite all the obvious other day to day police work to be overseen by the Chief, he insisted on involving himself in this case at every turn. Ferreira was a forty-year veteran, with his best police days behind him but he was well connected and that was a bigger asset than ability. The Captain's ideas were criticized and his plans for action delayed. Very soon he realized that real progress could only be made if he proceeded on his own course and brought the Chief on board only when necessary. This plan had yielded better results but the friction between the two men was growing. Captain De Klerk carefully logged his daily progress, or the lack of it, in preparation for the inevitable show-down.

The just-completed Kimberley area raids had been a success, due in large part to the quality of his old team back in

Kimberley who had conducted them. Even the Chief couldn't argue with success. While the Captain was in Kimberley the one part of the plan that was left to the Jo'burg team had been messed up. Surveillance of a courier named Jeff Smith was their job, in the hope that he would lead them to the suspected drop site and to some of the key players. But the Chief had intervened again and it was very questionable whether Smith's premature arrest was good work or incompetence.

Geordie McKay's entrance into the picture was a stroke of much needed luck on which the Captain hoped to capitalize. Smith could only be held for forty-eight hours before being charged with something, and that time was running out. Captain De Klerk was ninety percent certain of the identity of the Jo'burg organizer, he just needed McKay as a bait to blow the top off this thing. Thankfully the Chief had left early, complaining of high blood pressure levels again. To head off further friction the Captain had informed him, without drama, that they may have some routine stake-outs to do later. Although Sergeant Van de Merwe was far from his top choice, the Captain agreed to include him, to placate the Chief. It also avoided further questions from him that might have forced the Captain to lie, or reveal his true intentions.

Anna parked up the road and they walked to the security entrance at Jeppe. A heavily-armed policeman came to the barrier and greeted them in Afrikaans. Anna replied, also in Afrikaans, telling him they had a four o'clock appointment with Captain De Klerk. He went back into the guardhouse, came out with a clipboard list and spoke again to Anna. She thanked him and turned back towards her car.

"What's the story?" Geordie asked as they got out of earshot.

"Everything's fine," she replied. "He told us we can drive in and around the back to a side entrance, closer to the Captain's office."

After he checked the car trunk, the young policeman gave Anna a big salute and a smile as he waved them on. She thanked him through the open window.

"Geordie, you really need to work on your Afrikaans, it gets you easy access to lots of places," Anna said, as they drove through the large parking lot. "Maybe when we're in Cape Town at Christmas you can take your phrase books and tapes along, I'll help you with it."

"This isn't the kind of place I want to get into, but I know what you mean and that's a deal. Isn't this the building where Kaffirs, sorry, blacks keep getting pushed out of fourth floor windows, or is it "jump out" as they describe it?"

"This is it."

They found the side entrance and were directed to the fourth floor, As they went up in the elevator with three policemen, Geordie looked at Anna knowingly, "fourth floor eh!"

Geordie and Anna were shown into a stark room with a table in the center plus a few chairs. The two windows were unbarred and open a few inches at the bottom. Captain De Klerk, a big muscular Afrikaaner introduced himself in English. When he heard Anna's surname and accent, he switched to Afrikaans and the two of them conversed for a few minutes. Then a man entered who was introduced as Sergeant Van de Merwe, a case officer, accompanied by a female clerk with files and notepads.

Geordie and Anna were seated with their backs to the windows, the Captain facing them across the table, framed by the door behind him. The Sergeant sat slightly to the Captain's right and the clerk was at the end of the table on his left, notepad at the ready.

The Captain began again in English when everyone was seated.

"I want you to relax, Mr. McKay, you are not in any trouble. We appreciate your coming forward of your own free will. Your cooperation will be very helpful to us in resolving the outstanding issues of this case. After a few preliminary questions we will take a statement from you on the entire events that occurred in the Northern Cape Province, to the very best of your recollection. Miss Terblanche, you will have to leave at that point. We will take Mr. McKay back to his residence later. You did bring the evidence with you, Mr. McKay, I trust?"

Anna produced the green canvas sack from her shoulder bag and put it on the table in front of the Captain. He glared at it, then glared at Geordie.

"The seal is broken! How did this happen, Mr. McKay?"

"I didn't know what I had until I opened the bag, Sir. I'm sorry if I have done any harm by opening it."

"That's understandable, Mr. McKay," he replied, opening the string now and looking into the bag. "How many stones are there?"

"Five hundred and sixty-eight, Sir," Geordie replied.

"Thank you, Mr. McKay. Let the record show that fact. Sergeant, count these now in front of Mr. McKay and Miss Terblanche."

The Sergeant tipped out the diamonds carefully and began counting. Geordie noticed that Anna and the clerk were watching the counting too, somewhat agog, but the Captain never even glanced at them. He was looking at Geordie and their eyes met. Geordie held the stare for a moment, then looked back to the counting, but he could still feel the Captain's eyes on him.

"Could not Anna, Miss Terblanche, stay while I give my statement, Captain?" Geordie asked uncomfortably.

"We must follow procedures, Mr. McKay," came the Captain's reply. "Procedure requires only your presence."

"Five hundred and sixty-eight, Captain," the sergeant stated.

"Thank you, Sergeant. Now, take them to the vault and make sure you fill out all the paperwork. Meet us back here in five minutes. Mr. McKay, Miss Terblanche, you have five minutes to talk privately. There are soft drinks available at the end of the corridor. I then need only Mr. McKay back here. Miss Terblanche, you can proceed home. Thank you both."

"Can't I wait outside for him, Captain?" protested Anna.

"No, please. Our procedures must be followed. We will take good care of him and take him home later," the Captain added, in Afrikaans.

Out in the corridor Geordie sipped his coke nervously. Anna couldn't drink anything.

"It shouldn't take so long that I can't wait," she lamented. "Be sure to call me as soon as you know what time you'll be back, okay. I'll stay by the phone. If you can't phone, just get them to take you back to my place."

"It'll probably take a few hours, police are slow about everything. I'll be back in time to go out, though. We'll probably go down to Rosebank later and grab something to eat."

There wasn't much privacy in the corridor with the police standing around. Then they saw the Captain motioning to Geordie from down the hall. She fought back a tear as he got ready to leave.

"Don't worry, Anna, I'll be fine. Love you."

He hugged her and gave her a big kiss on the cheek. Anna watched him walk down the hall. He turned and waved from the Captain's door, then he was gone and the door closed behind him.

The young policeman was still on duty at the guard-gate and attempted to engage Anna in conversation, but to no avail. She drove away while he was still speaking.

◆

Back in the police station, Geordie was now alone in the room with Captain De Klerk, Sergeant Van de Merwe and Estelle, the secretary.

"Mr. McKay," began the Captain, "tell us the whole story of your trip to Taung. Try and put exact times on events, and names on the people you met, okay? Take your time."

Geordie began to recount his sales trip in the Western Transvaal, Northern Cape Province and the Kimberley area. He was asked to go back over some descriptions of the people at the mine and the layout.

"And are you absolutely sure, Mr. McKay, that you received no detailed information about a Jo'burg drop place and time?" asked the Captain.

"Absolutely, Sir. Per the letter, Van Rensburg was obviously just using me to get the package away quickly. Can I ask you a question, Captain?"

"Sure."

"Did that mine get raided and the people arrested?"

"Yes, they are in custody now."

"Well then," continued Geordie, "it's all wrapped up. Surely those people will tell you what you need to know."

Captain De Klerk shook his head.

"They are not telling us much. We need to catch the Jo'burg bosses red-handed and that's where you come in. We have very strong suspicions, but we lack hard evidence. The man that you were used as a replacement for is a courier, an Englishman. They always use foreigners for this work, it seems, Anyway, he was supposed to have been kept under surveillance, but my Chief and his fine men got carried away and arrested him. Nothing incriminating was found on him and he is not co-operating. We suspect that his Jo'burg drop was to be made within twenty-four hours after pick-up from Taung, which leaves us with little time. We need you Mr. McKay to help us this evening with a sting operation, if you don't mind."

The words resounded in Geordie's head like church bells.

"Me, Captain? But I know nothing of police work. Surely you can have one of your officers do this part."

"No, Mr. McKay, we cannot. We have to assume that the word has been passed to Jo'burg that you have the stones, you are the obvious delivery man now. Consider some other reasons Mr. McKay. Possession of illegal diamonds is a serious crime and we can make it stick on you if we wish. You have already admitted that you were carrying the merchandise to Jo'burg. I am being generous and here's more. There is a substantial reward on offer from DeBeers for information or help leading to the arrest and conviction of these criminal bosses. I will recommend that you get this reward in due course if you help us."

"Can I have a cup of coffee please?" Geordie asked quietly.

"Sure. Estelle, get us all coffee," the Captain ordered.

"Captain, I doubt if the Chief would approve of such hasty action," Van de Merwe cautioned.

"He already has, Sergeant."

The Captain raised the ante a little more. Twenty thousand Rand or more, in reward money was at stake. Men would be coming after Geordie for stealing their diamonds if they were allowed to regroup, and he would be an easy target. Geordie sat silently through all this, trying to find a way out, while still qualifying for the reward.

"Can I check on the men, Sir?" Van de Merwe asked.

"No need Sergeant, everything is taken care of."

The coffee came and they sat drinking it, each immersed in their own thoughts for the moment.

"What about the letter from the mine?" Geordie asked.

"I have it, thank you," replied Captain De Klerk. "It has no role to play in our plans for this evening."

"Will I be in danger if I do this?" Geordie asked again.

"Of course not, my people will be right there to protect you," the Captain assured him. "You'll be wired and we'll be listening and recording every word. It is a simple set-up to get suspects accepting the merchandise and therefore being caught in possession. The police burst in and arrest them. It'll be all over in time for dinner. Just routine, isn't that so, Sergeant?"

"Eh, yes Sir. Could I be excused for a minute Sir?"

"No, Sergeant. You might miss something important."

"But I don't know what to do or say," Geordie protested.

"I'll go through your lines with you beforehand," replied the Captain.

"Okay, I'll do it!" Geordie heard himself say.

"Good, very good," said the Captain. His strong voice echoed in Geordie's brain.

With that, the Captain picked up the telephone and spoke briefly into it in Afrikaans. A number of other men, presumably policemen, dressed in a mix of casual gear, with assorted weapons and equipment, now entered the room. One of them carried a green canvas bag like the one Geordie had been given at the mine in Taung, but with a wax seal now at the top.

After Estelle cleared the coffee cups and left the room, Captain De Klerk gathered everyone around the large table. He pulled out an assortment of maps, aerial photos and photographs of people.

"Gentlemen, this is Mr. McKay, he is going to help us. Now let's go over our plan and fit him into the picture. We leave in ten minutes so let's hurry."

"Maybe that is too rushed, Sir," the Sergeant persisted. "Why don't we wait longer, at least a few hours, to re-check our data?"

"Does the lioness giver her prey extra time when the pride is ready to strike, Sergeant?"

"No, Sir."

"And neither shall we, Sergeant. Chief Ferreira will be a happy man tomorrow morning when he sees our arrests. We are going into action, men. The time for discussion is over."

As his men re-checked their maps and equipment one last time, the Captain took Geordie to one side, where a first-aid kit lay open.

"Officer Sampz here will do a wiring and taping job on you while we go over your lines. You are to be the leading actor in our scene. Mr. McKay."

FIVE

The Friendly Plumber

As Geordie's taxi drove slowly up Houghton Road it stopped to let a van ahead of them pull into a driveway. Although his mind was racing in his attempts to remember all his lines, Geordie noticed the sign writing on the side of the van and looked back a second time as the taxi passed it. It was Mickey's plumbing van he thought, recognizing one of his Irish pals. Quite a short distance farther, the taxi stopped at the entrance to a large estate, with fancy iron gates adorned by eagle statues on either side.

"Here we are, Mr. McKay," shouted the driver. "You will need to speak to the security man inside the gate."

Geordie stepped out and walked slowly to the gate.

"Good evening," he said to the white man inside. "I'm here to see Mr. Botha."

"Is he expecting you? What time is your appointment?"

"Yes, he is expecting me, but not at any particular time." Geordie hesitated. "Just tell him Geordie McKay from Kimberley is here."

The man went back into the guardhouse to converse with a second man who picked up a phone and stood up, looking towards Geordie while speaking into the receiver. Although the evening was very warm both men wore jackets. Geordie shuddered to think what they had under those jackets.

The first security officer came back out.

"That's fine, sir. Walk through when I open the gate."

"Can I drive up in the taxi?" Geordie asked, showing his bandaged right ankle. "I had some trouble getting here and sprained it, can't walk much on it."

The man said nothing but went back into the guard house where he spoke again to his companion, then returned.

"Okay, sir, tell the taxi driver to stay in his car while he waits for you outside the house. Follow the driveway up to the right."

Geordie limped back to the taxi. They drove through the open gates and up the long driveway.

"Well done, Mr. McKay," officer Wyson complimented, smiling broadly as he drove the taxi, his white teeth shining from his black face. "Control said they heard your conversation loud and clear. Captain says keep it up, draw out the discussions with Botha to make him talk. Don't forget to unlatch the back of your seat so the men in the trunk of the car can slip out, and leave your door ajar. Here we are. Good luck, Mr. McKay."

Geordie adjusted his light sweater in an effort to make the listening device more comfortable. It made him feel hot. One of the policemen had lent it to him, at the insistence of the Captain, to cover the telltale wire marks under Geordie's shirt. The faked ankle injury had also accomplished its goal, even if the wrapping was so tight that it was actually painful.

The taxi pulled up just short of the front door, to reduce the amount of light it picked up from the porch. With brown briefcase in hand, Geordie limped up the steps and rang the bell. A few moments later the door was opened by a black servant girl.

"Good evening, *Baas*," she said, and showed Geordie into the large hallway. "Baas Botha is waiting for you. Follow me, please."

They walked down the main hallway, then made a left into another short hall. Geordie looked about at the big crystal chandelier that looked like Waterford, oriental rugs on the marble floor, oil paintings on the walls, carved wood and fancy furniture with many ivory ornaments sitting on top.

His limp was becoming so good that he looked like someone who really was hurt. The maid showed him into a huge room that was even more magnificently decorated than the hall. A man got up from a large desk at the far side of the room and came forward to meet Geordie.

"I am Botha," he said without smiling. "Elee, some tea for our guest, quickly."

"Yes, Baas."

Mr. Botha was a short portly man with old fashioned sideburns. His gray receding hairline displayed a tanned shiny scalp. He had a soft voice and a weak handshake, totally unlike the big rugged men at the mine. On the end of his nose sat a pair of bifocal, gold-rimmed glasses, over the top of which he glared out at his guest. Geordie took an instant dislike to the man.

"Please sit there, Mr. McKay," Botha said and pointed to a simple straight-backed chair facing the desk. Geordie hobbled over to the chair, while mentioning that he had a sprained ankle. Botha offered no sympathy, retreating to his own chair.

As Geordie sat down and put his briefcase on the floor beside him the maid came back in carrying a silver tray on which she had a silver teapot, two china cups and saucer, plus a silver sugar bowl, complete with silver tongs. She sat it down on the corner of the desk and poured two cups of the hot steaming tea. Without asking anyone, she poured milk in each. Then she put two cubes in one cup and sat it in front of Mr. Botha.

"No sugar for me," Geordie interrupted her as she reached again for the tongs.

"That will be all, Elee," Botha said. "Now go immediately to your room, we have business to discuss."

"Yes, *Baas* Botha. Good night, *Baas*," she addressed Geordie as she swept past him. "Good night, *Baas* Botha, Sir."

Geordie turned to look at the room and saw Elee leave by a swing door, probably through the kitchen. He also now realized that one of the jacket-clad security brigade had entered the room. The man closed the door behind him and walked forward to a point about twenty feet from the desk.

"Nice place you have here," Geordie remarked, as he sipped his tea. He had left the saucer on the table and held the cup between both hands, like one does on a cold morning. Geordie was not cold though, he was trying to calm himself and not show the nervous fear he felt in his stomach.

Mr. Botha opened the business discussion with an attempt at friendliness.

"I don't know you Mr. McKay, but I had a message that you are assisting us by delivering a gravel sample to me from the Olantsfontein mine at Taung. Is this correct?"

"Eh, yes, kind of," responded Geordie.

"I assume Meneer Van Rensburg sent a letter to me, along with the samples, right?"

"No, he didn't send any letter. Just this bag of diamonds."

"You mean samples, don't you, Mr. McKay. Let me have the samples please?"

Geordie put the briefcase on his knees and removed the green canvas bag, held it up, then put it back in the case.

Botha looked past Geordie, to his security guard, moved the glasses on his nose with obvious irritation, but managed to continue in the same tone of voice. "I'm a busy man Mr. McKay. Please don't play games with me. You will be paid for your help, once you give me my merchandise."

Geordie could hear the man behind him shifting his stance. Captain De Klerk's plan had not prepared him for this complication, so Geordie played for time and a way to convey a message through to his listeners. Standing up, he moved his chair to one side allowing him to see Botha and the guard without having to turn his head.

"I don't like having my back to people, it's not polite," Geordie said. "Mr. Botha, if you wish to have your associate here then he might as well join in the discussion."

"He is fine where he is, Mr. McKay," replied Botha sharply. "Now, give me my merchandise so that you can collect your reward and leave."

With that, Botha opened a briefcase on his desk and took out some American dollars.

"Here Mr. McKay. Five crisp hundred dollar bills. Now, off you go about your business."

"I—, I can't accept that Mr. Botha."

Botha removed the glasses now. He slapped his palms on the desk top.

"My patience is wearing thin Mr. McKay. I have a lot of important business to attend to. What exactly do you want from me, *Meneer*, in order for you to hand over my property?"

Geordie cleared his now dry throat in an effort to avoid his upcoming demand from disintegrating into a croak.

"How about ten thousand dollars Mr. Botha?"

"Ten thousand dollars!" Botha repeated, enraged. "*Meneer*, I don't have to give you one damn rand if I so choose. Instead of behaving like a grateful messenger and going off happy with your five hundred dollars, you come in here all high and mighty and demand a fortune. This is my property that you are trying to sell me and you have come onto my estate, alone, except for a Kaffir outside in a taxi. Don't make demands on me *Meneer* of I'll—."

Botha trailed off without finishing his threat, took a moment to compose himself, then continued. "Mr. McKay, why should I pay you ten thousand dollars for my merchandise when I can simply take it from you here and now?"

"Because—because I know that bag contains a fortune in diamonds, and I can forget I ever saw them or that I carried them out of the mine just before it was raided by police. If you were to harm me the taxi driver will report it, I told him I might be in danger here. You would have to deal with him then too, not to mention my attorney."

"Your attorney, Mr. McKay?" asked Botha with surprise.

"Yes. You see, I have left a very revealing letter with my attorney which he will pass to the police if I don't return safe and sound this evening."

Botha did not answer. He picked up the phone and dialed a number. Geordie listened intently as the man spoke into the receiver in Afrikaans. The word dollar was mentioned, as was Geordie's name and that of Smith.

Geordie seized the moment. "If you need to get your boss here to complete this deal, then bring him on."

"My associates don't think much of this stunt you are pulling, Mr. McKay. They will be—?"

Botha finished abruptly, leaving the rest of the sentence for Geordie's imagination. Instead, he opened the briefcase again, took out two bundles of green cash which he laid on the desk top.

"Here is your money, McKay," he hissed. "Now give me my samples."

Geordie was at a crossroads. He had to proceed in some form. He desperately wanted to buy time but he didn't know how. His move to pick up the cash was blocked by Botha.

"The bag first, McKay."

"How do I know there is ten thousand dollars in those bundles, Mr. Botha? I'd like to count them first."

"How do I know if the bag contains everything it's supposed to?" Botha retorted. "You can count your money while I check the merchandise."

Geordie fished out the bag and held it out towards Botha, while picking up the cash with his free hand. Botha grabbed the bag from his hand and began to examine the wax seal. Geordie thought he should in turn examine the money. The notes were dollars; twenties, fifties and hundreds. He was flipping though the first bundle, copying what he had seen mobsters do in movies, when he stole a glance at Botha.

Mr. Botha had opened the bag and was slowly tipping the contents onto a tray or a pan, which was on a side table behind the desk.

The ringing of the desktop telephone interrupted both men. Geordie waited for Botha to answer it before looking up. Botha was barking into it in obvious annoyance at being disturbed from his work. Then he fell silent and listened. Geordie looked away for a moment and when he looked back, the expression on Botha's face had changed dramatically. He could feel the anger being directed towards him from Botha's eyes. Despite this, Geordie forced himself to count the cash, inaccurately, but well enough to establish that the two bundles were each substantially shy of the five thousand expected.

When Botha put the phone down loudly, Geordie chose the moment to force the direction of conversation.

"Hey, Mr. Botha, you have shortchanged me here by two thousand in each bundle. That's four grand shy, pal. What's your game?"

"That's the least of your problems, *Meneer*," Botha shouted. "Van—, a trusted friend in high places has just told me that you are an imposter, McKay."

◆

The great Jo'burg skyline became bigger and bigger to the occupants of the white Mercedes, as it sped down the freeway from Pretoria. The older man checked his watch, then spoke.

"Call him again, Louis, I want to make sure he stalls things till we get there."

Louis tried, no answer. "That's strange. Usually security

answers, even when Botha will not. What do you make of it, Martin?"

"I think he's angry with us, that we are pushing in on his meeting. At least he will know from our earlier call to security that we are on our way."

"He should have told you earlier about this meeting, Martin," Louis pressed. "I don't think he should be handling these kinds of situations anymore. He's lost his nerve. This whole thing of using an outsider as messenger is the wrong plan. No matter what promise the messenger guy makes or what money he is paid, the fact is that he is a security risk. Van Rensburg should have done the job himself and to hell with the mine, it's gone now anyway and so is he. I think it's time for management changes."

"You are right about most of what you say," Martin answered, "and I know you want that job. Maybe the time has come for Botha to move over. Right now though, our priorities are to close all the loose ends, cut our losses and lay low. De Klerk is out to burst this whole thing open. But he can and will be muzzled, I have taken steps on this already."

"What about this messenger, McKay?" Louis asked.

"It depends what he knows. A quick purchase of some equipment from him might be fine, as long as he suspects nothing. We don't know if he went to Boer of not. If we can control him, fine. If not, then he may have to be removed."

♦

A strange silence followed Botha's accusation. Geordie stared him back, then stood up, facing the desk.

"Botha, that's the oldest trick in the book to get out of paying. I'm leaving with my merchandise and you can pay double later."

Botha's hand was now emerging from under the table and once Geordie glimpsed the metal he didn't second guess. He flung himself immediately at Botha, while the security guard behind him fumbled under his jacket. Geordie's superior size and weight floored his target in typical rugby fashion. Botha's gun was now in the grip of both men, with Geordie fighting to pin his victim in front of himself, as a shield. As they rolled on the floor, the gun fired into the ceiling.

"Shoot him Willy, shoot," Botha yelled.

Willy took aim, and just as all hell broke loose in the hallway, he fired. Geordie saw the flash, then saw the gunman turn his attention in that direction. Tightening his grip on Botha, he pulled him towards the nearest door, the one he had seen the maid exit earlier. The lights cut off, the sudden darkness disorientating Geordie. Botha was on the floor under him. He reached to get a better grip on his captive, only now hearing the man's choking throaty breathing. The sudden realization that Botha may have caught a bullet threw a panic into Geordie. He released his grip on the injured man, who crumpled onto the floor in a croaking, unmoving heap. Botha was probably dying, he thought but he couldn't help him and would go the same route himself if he didn't find a way to escape.

Now on his hands and knees Geordie made his way in the darkness towards the exit door as he remembered it. Something banged against his knees. Feeling its shape, he assumed it to be his briefcase and took it with him. A slight breeze blew on his face, he followed it till his head hit against a wooden door. It turned out to be a swing door and Geordie went through without hesitation, leaving the bedlam of the other room behind.

He figured he was in the kitchen and kept crawling in the direction of the breeze he felt on his face, hoping it would lead to the outside. He could hear gunfire somewhere round the front now also. Best to make for the safety of the back yard, he thought, as he exited through a screened door into the sticky night air that was now loaded with the smell of gunpowder. In the darkness Geordie stumbled and fell into some pungent flowering bushes. The ankle was really sore now. Time to get the damn bandages off. He was peeling off the layers when he heard the familiar voice. Van de Merwe was talking to another man as they came towards his hiding spot.

"It's no skin off my nose if Botha dies, he would turn any of us in if it saved his hide. You heard him almost tell on us before the shooting started. The boss is right. McKay must not get out of here alive either."

Before he heard this, Geordie had been in the process of getting up to go to them, but now gagged himself at the last moment. The noise got their attention just as their radio crackled into life. A voice called for immediate help after being hit. Van's companion responded to the man by name, saying he was on his way. Van shone his beam in a quick sweep around the bushes, before yielding to his companion's call.

In his hideout Geordie's shock numbed him for a few moments. Then, his flight button at full throttle, he rushed out of the bushes in a headlong run towards the back of the garden with bandages trailing behind him. Luckily, his course was obstacle free. As Geordie's eyes became accustomed to the darkness, he found a place farther back where he could jump over the fence from a tree branch on his side. In the next garden he remembered the bandages, the listening device, and the briefcase which he still held. The bandages had already fallen off somewhere and he ripped the remains of the wires from his waist. He thought about discarding the case too, changed his mind and pressed ahead through the next garden and the next and the next after that. Finally out of breath, he took stock of himself in the darkness, felt for wounds, thankfully finding none. Somehow he needed to find a way to get back to Anna's house. She would know what to do. Figuring he was now far enough away from the action, Geordie ventured up slowly towards a large house. Maybe he could pay someone to take him out of here, he thought. There were lots of emergency sirens in the distance and all the local dogs were now barking and howling.

Closer to the house, Geordie saw a wonderful sight. There in the driveway was Mickey Kelly's plumbing van that he had seen earlier. His bravery returned and he walked quickly towards the van, climbed in and sat in the passenger seat.

Many minutes passed and Geordie's anxiety levels rose with each one. Finally, Mickey emerged from the house followed by a middle-aged woman in a flimsy housecoat. Geordie could hear Mickey's voice from the open van.

"The water will be fine now Ma'am. I've got another job to get to."

"Won't you stay to check that it is hot enough for my bath?" the woman pleaded. "You look like such a friendly plumber to me that I want you to be my special friend."

"I'm sure it'll be fine Ma'am. I'll try to drop by later on to check on you again."

"Oh My! Listen to those terrible sirens down the street. It must be an A.N.C. attack or something. You simply must stay to protect me, with my husband being away for the next few days, please?"

Mickey looked like his resolve was wavering. Geordie intervened.

"Mickey, come one, we've got another job waiting!" Geordie shouted.

The startled woman rushed back into the house. Mickey cautiously approached the van.

"It's me, Geordie. Come one, for Christ's sake."

"Jasus! Geordie! You gave me a hell of a fright. You look terrible, are you hurt?"

"I'm fine now that I've found you. Can you be a friendly plumber to me and take me over to Anna's in your van, right now. I'll explain later."

"Sure, no problem," Mickey answered, smiling.

Moments later the van pulled onto Houghton Road. They were heading away from the Botha house, but soon saw a police checkpoint up ahead.

"I've got to hide, Mickey," Geordie shouted and began climbing into the back of the van.

"Lie down and pull that tarp over you," Mickey called out. "There are about six cars ahead of us in the line yet."

When the van got to the checkpoint the policeman shone his light in and asked for Mickey's license. Mickey showed him his plumber's card too.

"Have you seen anything suspicious along Houghton Road, Sir?" the policeman asked.

"Apart from all the sires and racket you fellas are making, nothing but a blocked u-bend officer," Mickey joked, "and I've another one waiting on me now."

"Carry on, Sir. Keep those pipes clear."

The policeman smiled and waved the van through.

SIX

Dutch Courage

At another checkpoint nearby, a white Mercedes pulled up at the back of the long line of cars. Louis and Martin looked at each other nervously.

"Louis, walk up ahead and find out what the deal is. I'll drive and keep trying Botha on the telephone."

Louis hurried up the street in his smart business suit. The car had moved only a hundred feet by the time Louis returned.

He sat in and shook his head.

"All I can find out, Martin, is that the police are having a shootout with some gang at a house farther up Houghton Road. I could not get an address but I don't like it. Any answer from Botha?"

"No. Seeing as they are diverting traffic off Houghton Road, we can't get to the house without the risk of arousing suspicion. My gut feeling is that something has happened at Botha's house, Louis, and we need to get the hell out of here. What do you think?"

"I agree. I told the officer that we were rushing to see a dying relative and that we would need to make a u-turn."

Martin nodded and swung the Mercedes round quickly and raced away.

◆

The plumber's van eased off Jan Smuts Avenue cautiously, stopping short of the house for a few moments. Geordie scanned the car parking area carefully. He saw Anna's car, his own, plus two others he recognized, and nothing suspicious.

"Pull up to the front of the house, Mickey. Wait till I come back out to you, I think I'll need another lift from you, please?"

"No problem mate. Take your time," Mickey replied.

"By the way, Mickey, you're on a plumbing call. If anyone suspicious, like police come by, blow the horn to warn me."

Mickey nodded as Geordie headed for the front door, Thankfully it was Anna who answered his knock.

"Oh Geordie, I've been so worried," she cried, as she threw her arms around him. Then she hesitated as she saw the state he was in.

"What in the world happened to you? Are you Hurt? How on earth did you get so dirty? Is that blood I see, Oh God?"

"I'm fine, Sweetie, honest."

"Let's get you into the shower, Sweetheart," she urged. "You can tell me all about it later. Here, let me carry your briefcase."

She herded him through the hallway and up the stairs to her room. As soon as he got there he pulled his small suitcase from under her bed.

"I nearly got killed tonight, Anna. The police, who are supposed to be on my side, are in fact rotten and all on the take."

"What!"

"I'll just wash here at the sink so I can save time and tell you the whole story."

He ran the hot tap as she got him a washcloth and towel.

"The Captain cornered me into going through with his plan, to act as the courier and do the drop at the place in Houghton. I went along with it in the expectation that it was going to be quick and simple. He told me of a sizeable reward to be had from DeBeer's, which sounded like easy money. The police took me to the contact man's house, the fella called Botha. I even had a listening device taped on me. I played the part great and was getting lots of recorded evidence for them to use in court. Then Botha received a telephone call. He said an informant called Van, Sergeant Van de Merwe I think, told him I was a fake and then he pulled a gun out of a drawer. I rushed him and all hell broke loose.

Botha got shot by his own man who was trying to shoot me. The lights went out and the police began to break down the door. I just grabbed the briefcase and escaped through the kitchen to get out of the line of fire, with the intention of rejoining the police later. Then, when I was hiding in some bushes I overheard Van de Merwe telling another man that his boss, who as you know is the Captain, had given them instructions that me and Botha were both to be killed in the raid. That's when I decided to get the hell outa there."

Geordie's body shook and he dropped his wash towel.

"Let me sponge you down, Sweetheart, while you continue the story," Anna said softly.

"That bloody Sergeant and his Captain must be in on this. His men or someone else cut off the lights, and bullets flew everywhere. They got Botha all right, poor bastard. There was a hell of a gunbattle going on behind me as I ran from garden to garden. Eventually I found myself in the back of a house where Mickey Kelly's plumbing van was parked. He was on a repair job, thank God. Mickey drove me out through a police cordon in the plumbing van and me under a tarpaulin in the back. He's outside now waiting for me. Christ, Anna, I came within inches of being killed."

He sobbed now as the realization of the facts sunk in. She soothed him as she finished washing down her naked, crying Geordie. Then she gently towelled him dry.

"What do I do now?" he asked. I can't stay around Jo'burg, that's for sure. I've got both police and the thugs after me."

"I know Mr. Goldstein will help us straighten out this new mess but we have to keep you safe till that can be done. You could go down to my parents' place in The Free State perhaps, or go to Cape Town early."

"Maybe I'm not safe anywhere in South Africa. This thing is big, Anna. You should have seen all the money these guys had on the table, I would rather be out of here till the dust settles."

"But it's very costly to fly out of this country just like that, and where would you go?"

By now he had a shirt on and was stepping into a pair of dark pants.

"Remember, I've got a return ticket to Ireland that I can use any time. And in the confusion I grabbed Botha's briefcase instead of mine. I don't even know how or why I took it but it's full of American dollars, which I feel are due me for risking my life there. The police will have the ten thousand Botha took out of it and they will have their diamonds back once they finish sweeping the floor."

Anna pulled out the case as Geordie put on his shoes, laid it on the bed and unlatched it.

"God Almighty!"

They both stared in amazement into the case at the neat bundles of dollar bills.

"See what I mean, Anna! This thing is huge. There's thousands and thousands in that case. I've got to get out of here and fast."

From downstairs someone was calling Anna's name for an urgent telephone call.

"Thanks, Peter, I'll be right down," Anna responded.

Geordie stood at the door listening, as she answered the phone.

"Yes, this is Anna Terblanche. Yes, Captain De Klerk, I remember you. No, I haven't seen him. Isn't he with you? What do you mean you have lost him? Okay, I'll be waiting on your call in five minutes."

By the time she got back to the room Geordie had the briefcase closed again and was packing the last of his clothes in the suitcase.

"I heard all I need to hear. It's just as I suspected. There's no choice. We've got to get out of here fast."

"The Captain is calling me back in five minutes. He'll be immediately suspicious if I'm not here to take the call. I need to stay here and hold the fort. You said Mickey is outside in the van. He'll take you to the airport. There may well be police on their way here already. I'll string them along into thinking that you will come back here and give you more time to get away. Write down an address in Ireland where I can contact you."

Anna sobbed as he wrote down the details.

"This is my friend Joe, in Galway. I'm putting G.M.K. after his name as a code, rather than doing care-of. He will know to keep anything for me that has these initials after his name. Let's do the same for you here.

Anna wrote down her friend Liz's address followed by the initials A.N.T.

"You remember Liz. She lives just up the road from here.

This is her phone number too. Call me as soon as you can just to say you're okay. I'll be at Liz's Sunday evening in case you can't call before then. Oh Geordie, this is terrible."

"I don't know how this is going to pan out, Sweetie, but we mustn't lose each other through this, no matter what," Geordie responded.

They hugged, kissed and sobbed for a few moments against each other.

"Don't say good bye Geordie, don't say it. Just go, now. Be careful. Leave all those dirty clothes here, I'll hide them and have them laundered later. Please go. Hurry."

One final hug and she pushed him towards the door. A moment later he was gone and she listened to the van pull away while tears ran down her cheeks.

Geordie didn't go into any details with Mickey about his predicament during the ride to the airport, not out of any mistrust, he just didn't want to put his friend in any danger.

"When does Tom finish that construction job in Durban, Mickey?"

"Today or tomorrow, I think. Then he's staying on there for the weekend 'craic', you know how Tom is."

"When he gets back tell him I've had to leave town for a while. Make sure one of you contacts Anna in the next few days, she may need your help and support while I'm away."

"Consider it done."

As they rode on, Geordie felt again for his passport and

wallet. They reached the international departures area without incident, before Mickey spoke.

"Seeing as you're going back home, Geordie, I'd better come in and have a drink with you and see you off."

"No Mickey, I can't this time. Have a drink for me in Rosebank on the way back."

"Well then, put it there and good luck."

They shook hands warmly. Geordie gave his pal a big hug too, before he left.

"Thanks a million, Mickey. You saved my life tonight. I'll be back before you know it. Keep everything hush-hush about tonight, all right?"

The British Airways ticket counter was one of the first Geordie saw, and he rushed over to speak with the girl on duty there.

"What time does the London flight leave please?"

"Sorry Sir, all our U.K. flights have gone a little while ago. Tomorrow evening before the next ones. Were you booked to fly this evening, Sir?"

"No, but I've got to get over there tonight. Are there any other possibilities, Miss? I've got an open return ticket here in my passport."

"Unless you have an emergency, sir, or we have messed you up I can't put you with another carrier. Even then the choice would only be to the Continent."

"I have an emergency, Miss," he lied. "My, my mother had a stroke today. They called me from home a while ago. I came straight here from work. Please, Miss, please sort something out for me? I only need to get to London, that's where she is."

"I'm sorry to hear about your mum, Sir. We are supposed to have a letter from a doctor or a hospital."

"Please Miss, I'll get that to you later, please?"

She pressed some keys on the computer and waited. Geordie struggled to remain calm while the machine bleeped and squawked.

"Let me see your ticket and I'll try for you. Mr. McKay, the computer is showing that I could get you into Amsterdam on KLM, with a British Airways connection to London, without making any changes in ticket cost."

"Yes, Yes. That'll be fine. Thank you, Miss. You're an angel."

"You'll have to run for it, they are getting ready to leave. Pop these tags on and carry your bags through as hand luggage. I'll call the gate to tell them you are coming. Straight down that way to A6, Mr. McKay, and hurry. I hope your mum gets better soon. Don't forget the letter, to any British Airways office."

"Thank you again, Miss," Geordie answered sheepishly and hurried away. He knew his mother would give him a thick ear for that lie.

A half-hour later Geordie was airborne above Jo'burg and away from all the dangers it now held for him. His travelling companion was an elderly Dutch lady who couldn't speak a word of English. Thank God, he thought. The flight was wonderful. He ate and drank everything they brought to him and he even watched a Robert Redford movie in Dutch. Countless times Geordie had to look at the flight magazine and rejoice at the distance that was steadily being put between him and Jo'burg on that curved line representing the flight path to Amsterdam. At some stage he fell asleep and awoke with a start as they touched down. The old lady smiled benignly at him as she pointed through the window into the early morning mist.

"Amsterdam," she said proudly.

His stomach began to knot again as he struggled to figure out what he should do in the airport. Here he was in one of the drug capitals of the world with a case full of American dollars and the strong possibility that the police were waiting for him. He didn't think he had done anything wrong by running, but he wasn't sure. Carrying money into another country like he was doing, was probably an offence for sure, he thought. Did he have to go through customs here or not? His palms were sweating and he couldn't think. Why didn't he tell the British Airways girl a Dublin destination instead of London? Assuming he got through Amsterdam okay then he had to face the authorities in London, and with the Northern Ireland troubles Irish people were heavily scrutinized there.

His thoughts were interrupted by the old Dutch lady, who was talking to him again. Eventually he got the message that she was stiff after the long flight. She needed some help getting up and walking out of the plane. Yes, of course, he would help her. It then suddenly dawned on him. Yes, he would help her all the way through passport control or whatever else they had to go through. She took his arm and off they went. A stewardess interpreted the old lady's words for Geordie as they left the plane. Her son was meeting her. Geordie found out that he needed to follow the signs for transit passengers for his connecting London flight, and he could go through customs and passport control there. He noticed some officious looking gentlemen around the gate area, so he kept his head down and nodded in understanding as 'grandma' talked on. He took her to the passport control queue, then doubled back quickly to the transit area so that he kept with his crowd.

On the departures board he noticed that British Airways had a Dublin connection also and approached the nearby B.A. desk.

"How can I help you, Sir?" the lady asked, in English.

"Miss, I've just realized that they messed up my ticket in the rush in Jo'burg. They have me connecting into London instead of Dublin. Can you correct it for me?"

"I'm sorry for the mistake, sir. We should be able to help you and I know there is room on the Dublin flight but we haven't much time. Of course, your luggage will go to London, sir."

"No Miss, I have it here. I carried it on as I was in such a rush."

"Great." Viewing his ticket, she went on. "Let me see now, Mr. McKay. The Dublin flight leaves in fifteen minutes. You should easily be able to get across to it in time, but don't delay. There is a slight difference in cost but we won't worry about that, seeing as we messed you up. Here is your Dublin boarding pass, and thank you for flying British Airways."

"You're welcome, indeed. Thanks a million, Miss."

Once in route to Dublin Geordie was able to relax a little. Only one more leg in the journey to go, he thought as he savored his gin and tonic. He bought a bottle of duty free whiskey for his friend Joe and some perfume for his mother.

In Dublin he was much more confident at the passport control counter. The examining officer asked him about his visit and he trotted out the lie again, even more smoothly. The man sent him on his way with a wish and a prayer for his mother's speedy recovery! A female customs agent called him to one side as he walked through the green section. His heart sank at the fear of being caught at the last hurdle, but he managed to keep his cool and smiled sweetly at her. She was only interested in the contents of the duty free carrier bag that he had been given on the plane and moments later he was on his way.

As he exited the control area, into the crowds waiting to greet their returning loved ones, Geordie had to fight the urge to shout out with delight and relief. Once in his rental car and on his way he could hold it no longer. He let out a massive 'Yah-Hoo' into the cold Dublin November air.

SEVEN

The Aftermath

Captain De Klerk had never been as angry in front of his men. The entire sting had been a disaster. Mr. Botha and another man were dead, two of his own men had been seriously wounded and on top of all that Geordie McKay had apparently disappeared into thin air. Clean-up operations were in full swing, covering a mile radius from the site. In order to get all this extra manpower the Captain had to call Chief Ferreira for authorization and now had to contend with him too, as if he didn't have enough on his plate.

A preliminary investigation had already begun, to piece together the chain of events that led to the disintegration of the Captain's carefully laid plans. Technicians were at work trying to recover the missing parts of the taped discussion between McKay and Botha before the firing erupted. He himself had been listening to the whole thing from the control van down the street when the quality of reception deteriorated. The telephone call to Botha was the spark but there was no way to retrieve that unless Botha was recording his own calls. To the Captain's own ears Botha told McKay that an informer named Van fingered him as an imposter. Others disagreed with him on what actual words were said and it was not very important right now other than it gave the Captain a bad feeling about Van de Merwe. There were millions of people called Van in South Africa, assuming that is what the dead man said. McKay was the only person alive who could clear up that question. The gun found beside the body belonged to Botha and had only fired one bullet, and that was into the ceiling. An educated guess had Botha reaching for the gun at the time he was tackled by McKay. The dead bodyguard may well have shot his own boss by mistake while trying to shoot McKay. Ballistics tests would reveal that in due course. The four-man assault team led by Van should have been in a better position to act quicker and help McKay when the sudden crisis occurred. Officer Wyson was in the hospital and both Van's and Boote's explanations came up short in the Captain's mind. Indeed the back up team led by the Captain himself had considerable difficulty in gaining entry to the estate, losing valuable time in a shootout with the gatehouse security guards.

He was pretty sure McKay had run in panic and would come forward soon. Maybe calling Miss Terblanche on the phone was a mistake but that was the obvious place for the boy to make for. His men had her house under surveillance and were to call in as soon as McKay showed up there. The Chief had been surprisingly nice about the whole debacle, had even called him twice and offered more help if needed. No doubt that attitude would change as the facts of the evening came to light. One thing was sure in his mind, Van de Merwe had to be dropped from this case immediately, whether the Chief liked it or not. It was not beyond the realm of possibility that Van or someone else involved in the case was indeed an informant. For now the Captain decided to keep these suspicions to himself and seek to placate the Chief in the face of the expected criticism of his handling of the operation.

◆

Cleaning up and removing all traces of Geordie's visit kept Anna busy and her mind occupied for a while after he left. Once she was satisfied with the room she joined her housemates watching television. With the house being so big, the earlier commotion in her room hadn't drawn any attention. She forgot that Thursday was 'Dallas' night so everybody was engrossed in the American soap opera series, hardly noticing her entrance.

But tonight, J.R. and company couldn't seduce Anna. She made tea and took it to her room, to the welcome darkness.

Her head was full of questions.

Where was Geordie now? Did he get away all right? Should she call the airport? What about calling Mr. Goldstein or Captain De Klerk?

The noise of a car in the driveway caught her attention. She could see no lights. It cruised around the side where Geordie's car was parked. A flashlight beam was shone on the number plate and into the vehicle. Nobody got out and she couldn't see much with the outside house lights being off. She thought about turning them on but decided against it. The car went back out the driveway but not all the way into the street. All Anna knew for sure was that there was no police insignia on it, but it was them, she just knew it. What if someone called the police about a prowler? Peter would call if she asked him. No, it would just give them a perfect excuse to come snooping around and could easily upset her housemates. She mused about the contradiction of sharing her day to day living with people while not having a close relationship with them. The commune had to be kept out of this affair.

She resisted the urge to make any telephone calls in case the line was being monitored. She'd just go to work as usual the next day and arouse no suspicions.

◆

The Chief walked into the Captain's office at 6 A.M., to his obvious surprise.

"Morning Captain. I won't use the word 'good'."

"You're in early, Sir."

"Have you seen this morning's paper, Captain? The Press make us sound like bumbling idiots."

"I haven't seen it, Sir. I wouldn't have read it even if I had the time. All they want is sensationalism and they were upset with us because we kept them back so far from the scene last night."

"The Cabinet politicians that I have to answer to, do read it, and will drag me over the coals. Tell me in detail exactly what happened so that I can at least defend you if they get nasty about it."

The Captain painfully recounted the sequence of events, citing simple bad luck as their main downfall. Contributing factors were; McKay's wire problems resulting in patchy recordings, his men's uncertainty till they heard shots, the power outage and his own problems gaining access to the property. No doubt there would be a row later about the demolition of the main gate and the near wrecking of the big police van in the process, but for now he left that out. His suspicion of Van de Merwe's actions and the disputed mention of his name by Botha were also omitted.

McKay's disappearance seemed to anger the Chief more than the deaths of two civilians and the wounding of two of his officers. He insisted that the search area be widened and even argued that McKay's running away constituted a crime, thus necessitating that he be hunted down like a regular criminal.

The fact that the stones and ten thousand dollars were recovered at the scene did not have the expected pacifying effect on his boss, so the Captain took the lashes till the Chief burned himself out. Yes, he would watch bus and train terminals and the airport and report personally on the search progress later in the day or with any breakthroughs, as they occurred.

◆

In the morning there was no sign of the watchers, despite Anna's searching looks. The newspapers covered the story of the previous night with a few paragraphs on the inside pages under the heading,— 'Two dead In Botched Diamond Bust'—. No names were given and there were no details like those Geordie had described. Just routine press coverage, but highly critical of the police performance.

Mr. Goldstein was already in his office when Anna arrived.

"Good morning, Anna," he spoke as she entered the main hallway.

"Morning Sir. How did you know it was me?"

"Nobody else arrives at seven-fifteen," he said.

She was startled a little by the sight of him in his court robes.

"Oh, I completely forgot about the Krugersdorp case being up today. Do you have everything you need?"

"Yes. I'm reading through what you typed yesterday. I'll be finished in a few minutes."

Anna busied herself making coffee and was pouring out two mugs when Mr. Goldstein walked into the kitchenette.

"It sure smells good in here, Anna."

He sat at the small table and reached for one of the mugs. Anna took the cue and sat too. Both drank silently for a moment. She wanted to speak but held back, more from habit and respect. He opened the conversation.

"From what I saw in the paper the police operation didn't go well. Is Geordie okay?"

"Yes, but I'm so worried that I can't see straight. He's lucky to be alive."

Anna struggled to remain composed.

"Where is he now?"

"I don't know, hiding somewhere. He said the police tried to kill him during the raid. What's happening Mr. Goldstein? This has turned into some kind of nightmare."

"I'll call Captain De Klerk just now and see if he can give you some answers. Geordie shouldn't be running, he has nothing to run from. What is he going to do next? Can you tell me any more?"

"He understands all that, but when he sees that both sides are after him logic goes out the window. I feel responsible for putting him in danger."

"You and me both. But I'm sure we can resolve this quickly and safely. Let's hear what the Captain has to say first. With me being in court today there isn't a lot for you to do here. Take the day off, it's Friday anyway."

"I was planning to get our files updated while you were out and I need something to keep my mind occupied. I'll stay till lunchtime anyway, thanks."

"It's after seven-thirty now. Let's try the Captain from my office, follow me," Mr. Goldstein said, leading the way.

The Captain was in and the call was put straight through. He was in a foul mood.

"Morning Captain, Harold Goldstein here. I've got Anna Terblanche, Geordie McKay's girlfriend, sitting here in my office. Can you give us an update on the events of last night?"

"Hello, Mr. Goldstein. Yes, I'll be happy to update you both. Investigations are continuing so I'm not at liberty to go into great detail. My men had everything under control until forced into a confrontation by a turn of events that resulted in two of my men being seriously wounded and two civilians being killed. A number of arrests were made and follow-up operations are now in progress. Mr. McKay disappeared during the confrontation. It is imperative that he comes forward immediately to clear up any suspicions surrounding his disappearance. Does Miss Terblanche know where he is at present?"

"Thank you, Captain. She doesn't know Geordie's whereabouts, either. I have you on speaker phone so we can all speak."

"Anna here, Captain De Klerk. He has called me. Out of pure luck he was not hurt in the gunbattle. Yes he did run, he ran for his life. You should not have put him in the line of fire like that Captain. As far as we are concerned, the police actions were dangerous. Geordie was used like fishing bait which can be devoured or discarded once it has served its purpose. We are angry and have lost our trust in your police until you prove to us that you can be trusted."

"I understand your feelings, Miss Terblanche. First of all let me say that I'm very glad that Geordie did not get hurt. I'm a father as well as being a police officer, I have a son close to his age. Obviously things did not turn out the way we planned. An internal assessment of the procedures used is now taking place and I can assure you that action will be taken against anyone who violated our set rules for this type of operation. However, that doesn't change the fact that I need Geordie to come forward. I will personally guarantee his safety."

"As I told you earlier, I don't know where he is and I'm not sure when I'll hear from him next. People will be coming into work here any minute, Captain, so I must go."

"Can you come to my office today Miss Terblanche and I'll explain to you in detail how he can come forward in safety? I would also like the opportunity to regain your trust. What time suits you?"

"Well, I suppose it wouldn't do any harm to hear what you have to say and Mr. Goldstein has kindly given me some time off today. Two o'clock if that's okay with you."

"Two it is. Goodbye, Miss Terblanche, Mr. Goldstein."

After the Captain was gone, Anna turned to Mr. Goldstein.

"What did you make of all that, Mr. Goldstein?"

"I think the Captain sounds sincere. In fact I know he is a sincere and honest man. His men got carried away during the raid, they didn't mean any harm to befall Geordie. If the Captain says he can guarantee his safety on coming forward, then we've got to at least look at it. He can't hide for long and the diamond smugglers will be after him also, to recover their money and merchandise. My son Mervin works in the diamond business. It is a strange and tightly knit world, believe me, and that's the legitimate one. Where do you think Geordie will go?"

"I think he'll go where he knows best. He said he was going back home to Ireland."

"All his folks live there don't they? What part of the country is he from? Have you been over there with him?"

"No, I've never been there. We've talked about going, that's all. It's supposed to be beautiful. His family live on the west coast near some spectacular bay. Geordie often sings about it when he gets going, at one of the Irish parties with his friends."

"That's probably Galway Bay then, County Galway."

"I'm sure that's it. Have you ever been there yourself?"

"Yes I have and it is indeed lovely. We had a wonderful holiday there some years ago. Great people, great scenery, beautiful old castles. You should go when you get the chance. Of course, it is not hot and sunny like here, more like a damp cool Cape climate. But it definitely is a wonderful country well worth visiting. Gosh, look at the time. I went off on a tangent there. I had better make tracks for the Krugersdorp courthouse. Are you going to tell the Captain where Geordie is going?"

"Not today at least. I'm very confused about everything and I really don't trust the police right now. This weekend I need to figure it all out and get my head straight. I wish Geordie had never got caught up in this Kimberley mine stuff."

"Don't we all," Mr. Goldstein added softly.

A few minutes later he was gone, leaving Anna to her own thoughts and her cold coffee. Her co-workers began to arrive and at least managed to divert her attention with the usual office banter. Then she busied herself with work, taking advantage of Mr. Goldstein's absence to get his office and files tidied up. The receptionist took Mr. Goldstein's messages except where clients needed something specific. About eleven she buzzed Anna, asking her to speak to a man who had called three times.

"Hello, Mr. Goldstein's office," Anna spoke, into the phone.

"I'm looking for Goldstein. Where the hell is he?" a man answered.

"This is his secretary. Mr. Goldstein is in court all day. Can I help?"

"What's your name?"

"Anna Terblanche."

"I'll just call him back later."

The caller hung up without giving Anna the chance to respond. Moments later the phone rang again.

"Overseas call, Anna," the receptionist told her.

It was Geordie's voice. "Anna is that you?"

"Geordie! How are you, where are you? It's so good to hear your voice."

"I'm in Ireland. I'm fine. How are you doing?"

"I'm fine now, knowing you're okay. Hang on a second while I close the door. You couldn't have called at a better time. Mr. Goldstein is in court all day. I'm just tidying the place up before I leave at lunchtime. He gave me the rest of the day off. It's a lot safer calling me here than at the house. Tell me everything that happened after you left yesterday."

"Before I get to that, write down this number. I'll be staying with Joe, my old college pal in Galway City, from Saturday night on."

He called out the numbers and Anna wrote them down.

"I've got that, Geordie. Now go on with your story."

"Well, I spun a yarn to the British Airways girl at Jo'burg airport and she got me on a KLM flight to Amsterdam, where

I picked up a British Airways connection to Dublin. I had some hairy moments with customs, you know, with that briefcase and all, but everything went smoothly in the end. I'm safe but I'm worried about you and I don't think I did the right thing leaving you behind."

"I'll be fine and we'll get this sorted out quickly. By the way, the Daily Mail carried a story on the Houghton raid. Very vague. Two dead, two wounded. Captain De Klerk spoke to me on the phone this morning. He is pissed with you, thinks you ran out on him. How dare he? I gave him a piece of my mind. Anyway, he then changed his tune a bit and asked to meet with me this afternoon to discuss how you could be protected in any deal, and he thinks he can restore our trust in the police. Don't worry, I didn't tell him where you went and I won't."

"Good. I don't trust any of them after what happened but I suppose we'll have to cut a deal at some stage."

"All I'm going to do for now is hear what he has to say and try to figure out who is what in the puzzle."

"Don't let Van de Merwe be at your meeting. He's definitely in my bad books after what he tried."

"I'll meet only with the Captain, and even then, with a lot of suspicion of him. Take good care of yourself, Darling, I'm missing you already."

"Likewise, Sweetheart. You must be very careful and be on your guard. Don't hesitate to call Tom or Mickey if you need anything. I love you."

"Love you, too. Bye."

"Bye-bye."

◆

Anna finished her work in short order, tidied her own office and left. Now that she knew Geordie was safe, she was happy. She had plenty of time before her meeting and decided to treat herself to lunch at a Hyde Park deli on the way home. Earlier in the morning she hadn't been able to eat but now she was ravenous. Her mind was clear and focused as she drove home to freshen up ahead of her show-down with the Captain.

The maid came into the hall when she heard Anna walk in.

"What is it, Muti, you look upset?" Anna asked.

"Yes, Miss. Some policemen came. I had to show them your room, Miss. They made a mess searching it. I have cleaned up since they left. They asked me about Mr. Geordie and gave me this number to call if I saw him here. They opened his car also, Miss. There was nothing I could do."

"Thank you, Muti. Let me have that piece of paper and I will check into it. How many were there and did they wear uniforms?"

"No uniforms, Miss, but they wore guns. There were two, two big men, white men, Miss. They asked me for my passbook first, then about you. Their car had no signs on it but they were police for sure. Here is the number they gave me and the registration number which I took off their car."

The room looked fine at first glance. Muti had folded her clothes and tidied as best she could. However, once Anna checked drawers and the wardrobe she could tell immediately that the room had been disturbed. Nothing was missing as far as Anna could determine but that did little to abate her anger over this invasion of her privacy. The Captain would feel the brunt of her anger later.

The key to Geordie's car was gone. She went out to check the vehicle herself. Some stuff was pulled out of the glove compartment and the trunk was left open. The key was thrown on the driver's seat, with the door still open. Muti said that as far as she could tell the men took nothing from the car.

Back upstairs, Anna touched up her make-up tearfully. The bastards had even gone through her underwear. She felt violated and couldn't wear anything they had handled till it was washed and ironed again. She found an outfit that was still unopened from the dry cleaners and wore that. Muti offered to stay longer to rewash and iron the clothes.

Armed with the crumpled piece of paper and her pent-up anger, Anna drove out onto Jan Smuts Avenue. Captain De Klerk at Jeppe police station was going to see a different side of Anna Terblanche today and feel the lashes from her tongue.

EIGHT

The Auld Sad

Geordie was the first to admit it, he was greatly relieved at being back in Ireland. After calling Anna at her office, he had made a beeline from Dublin airport for the West Coast in his rented car. Once he cleared the Dublin city limits he began to enjoy the ride. Even for November, the countryside looked good. Must have been a damp year, he thought.

Flicking through the radio channels, Geordie recognized the voices, the shows and even the adverts. It was as if Ireland had stood still while he had been away. He could picture the typical conversation that would occur if he walked into one of his local village pubs and found himself sitting with any of the farmers at the bar. After the usual mandatory weather talk, the next question would be obvious.

"Where are you now, Geordie?"

Geordie's answer of Africa wouldn't raise an eyebrow higher than if he named a local town fifty miles away. They might mention something about it being hot there, or ask if he sees Father Kenny often, as he is with the missions there. Geordie would promise to keep an eye out for him, rather than risk embarassing them by trying to explain the vastness of the African continent and the fact that Africa doesn't have large settled Irish communities like they do in London or Manchester. If an immigrant returned from Mars and was daft enough to discuss it on the bar stool, some smart aleck would know someone who had been there first and probably married into money there.

The frequent road signs for ancient castles and battle sites flashed images into Geordie's brain. Bodenstown, where Wolfe Tone is buried. Hill of Tara where the ancient high kings of Ireland sat. The River Boyne, where the decisive battle was lost by seventeenth century Catholics and which was still today at the heart of the hatred that was causing endless misery to the entire island and shaming Ireland before the television screens of the world.

The rental car wound its way through little towns whose streets were built for donkey and cart traffic, not for lines of cars and massive juggernaut trucks rushing products to the markets of Paris or Brussels. Geordie had a weakness for horse racing when he had lived in Ireland. In the Curragh, Ireland's thoroughbred horse country, he stopped to watch the stable boys riding out their horses in groups of three, their hot breaths steaming the frosty morning air, within a stone's throw of the highway. Memories of the Galway Races held every summer, flooded back. Long crowded bar counters with pints of stout lined on top, ten deep, and thirsty punters ten deep in front of them, consuming the pints as fast as they could be pulled.

Geordie had arrived into Athlone, a town in the center of Ireland, straddling the great river Shannon which splits the Irish plains. All this nostalgia had got to him, he needed some air and refreshment. A brisk walk along the riverfront put an edge on his thirst. The Bridge Pub looked too inviting to pass, especially when it started to drizzle. It gladdened his heart to see a dozen or so customers sitting at a bar with big black pints of stout in front of them. Taking his place among them he quickly sucked down the first one.

The old man sitting next to Geordie spoke.

"If you'd written your initials on the cream of that pint son, you'd still be able to read them, you drank it so quick."

"I've ridden a long way for that black beauty."

"Amerikay?"

"No, Africa."

"You're not a priest, are you?"

"I'm not indeed, but I'll take that as a compliment."

"The clergy can be very fond of their porter," the man continued. "A fella told me it's because the creamy head reminds them of the bishops collar. He might be right."

"You don't say."

Geordie endured more stimulating conversation from this 'boodan' in order to sink a few more pints. The drive later through the central bogs would be wet and foggy, but this tourist was happy, happy to forget his recent ordeal for a few hours and enjoy the peace and tranquility of the 'auld sod'.

Geordie's mother got a frightful surprise when he walked in that afternoon, and more out of habit than suspicion, had asked if there was anything wrong. There was absolutely no need to worry the old lady with his trouble so he had concocted a suitable alibi.

"Mother, the company sent me over to check out some machinery applications here and in England. I'm looking at what modifications would make them more useful for the Southern African market. I didn't call, because I wanted to surprise you."

"Well, I'm glad you're finally doing something that's connected with your engineering background rather than just being a travelling salesman. I hate telling people than you're a traveller for machinery, with all the education you have. Your poor father would turn in his grave if he knew. At least I can tell Delia something better the next time I meet her and she will spread the word of your promotion. She always asks about you, with you having been a classmate of her Seamus."

"Let's not get into the old argument again about wasted education. Sales is where it's at in today's world, Mother. I would have rotted in that cement factory waiting to rise to senior engineer. It would have taken fifteen or twenty years. This present assignment is not a promotion or a total deviation away from sales and it's supposed to be a secret. Look, if you want to tell Delia or her teacher son Seamus something to make them choke on, tell them this. Yes I have been promoted, I'm 'An International Entrepreneur and Industrialist', requiring regular travel between the major capitals of the world. That'll shut them up for a while. By the way, Mother, I want you to keep it quiet about me being over here. If anyone calls asking my whereabouts just say I am travelling overseas on business, okay?"

"You and your big words and big ideas, Geordie. I hope Delia doesn't swallow her false teeth trying to repeat that story. Now, let me make some tea and a sandwich for you, if I knew you were corning I'd have made something special for you."

Geordie stayed overnight, leaving supposedly for England the next morning but actually for Galway City to stay with his pal, Joe. It was only sixty miles away but in Ireland that's a lot and his mother never went there, so he might as well be in London. It was a perfect hideout.

He was looking forward to the scenic drive to Galway. The trip took him along the shore of the massive Lough Corrib, with the mountains in the distance on all sides. It was an unseasonably mild Irish day for November with occasional sunshine. Even though he had seen them a thousand times he had to stop often and get out to enjoy the sights. He wished Anna was there, he would have to bring her someday, soon. The cloud and mist, mixed with the sunlight made for some real picture postcard scenes. Geordie had often in the past tried to capture it on film, but it was illusive.

Later, he was stopped at one of these special viewing spots when the two elderly American tourists joined him. Leaning against the car Geordie marvelled at the pockets of sunlight racing from mountain to mountain as the clouds and mist shifted. They spoke to each other briefly, then stood side by side enjoying the scenery.

"We're surprised to see an Irishman doing what us tourists do," the Yank observed.

"One can never get enough of this," Geordie replied. "So many of us are only visitors here now, having to live and work overseas. The great tragedy of modern Ireland is her inability to provide for her young and growing population. When we make it back we have to fill up on her natural beauty, I don't know how else to explain it."

They all gazed out on the tranquil water at the numerous islands.

"Gosh, Eva, I can see the ruins of a castle over on one of those islands. Here, take a look with the binoculars."

As the woman struggled to line herself up and move her plastic rainhood out of the way, the old man spoke to Geordie again.

"You know, we've had such a good time on this trip, all

unplanned, that we're thinking of staying on a bit longer. Where would you, as a native, suggest we visit?"

"Tell me where you've been to date," replied Geordie.

"We flew into Shannon and had a helluva time to get used to this little car and driving on the left. After seeing these cute little roads and the price of gas I'm sure glad I'm not driving my Lincoln here. Anyway, we did the Ring of Kerry first. It was great but so full of Americans on tour buses, I was half expecting to run into someone I knew. Next we took in the Rock of Cashel and Limerick city, and of course the cliffs of Moher. After that we weren't sure, so we decided to continue up the west coast and just wander about. I'd sure appreciate any suggestions you might have."

Geordie thought about it for a moment before replying.

"You've done the standard tourist bit to date, but luckily you've found the real Ireland now. It's not as well marked out so you'll have to work at it. Don't just drive the coast roads. Cut inland like you have here, for example, drive over those mountains there on your way to Connemara. We get no snow here and not much frost till after Christmas, so the mountain roads are no problem and they're all paved. Zig-zag your way up through Galway, Mayo, Sligo and all the way to Donegal if you've got the time. You'll see the best combination of scenery that way. Don't stop to eat at hotels where you see tour buses, go instead to small pubs and if possible, develop a taste for the black stout, Guinness of Murphy's. Ask and you shall receive, you're in the friendliest country in the world."

"Thank you very much. I'm Marv Donohoo by the way, this is my wife Eva."

"Geordie McKay."

After the couple went on their way, Geordie stayed on a while, engrossed in the scene, till a shower of rain forced him back into the car.

While sitting there, the brown briefcase caught his eye, poking out from behind the seat. The first thing Geordie needed to do in Galway was to put the money in a safe place. At his mother's house he had finally had a chance to count it. One hundred and eighty thousand dollars! Here he sat in the rain in his car at a picturesque picnic stop in Galway, looking at it again. He had borrowed a canvas hold-all from his mother with the intention of putting the money in it and dumping the briefcase. The bag would be far less conspicuous to put in one of those luggage lockers at the train station in Galway.

This was as good a time as any to make the transfer and he quickly accomplished it. Now the empty case lay open on his lap. It was in good condition, not a real expensive type but not cheap either. He would give it to someone rather than just throw it away, he thought, as he rubbed his hand along the leather lining. It had a pouch inside for the lid for papers. A tug of the holding strap and it opened, showing a single sheet of white paper, folded. It was a memo of some type in Afrikaans. Another hasp then caught Geordie's eye. When he opened it the entire pouch area flopped down revealing more typed sheets, about ten. They were in Afrikaans also but these were in list form. He felt around the leather again, no more hidden compartments. Putting the memo and list carefully to one side he put the money back in the briefcase and then put the entire case in the hold-all. This baby was too valuable to dump, he decided. The big bag was put in the trunk of the car alongside his suitcase of clothes.

In Oughterard Geordie stopped at one of his favorite pubs for lunch. It was a bit early but he just had to sit and study the new-found documents, which he felt sure contained some intriguing and significant information.

◆

Anna drove directly to the security barrier at Jeppe and moments later was on her way to the parking spot near the Captain's office. This time she was directed to the other end of the fourth floor corridor. Finding no secretary in the outer office and hearing voices inside, she knocked at the door. It was the Captain himself that opened it. He immediately recognized her and apologized for not being quite ready. His company in the room was non other than Sergeant Van de Merwe and she could tell that the two men had been arguing.

"The Sergeant was just about to leave," Captain De Klerk said.

"I intend to take this up with the Chief, Captain," Van said. "I won't stand for it."

Van didn't even acknowledge Anna's presence. She broke into the tension as Van edged towards the door.

"I've got something to say to both of you right now. A little while ago I came home from work, before coming here, to find that my room had been searched, plus Geordie McKay's car, which is parked at my house. According to our maid, the culprits were two policemen in plain clothes. I demand an explanation, an apology and an absolute assurance that nothing like this will happen again, or I'm walking out of here and to hell with any further cooperation from me."

Captain De Klerk answered immediately.

"I gave no authorization for any search, I am indeed sorry. Are you sure that these people were police?"

"Yes. How about you Sergeant, do you know anything about this search, that the Captain here has no knowledge of?"

"Of course not," Van snapped.

Anna continued. "Captain, one of the men gave our maid this piece of paper with a phone number on it. I established on my way up here that the number is one of your Jeppe numbers. Captain, the other number written here is the registration plate number of the car that the men arrived in. Does this jog your memory?"

"This is the registration of one of our division cars! If I'm not mistaken it is the one you've been driving, Sergeant."

"Could I have a word with you alone, Sir?" Van asked, quietly.

"No Sergeant. You will say what you have to say here in front of Miss Terblanche. Out with it man."

After a pause Van answered. "It was just a routine check, Sir."

Anna turned on the sergeant, who was edging towards the door.

"Does routine mean pulling my clothes out of the drawers and the moving of furniture, Sergeant?"

Captain De Klerk had moved to cut off Van's escape. He glared at his sergeant, then addressed Anna.

"Miss, I obviously do owe you an apology for this unwarranted action by my department. Now, Sergeant, what reason did you have for conducting this search and did you remove any of her property?"

"Eh, we had an anonymous tip, Sir. In the heat of the moment we forgot to clear it with you. Nothing was found. I'm sorry we messed up your place, Miss."

"Go to your office, Sergeant, and wait for me there. You are off this case, do you understand, Sergeant? Off completely. Get your full report of this unauthorized search ready for me and get your partner to your office, too. Now get the hell out of here."

After Van left there was a long silence while the Captain tidied his desk, as a means of allowing himself time to cool off. Anna waited for him to reopen the dialogue.

"Again, Miss Terblanche, I offer my sincere apologies. I hope you saw from what happened just now that l had no knowledge of this, and will not tolerate such action. The sergeant will be suspended, his companion too. Ironically, I asked you to come here in order to gain your trust. I haven't made much of a start, have I? From now on I'll take personal responsibility for insuring that you don't get bothered by my men again. On that basis, can we still talk about how Mr. McKay can come forward in safety and help us?"

"I'm listening Captain," Anna answered.

◆

Once settled in a snug corner with a pint of stout Geordie took out the typed sheets for closer inspection. It was at times like this he regretted not having made an effort to learn Afrikaans. He scanned the memo sheet first, word by word and line by line. It was quite formal, addressed "Gentlemen" and signed only by the initials C.B. His scanning revealed some identifiable words; "Kuruman, Taung, Hotazel, Kimberley". All towns in the Northern Cape Province-Western Transvaal area. Also the words "police, mine diggings, danger, stones" were familiar. The memo was dated September and it was now mid November. What did it mean, he muttered aloud, drinking deep from his pint? His guess was that it contained some kind of statement about police activity and its effect on mining operations. The other pages were stapled together, dated September also and containing a shortened version of the memo before going into a list format. At the top was a heading in large letters – Kimberley File.

Geordie scoured the list carefully. It contained surnames, addresses and telephone numbers. Van Rensburg was near the top and Geordie recognized the Kimberley area code. The name had a dot before it as did the other five names at the top of the list. These probably denoted mining sites as all were rural numbers in the same area. Further down, the numbers were almost exclusively Johannesburg. He saw Smith! Would that be the courier arrested and whose non appearance pulled Geordie into the picture. Botha was there too. Two other names caught his attention, Goldstein and Van de Merwe. He had suspected the sergeant already because of the shooting, but was Anna's boss involved in this ring?

Geordie finished his pint and began another while he mulled over his findings. Nobody on the list was given a title. The best assumption he could make was that these were important links in the chain and that only key personnel had this list to use in an emergency. Could the loss of this be even more damaging to their entire operation than the loss of the money?

Just then the waitress brought Geordie a plot of steaming cockles and mussels, plus a large plate of the legendary Irish brown soda bread. Geordie could always think better on a full stomach and he ripped into the food.

How weird to find the file, he thought, as he munched the seafood. Was he stupid not to have found them earlier? Hell, he could hardly have flung the briefcase open on the plane to search it. He thanked God he didn't find it then, as he would surely have been even more on edge going through customs in Dublin. No fault, no fault, he assured himself. He tried to place his current South African time. Wasn't Anna meeting with De Klerk Friday afternoon? It was a pity she didn't have this new information prior to that meeting. Now that he had it, she needed to know, too, and quickly he decided. She may be in more danger than he figured before!

Without finishing his food, Geordie headed for the telephone booth in the corner of the pub. It would be Saturday evening in Jo'burg, he calculated.

Getting through was easy and Peter answered the phone.

"Anna? Yes, I think she just came in. Hold please."

On hearing her hello, Geordie shouted into the phone.

"Hi, Sweetheart, how are you?"

Anna was overjoyed. "This is a wonderful surprise, Geordie. I'm fine, all the better for hearing from you. Is everything okay?"

"Sure. I have very important news for you and I want to hear about your meeting yesterday. I'll call you in five minutes, per our plan."

Five minutes later Geordie called Anna at Liz's house.

"Anna, is that you?" he asked timidly.

"Of course, Geordie. You're in a pub aren't you? I can hear it, and I'll bet you're drinking that black porter by the gallon."

"I had to have a drop to steady my nerves."

"Cut out the background noise if you can, so I can hear you better. I can talk freely now."

Geordie closed the telephone booth door, being careful to lock his pint inside with him. The line was much better for both of them now.

"What's the important news, Sweetie?" Anna beat him to the question.

"Guess what I found in the briefcase."

"I can't guess at a time like this, just tell me."

"Today I finally had a chance to take a good look in Botha's briefcase, I was getting ready to throw it away."

"Tell me or I'll hit you down the phone."

"Well, I pulled the inside flap down and found a memo and a file marked Kimberley."

"What does it say?"

"Anna, it's in Afrikaans. My Afrikaans is only slightly better than that of the barman here. I'm not sure exactly but I think I can give you the gist of it. The memo seems like a warning of sorts, or instructions about police activity. The list contains a bunch of surnames, addresses and telephone numbers. Six are in the Kimberley area, including Van Rensburg. Probably the various diggings that produce the diamonds. The rest, I think are members of the group in the Jo'burg area, like Botha, whose name is one of them."

"Wow! I'll bet they're upset about losing that."

"There are other names of interest. How about Van de Merwe and Goldstein?"

"God Almighty!" Anna gasped.

He heard the phone drop, followed by the moving of furniture before Anna came back on.

"I'm okay now Geordie that I'm sitting down," she said softly.

"While you are catching your breath Anna, let me tell you what I make of it. Van de Merwe I'm not surprised about, obviously. The only reason I can figure for his late warning to Botha is lack of opportunity or maybe some internal squabble. He may well have set Botha up on purpose and thereby eliminate him from the picture, like he said that night. If he had got rid of Botha and me at the same time, he would be a hero to his partners, and be a step up the ladder, all at the same time. Of course, De Klerk didn't tell anyone the details of the Jo'burg raid till the last moment. I remember the sergeant suggesting they wait a few hours but he was turned down by the Captain. Now, Goldstein is a fairly common name, it is probably not your Mr. Goldstein. Do you want the telephone numbers that go with the names?"

"Yes please."

Anna repeated the numbers back aloud.

"That's not Harold Goldstein's number. There is something familiar about it but I don't know what it is. I'm sure the police would love to get their hands on that file, but can we trust them now?"

"How did your meeting with Captain De Klerk go yesterday, Anna?" Geordie asked, changing the subject.

"More trouble, unfortunately. Well, shortly after you called me on Friday I went home to change clothes only to find that my room had been searched. The maid was sure they were police. Captain De Klerk was waiting for me at Jeppe at two o'clock, as arranged, so I barged into his office in a rage. Van was with him and I could tell they had just had a row, probably about the terrible mess that the raid turned into. I was real angry and accused them of the search. It shocked the Captain when I produced a slip of paper with Sergeant Van de Merwe's registration number on it, that Muti had written down. He made the sergeant admit his part in the search, there and then in front of me. At first Van tried to deny it but couldn't in the face of the evidence. Then the Captain angrily sent him away. He will be suspended, I think. We then finally got into the details of how you could come forward in safety. But let's just leave that for now, in the light of what you have told me tonight.

We can't take it any further till we figure out more of this puzzle and are sure of who we can trust. I'm scared, Geordie. You're definitely in danger from these people and you're much safer where you are. By the way, Captain De Klerk knew that you were in Ireland. He said he found out yesterday from flight records that you had flown to Holland. I asked him whether he intended to try and have you picked up over there by the police. He said no, because you did nothing wrong, and he wants your cooperation later. He seems okay really, probably a good honest policeman, but we need to prove that to ourselves. There is just so much to absorb. We need some time to think our plan through. Post me a copy of what you have by express mail to this address here like we arranged. I'll check the phone numbers out in the meantime. Can you call me here on Monday evening at eight?"

"You must be very careful, Anna, they may come after you, with me out of their reach. Change your routine and always try to have someone with you. I feel bad about leaving you there on your own."

"I'll be careful. Now that Van knows there is nothing of interest hidden in my room, or your car, they searched that, too, by the way, and after his formal reprimand and suspension, he shouldn't bother me. On Monday I'll be able to check on some things. Bye bye, Darling, take care."

Geordie had a last minute request.

"Will you call Pat at my work soon? Tell him my mother took ill and I had to fly home suddenly. Ask him to keep an eye on my current sales deals for me and to tell the boss I'll be in touch soon. Take care of yourself, Sweetheart, I'll talk to you soon. Love you."

After the conversation Anna remained at Liz's, talking with her girlfriend for a while, but still got home in time for rusks and coffee. She felt it was important to keep a cozy commune ambience during this trouble even if she couldn't confide in her co-dwellers.

Geordie finished his now discolored pint, paid his bill and headed for Galway. On the way, he got three copies of the file made, posting one to Anna with a cute card. He took some spending money from the case, left the original file in it and stashed the hold-all with the man at the luggage counter in the Galway city train station, who gave him a redemption ticket. It was a big relief to be rid of the bag. If only the ticket man knew what he was storing for a few shillings a week, Geordie smiled, as he headed for his friend Joe's house. The "craic would be ninety" in Galway over the weekend and he would now be able to enjoy it. He tuned the radio to Radio Na Gaelthacta and turned up the volume.

The traditional Irish jigs and reels blasted out and Geordie's foot was tapping. Yes, despite everything it was good to be home.

NINE

Visitors from Across the Pond

November is a quiet time of year for the ferry sailings between England and Ireland. The summer tourist season is over and the Christmas rush has not yet started. But with an immigrant population many times its own, Ireland has a thriving import-export business in people. Add to that the stormy reputation of the Irish Sea crossing in the winter, and the shortest route, namely Holyhead to Dun Laoghaire maintains the heaviest traffic. The Saint Brendan docked in Dun Laoghaire in the middle of the afternoon. Shortly afterwards cars and trucks began streaming from its belly.

Nigel Smyth, known as Snotty to his friends and enemies alike, because of his nasal discharges, and Patrick Jones, without any Irish ancestry but nevertheless nicknamed Paddy, were average London thugs. Both had served time 'At Her

Majesty's Pleasure' in Worm-wood Scrubbs prison, for petty offences and actually met there. Both despised their nicknames, to which they were subjected constantly while 'doing porridge'. Their friendship began with an agreement not to call each other by nicknames. On their release they formed a team, doing small-time subcontract jobs from their East End London base. Their resume included extortion, robbery, various minder jobs, arson, and two hits. Both hits were for their main client, a leading London hoodlum called Big Larry Porter. One hit was an unwanted competing girlfriend contracted by the man's wife, the other was a shopkeeper too far behind in protection payments.

They had never worked in Ireland and weren't too enthusiastic when Larry called, but it sounded simple enough and they trusted Larry.

Find this Geordie McKay geezer in or around Galway, recover a briefcase with documents for South African clients of Larry's, dispose of the guy and leave. One of the main reasons they hadn't been back to prison was their choice of jobs, and Ireland was not appealing. Guns were impossible to pick up there and the IRA were into most avenues of the crime business. Larry assured them that this job had no IRA complications, it was paying top money plus an all expenses paid trip, very attractive with Christmas round the corner.

Mavis and Vicky were delighted to be offered a free trip to Ireland, to make up a happy foursome. They knew Nigel and

Patrick were in the rackets but that was none of their business. Free food and drink and lodgings for a week, in return for 'a bit of how's your father' was a nice break from walking the streets, with the promise of a bonus thrown in.

Over for a wedding is what Patrick told the police and customs people as they drove through without incident. Once out of the port they headed for Galway and booked into a small hotel in the Salthill resort area of the city, facing the ocean. The plan was to leave the girls based there, with their English registered car. Patrick had a rental car booked to pick up the next morning which would be their operations vehicle. They would carry some clothes in it in case they had to stay somewhere else during the job, but planned to come back to base and stay with the girls if possible. Of course they would also carry some of their weapons. Under the floor of the luggage compartment of their own car they had a concealed space for their hardware. On this type of job they weren't sure what to bring so they brought a selection. Their favorite pistols, sawn-off shotgun, an Uzi, a good supply of assorted ammunition, spare pistol and a small repair kit.

It was Sunday night, with fine weather for November. They decided to do the tourist bit. Following directions given at the hotel they drove around for a while, to get the lie of the land and check out some eating and drinking establishments. The promenade area was pretty quiet with a lot of places closed for the season. Anything with a bar connection was open. Someone told them of a bar on the Connemara Road that had music and food, so they headed there.

It turned out to be Traditional Irish Music and it was going in full swing when they arrived. Paddy and Snotty were not too keen on it, but the girls had a few vodkas in them by now and liked the action. Their meal and the whole evening turned out great. Mavis and Vicky had a blast and even danced jigs with American tourists and members of a local football team. The two plebs were shamed into action to prevent any propositioning from starting. The later it got, the higher the tempo of the action became. It was going full blast when the happy foursome left, even though it was well past closing time. Back at the hotel the two 'working girls' put their lads through another vigorous workout, till the early hours.

Morning brought rain and hangovers. The girls were left to sleep while the rented car was picked up, without any hassles. They drove both vehicles to an isolated spot overlooking the Atlantic where they transferred the weapons. Breakfast was slow, but so was everything on a wet Monday in Galway. Back in the rented car they smoked duty free cigars as they looked over a map of the area and planned. Their information was that McKay had grown up near Galway and had gone to university there, quite recently. Chances were he would surface in the bars frequented by the student crowd. They marked out a two square mile area around the university and concocted a story to tell as a cover.

It was nearly noon when they got back to the hotel and the girls were still sleeping. Hot tea finally coaxed them up so they could be told where to hang out while the two "businessmen" were taking care of business. After looking out at the rain, the two girls got back into bed, one bed. Paddy was disgusted, and told them to catch up on all their beauty sleep, which would take a long time.

The two men headed into the city in their rented Ford.

Galway is an attractive city, perched on the rugged west coast of Ireland. By world standards it is a small city, but that is one of Galway's charms. It was an obvious settlement choice for the ancient Irish Celts, commanding as it does the estuary of the mighty river Corrib, as it empties itself into the Atlantic Ocean via Galway Bay. Like most of Ireland's old cities, Galway's thick solid stone city walls, castles and towers have withstood the ravages of time and centuries of warfare.

The modern Galway is a rich blend of this history, clean new industries, and strong tourism revenues. With a university and other colleges, the student population is a significant and appreciated part of the city economy.

This was the vibrant scene that Geordie McKay had entered some years earlier, to study engineering but learn a whole lot more in the process, like how to obtain a hundred pint barrel of porter for a party with only a pound note in his pocket. Galway formed such strong bonds with its student visitors that countless numbers of them stayed on permanently after finishing College. Geordie's pal, Joe, and his two housemates were part of that community. They worked at good jobs but lived like students. It was inevitable that Geordie's homecoming weekend would be spent on the wild side. Being only out of college a few years, Geordie knew lots of students, and of course the ex-students.

On Saturday evening Joe and Geordie made an early start, visiting favorite bars while checking out where the parties were happening. Later they went to a raucous music 'seisiun' of Irish Traditional Music. It was so crowded that people hardly had enough elbow room to drink their pints. The 'craic' was great and Geordie was surprised how many people he met whom he recognized and who remembered him. Joe was chatting up some American girls, then moved on to three Danes who were drinking pints. They took the Danes to a party later. One of them had the hots for Geordie and he was responding well to treatment as the kegs of stout were consumed. Eventually she and the other two feel asleep on their seats. Joe was lamenting the lost opportunity and Geordie commiserated with him but he was glad really, he still had a lot on his mind.

On Sunday Joe took him to Spidal to watch Joe's pal in a Hurling match. It was another good day. This time they limited the stout intake, getting back to the house in Galway at a reasonable time for a much needed early night.

Geordie had the house to himself Monday, once the others went to work. He slept on a short while. Then he went to the local shop for the newspaper, picking up notepaper, pen, pad and envelopes. It was raining, a perfect time to sit and figure out his strategies. Over boiled eggs, toast and a large pot of hot tea he began work. He had always found that putting things down on paper got his thought processes going.

His first list comprised the events to date as they occurred, the next one listed the people involved. He then tried to put himself in the place of the ring leaders. What would they do, what would they be satisfied with? Obviously they wanted their file back and probably the money too, in that order. They might not even know the exact amount of money missing, with Botha dead. They may or may not know the circumstances by which Geordie stumbled into this and would it matter to them if they did? There were huge sums of money involved, and probably some highly respected people who didn't want to be exposed as criminals. How ruthless would they be, how far would they go, what was the chink in the armour that might cause them to walk away and leave be what had happened?

Then there was his and Anna's perspectives. They should be going to Cape Town shortly for three weeks vacation over Christmas which they had been looking forward to. Now, that trip was totally up in the air. His job was fairly secure so long as he didn't take too much time off but he wouldn't be paid for this forced vacation.

Anna was an innocent party dragged into this by her relationship with him. She loved her job and Jo'burg dearly. It was very unlikely that the Goldstein on the list was her boss.

Nevertheless she was definitely in the front line and therefore in danger, the degree of danger being difficult to gauge. Geordie felt sure that Van de Merwe was not out of the picture even if he was suspended from duty. The fact that he was ready to kill once meant that he could be expected to do so again. The Captain could possibly be involved too, or he could be the good guy Anna thought he was.

Another mug of steaming tea and Geordie started on his most difficult list, their choices. It seemed to him that time was more on the side of the criminals. He and Anna both had careers to build and couldn't afford to lose their jobs. It was pointless at this stage wishing or hoping it never happened. Run! It looked terrible on the page but it was a real option. It meant leaving South Africa which he didn't want to do, and he would have a hard time convincing Anna to go. Though he loved Ireland, he had purposefully left it to seek out warmer climates and South Africa definitely had that, plus opportunity. America would be nice but so difficult to get into, especially for Anna, with South Africa being the international outcast because of apartheid.

Leaving without Anna was something he didn't want to think about. He had to admit that he was in pretty deep, if missing her was a measure of it. To take the police at their word, they simply wanted to catch and convict the players in the diamond smuggling operation. Botha was dead, and his bodyguard who saw the case of dollars was probably the other dead civilian, so the police likely didn't even know of the existence of the briefcase. Taking money from thieves didn't feel like a crime to Geordie. The file copy he sent Anna would be very valuable to the police in catching the ring leaders. Geordie had already helped the police once, and Captain De Klerk had told Anna that he had done nothing wrong. They couldn't expect him to solve the whole case for them. If the police had the Kimberley File, could Geordie and Anna make their exit from the scene? The thugs wanted the list too and would probably pay for it again, but trying that sale would be breaking the law, not to mention putting himself and Anna in further danger.

Geordie was the leading actor of the play but he could not exit this scene at the stroke of a pen. He spread out the sheets of paper in front of him and played out the competing scenarios in his head. It was the feeling of hunger that reminded him to look at his watch. It was evening in South Africa, time to call Anna. His call went straight through. A girl's voice at the other end answered.

"Anna? Is that you?"

"Yes Geordie, surely you recognize my voice."

"I wasn't expecting you to answer the phone, that's all. You caught me by surprise. You sound great, is everything fine with you, Sweetie?"

"Yes, I managed to get some things sorted out in my head and get myself focused since we last talked."

"Good. Me too. Great minds think alike, eh?" Geordie answered.

"I had the office to myself again today. Mr. Goldstein is

back in Krugersdorp at the murder trial and will probably be there all week. He was in the office this morning when I went in but I spoke to him only briefly before he left. I was going to call in sick till I had my heart to heart talk with myself, then I went in only at eight o'clock so I wouldn't get tied up in discussion with him about you, and this case."

"Did you manage to find out anything from the numbers I gave you?" Geordie asked.

"Yes indeed. Calling from an attorney's office I can get access to information that the general public cannot get. Van de Merwe's number turns out to be a second line he has to his house, so that is definitely our Van. I have Mr. Goldstein's home number here on file which I checked, it's definitely not his. I looked for a second line and found nothing. Then I noticed his son Mervin's number on file. Mervin works in the diamond trade, at one of the big diamond cutting and dealing companies. Mr. Goldstein had told me himself that Mervin worked there but I had forgotten. I tried the number you gave me and asked for him. The lady who answered, his wife I presume, was suspicious of a girl calling on this private line, as she called it. I did succeed in getting her to give me his work number which matched with the one I already had."

"So, Mervin Goldstein is in this too! It seems like a good fit. Get someone from the trade who has the contacts and the cover to sell the merchandise. Are you upset about this news?" Geordie asked.

"Yes, for Mr. Goldstein's sake. He has often spoken about

how proud he is of his son and in true Jewish fashion, proud of all the money he has made. I have nothing to indicate that Mr. Goldstein is involved and I don't think he is but I cannot rule it out. Assuming he isn't, I still can't talk to him about details, in case he might be innocently discussing it with Mervin. That news will hurt him deeply. The sun shines from that boy's eyes as far as he is concerned. There is the possibility that my Mr. Goldstein is involved too, but I just can't bear to think of that right now."

"You'll hardly have received the copies yet?"

"No, nothing yet. But I did manage to establish that Captain De Klerk has only one home line and I have that number, too. When I get the file I will check the number against it. By the way, the Captain called me at work today to ask how I was. He confirmed to me that Van has been suspended, both he and his partner. The Captain also told me where he jogs a few mornings a week, close by here, and suggested that I can reach him easily there without drawing any attention. I may jog with him tomorrow morning to try to find out more about how he thinks. My gut feeling still is that he is okay. What have you been up to, Geordie?"

"I visited with my mother and stayed one night. She thinks I'm in England on business now, I've spent the weekend with Joe. It was fun. I have missed you, though. It'd be nice if you were here, too, Anna."

"I'd just be in the way with all your old girlfriends around. I wish we could bring this whole thing out in the open somehow and then back out of it. Let the police finish it, it's their job. We're supposed to be in Cape Town in a few weeks and at this stage I'm beginning to doubt if we'll make it."

"Don't think that way, Anna. Continue with the plan that we have, We've got to make things happen and I desperately want to get to the Cape. I've been thinking, too. This whole business might well cause us to both have to switch jobs and move out of Jo'burg, maybe even out of South Africa for a while."

"I don't want to think about that either, but it's not the end of the world if that happens. Don't go blaming yourself for getting me into this, or thinking of it as a way to dump me, Geordie McKay. Whatever else about it, it has been the most exciting thing that every happened to us, me at least. It'll work out somehow and will make a good fireside story to your grandchildren. Geordie, I'll call you in Galway as soon as I get the list and decipher it. Is the morning the best time, after your friends are gone to work?"

"Yes."

They said their goodbye's and sweet nothings. Anna went back to her commune and Geordie made himself some late lunch.

TEN

A Winner at Galway Races

The crowd in the Keys bar were not impressed with the two overdressed Englishmen. Patrick had the idea to change into something more casual, but had left their clothes in the other car. There was no answer from the girls at the hotel so they decided to buy some clothes. A small clothes shop on a side street was chosen. The young assistant was told a story about their getting a few days off while waiting on a ship. He advised them of the styles being worn by students and older ex-students alike. Fifteen minutes later the two were back on the bar scene having put their stuffy clothes in the car. The only problem was that these tight jeans did not accommodate the carrying of a gun, so they had to proceed unarmed. Nigel chuckled at Patrick's name being shortened to Pat by the Irish but he had to admit that Pat was getting their ear. They were told about a few McKay's that didn't sound like their man. Pat's last name, Jones, they assured him was indeed Irish, and had roots there in Galway. The afternoon drunks would tell them anything to keep their interest, and keep the pints flowing. The ship story was modified to shipment by trucks when it became apparent that many of the pub patrons were part-time workers at the docks.

As the afternoon wore on Pat, as he had now come to accept, and Nigel became intoxicated. They couldn't switch to lemonade in these pubs and expect to be taken seriously so they decided to go eat instead. It would be a long evening and the food soakage would be needed. In the cafe a young man who was obviously a student served them and struck up a conversation. Once they relaxed, Pat threw out their big question. Yes, the student knew a Geordie McKay who had been ahead of him in college, and had gone to work in Africa. He then volunteered the news that Geordie was back on vacation at present, he had seen him with his own eyes. The pubs most likely to find him in were listed, with the Keys high on that list.

Shortly after the Englishmen left, Joe came into the same cafe with a girl from work. The waiter recognized him as a friend of Geordie's and told him of the two English friends who were in town and were hoping to surprise their pal. Joe thanked him, saying that he and Geordie would be in some of those same pubs later, where they could indeed meet some of these old friends. The men were described to him, so Joe could be in on the surprise later. Oddly enough, he and Geordie had planned to meet in the Skeff, a place they seldom went, but had done so because a college pal of Geordie's, Dave Long, usually drank there.

Geordie hit the Skeff about five-thirty. He was halfway into his first pint when Dave came in. Dave had made a simple choice to stay with the money, his father had a successful hardware business which he joined and would someday own.

Joe came in about the time Dave was ordering drinks, so he joined them over by the window.

After the usual chat about family health, how well fed they both looked, and so on, Dave wanted to talk of nothing else but Africa.

"Geordie," he begged, "please tell me what it's like there, really? We hear so much on the news about how the darkies are rioting and that it is all about to boil over into a huge civil war. I don't give a damn about all that shit, we have the same here in the North everyday. Mary and me are getting married next year, you remember Mary Burke?"

Geordie nodded.

"Anyway," Dave continued. "I want to take her to someplace special, and South Africa sounds like an exotic place, with all the wild animals and such. Give me some ideas about what you think would make a good trip."

Geordie took another long swig from his pint, composed himself for his speech, then launched into his tourist promotion.

"First, Dave, let me congratulate you on your future wedding. Another good man gone, but Mary's a nice girl, I remember her well. Obviously if I'm still there I'll be able to show you around Jo'burg, put you up if you want. To get the worry about the troubles out of the way, avoid going near townships or the homelands, same rules that apply in Northern Ireland here. You need to see Cape Town, Table Mountain, and that whole wine district around there. It's the most beautiful area I've ever spent time in. Fly in and rent a car at the airport. They'll give you the maps for the wine route and the garden route. Base yourself in Cape Town and travel out everyday. That way you get the best restaurants and stuff, I've got a good friend who lives there and would love to show you round provided you can buy the drink, which reminds me."

Joe got the hint and called for fresh pints. Geordie continued.

"After a week at the Cape fly to Jo'burg, it's too far to drive. I might be able to get you the loan of a car. Anyway, after seeing the gold museum and such, you need to head for the Kruger Park! It's a massive national park about the size of Wales, about four hours drive east of Jo'burg. They have great camps there, right in the middle of the wild. Of course they are protected by large fences and are like villages with chalet huts, restaurants and all of the mod cons, as they say here. You can lie in your bed with Mary and listen to the lions roar. That should give you the urge. If you can, visit the separate black country of Swaziland next door to the park. It's real nice and safe, and they have great outdoor markets there to buy souvenirs, it's worse than a fair day in Gort. I'll write down some notes for you on the different places I mentioned and drop it into the shop to you. Now, let's get on with the more important business of drinking a toast to your future bride."

"You didn't tell me very much about your sudden trip, Geordie but I know that you're not expecting out of town visitors to drop in," Joe cut in, with some concern in his voice.

"What are you talking about, Joe?"

"There are two Englishmen looking for you in town, making out to be friends of yours and wanting to surprise you. They're probably in the Keys Bar now."

Geordie swallowed hard, reached for his pint and gulped down some stout.

"This is bad news, Joe," he said.

Geordie motioned them closer and spoke softly.

"You're well in with the Gardai here, aren't you, Dave?"

"Sure. The Superintendent is a golfing pal of Daddy's and comes into the shop all the time, gets his 'super' discount. Got me out of a few scrapes, why?"

"I've something important to tell you both, very confidential and I'm going to need your help. Maybe even the help of your friend, the Super."

The lads both nodded their heads and leaned forward in anticipation. Geordie looked around, making sure they were out of the other customers hearing range before continuing.

"Well, to cut a long story short, here is my predicament. I stumbled onto a smuggling ring in South Africa, dealing in illicit diamonds. I then helped the police set a trap to catch the kingpins in the gang. The trap didn't work too well because one of the police was in cahoots with the smugglers, and I almost got shot. I just didn't feel safe there at present so I came here till the dust clears. There are other details and complications but that's the gist of it. Joe has just found out that two Englishmen are in town looking for me. Nobody knows I'm here, so there can be little doubt why they've come. They're after me."

"Holy shit," exclaimed the pair, chorus-like.

Dave regained enough composure to call for three pints. Secure in the knowledge that refreshments were on the way, he spoke.

"Surely they can be arrested for this, I can arrange a tip off."

"We need something stronger than that," Joe interjected, "like catching them in the act."

"I don't want to be shot at again. I haven't got nine lives you know," Geordie said, trying to lighten it up.

The pints arrived. Dave toasted Geordie's return and was into the familiar good health routine till he checked himself. They all took long swigs in search of inspiration.

"If we could find out the names of these Englishmen I could get them checked out," Dave suggested.

Geordie now took up the slack.

"Assuming they're here to harm me, then we must also assume that they have weapons with them. Guns are extremely difficult to get around here and with the troubles in the North the anti-terrorism laws are very wide reaching, right. If we could be sure they have guns, the Garda Special Branch would take care of them. I don't want to have to keep running while things are being sorted out in Africa."

"Could I pose as the local gun runner or something and find out that way?" Joe asked. "Better still, pose as the local IRA unit gun runner."

"You certainly look shifty enough, Joe," joked Dave.

"I think the IRA angle might scare them," Geordie said. "Maybe a combination like this. You're a local gun runner whose contacts informed you of their arrival in town. They need to buy some guns from you or you might pass the word to the IRA that they're here."

Joe nodded. "Excellent Geordie. That should stir them up enough to say something. Let me try it."

They talked some more about it and it was agreed to let Joe try. He was to arrange to meet the Englishmen at their car later that night to collect guns. If he was not back to the Skeff in two hours Dave would go looking for him.

Geordie switched to cidona while they waited on Joe. He needed to keep sober. Time seemed to stand still as they nervously watched television and chatted. Joe was back inside the hour.

"Went like a charm," Joe smiled. "Look, I even got a fifty pound deposit from them. They're London yobbos. Pretty drunk by now and very nervous about being in Ireland. The very mention of the IRA rattled them big time. They already have weapons and would only say they have a business associate to settle with. I think they hope to try and sub out the job to me later when we meet again. They've got a red Ford Fiesta parked in Eyre Square. I know they have guns in it and a few more at their hotel, somewhere in Salthill. Here is the registration number I jotted down from it, it's rented from Budget."

They talked over the details for a few minutes. Geordie was worried that it went too easy. The two men were already half drunk, according to Joe. After further discussion all three agreed that it was best to try to pass this one anonymously to the Gardai Special Branch and keep Geordie out of it completely. Dave went to the phone cubicle and called the Garda Superintendent at home.

Ten minutes later he was back, smiling.

"Lads, it's all taken care of. He will put it through the system as a tip off from an informant. My name will not appear at all and your names weren't even mentioned. Joe, go out and put a note on their car to the effect that you can't meet them tonight but will do so tomorrow night, same place, same time. We want them to head back to their hotel. They'll be stopped for a traffic violation and the Branch will be brought in at that point. Watch the paper, but you must still keep low,

Geordie. These fellows should get at least a few years on weapons charges alone, but they may not be alone."

"That's great, Dave. You can have the credit and I'll be content with keeping my scalp."

After a couple of drinks and a steak treat by Geordie, they got permission to go to the fourth floor of the building where they had a clear view of the Englishmen's car across from them in the lighted square.

Presently, the pair of Englishmen staggered up the street and sat on the hood of the Fiesta. It was a while before they spotted the note. Once they got it they seemed to argue about what to do. Finally they got into the car and drove out of the parking lot.

"I don't see any car following them, maybe there was a mix up?" Geordie said. He was worried.

Dave patted him on the back, with confident assurance.

"Trust the Gardai, Geordie. If we can't see them, then the Englishmen can't either. It's a done deal, believe me, the Super is sharp. It's like backing a dead cert at the Galway races, remember?"

"Dave, you never put me onto one of those," Geordie shot back, smiling.

"Well, this time I have, old buddy, old pal."

ELEVEN

A Girl With a Plan

Almost a whole week had passed since her involvement with the diamonds had begun, but with all that had happened it seemed much longer than that to Anna. She was used to Geordie being away on the road all week, but he was always back at the weekend. Now he was three thousand miles away and everything was a struggle for her. Just going into work was difficult. She was glad Mr. Goldstein was out of the office, but in his absence she had little work to do and was reduced to helping out on divorce work, which was a large part of their law practice.

There Anna was, trying to cope with an enormous problem while all these middle-aged people who should have more sense, were arguing over the dividing up of their money and property. From what she could see, the reasons behind most of the divorces were petty and the result was a self-inflicted sentence of bitterness and loneliness for many of the divorcees.

The Krugersdorp trial would end soon and Mr. Goldstein would then be back. He would be asking about Geordie's situation. Normally she would welcome his advice, as she did the previous week, but Mervin Goldstein's involvement changed all of that. It bothered her also to be using her position to obtain information that may end up hurting people she liked. But she had a higher duty to her own wellbeing and that of Geordie. At a time like this, she really needed people around that one could count on. She was hurting inside, trying to cope with it on her own.

Liz called as Anna got in from work on Wednesday, a package had arrived from Ireland. Anna rushed over. She had to be polite in opening the package there, so as not to offend Liz and was doubly pleased to see Geordie's card. It got her off the hook with Liz, who was wondering about the contents. Just some papers to be filed that Geordie took with him by mistake, she told Liz and went home. Instead of dinner with her co-dwellers at the commune, Anna excused herself politely and hurried to her room, retrieving Geordie's envelope where she had hidden it under her carpet.

The memo was largely as Geordie had described it. Originating in Jo'burg it referred to a reliable inside informant who had warned the writer of forthcoming police activity against the group's diamond operations. The writer instructed his managers to keep the reported diamond recoveries to the book average while remaining ready to send out 'other stock' at short notice, through their couriers. Coded warnings as practised were to be given just ahead of any raids, but would only be a few hours notice. The accompanying list had names and addresses of the directors of the diamond enterprise, prepared as a draft by Botha, marked 'original and only copy'. The last section caught her attention. Action was being planned to deal with the persons responsible for these recent interruptions in their business. Informants were now in position in high places, and were already supplying quality information, especially one code-named TAF.

◆

It was a beautiful morning at Jan Smuts Park. A thunderstorm during the night had rejuvenated the plants and grass after the previous day's heat, and another scorching day was on tap. After parking her bike, Anna limbered up, stretching and bending. There were quite a few people jogging already even though the sun was not yet up. Some runners nodded to her as they ran past. One handsome young man invited her to run with him. She declined but found herself looking after him, at his long tanned legs and shapely bottom.

Finally she saw her quarry approaching. She had been wondering earlier if she would recognize him in running gear but as soon as she spotted him she knew.

"Morning Captain, mind if I jog with you?"

"Morning Miss—Terblanche," he finally recalled.

They set off along the pathway at a steady pace. He did this all the time and could keep it up for ages despite a bit of puffing. Anna was fit but running was not her thing. At this pace she felt comfortable and many minutes passed while they ran along, side by side.

"How is Geordie doing?" the Captain asked.

"Fine, just fine."

"Are you busy at Mr. Goldstein's?"

"Yes. He is in Krugersdorp mostly at present, in court, on the big murder trial. I'm sure you know of it, Captain."

"I do. His client is the Randburg man in the Van Kloof love triangle killing. Is Mr. Goldstein going to get him off?"

"If anybody can, he can. If he's innocent, that is," Anna added.

"You had other business in mind to come jog with an overweight policeman?"

"Yes, I have some new thoughts and information that may be useful."

"Let's take a rest over here at this bench at the top of the hill. Now, Miss Terblanche, thoughts are all well and good but it is factual information that solves cases in my business."

"I understand fully. Before I offer my information I want to hear your views on some aspects of this 'Kimberley Case' as I call it. It is obvious to Geordie and I that this illicit diamond ring, pardon the pun, has some heavy hitters involved. Geordie stumbled onto it and his attempt to help the police almost got him killed. You yourself said that he has done nothing wrong. Yet, he will probably have to give up his job for safety reasons. This incident has disrupted his and my life. To help you further with it only adds to our risk and there is nothing in it for us except the good citizen award. That doesn't go far to pay the rent, or worse, God forbid. Are we not better just to walk away and get our lives back together somewhere else?"

The Captain answered immediately, as if he had been expecting to be questioned.

"There is always risk involved in this type of situation and it is not for me to tell you what you should do. Let me tell you briefly about the background of this case, off the record. Then you can make up your own mind. As you know, the diamond business is a very important part of the South African economy. Illicit trade harms the country in many ways. Quite some time ago it was decided at government level that these and other crime groups that harm the outside image of the country be stamped out. Major resources were made available and I was given the responsibility of cleaning up the illicit diamond trade. I have already been extensively involved in this kind of work with the Kimberley police. The Olantsfontein raid was one in a series that we have been carrying out. I don't mind telling you that our success has been limited. Our targets have been a step ahead of us. The incident with Geordie was a lucky break for us, which I was very eager to exploit, and it gave us valuable information into the workings of the crime organization.

It was unfortunate about the shooting in Houghton and I sympathize with Geordie's decision to run from the scene. The internal investigation is currently in progress into the events of that evening. I think Geordie can still be of great help to us in flushing out these people, but I have to tell you that there is danger involved, more danger than I had thought before. It is his, and your decision to make.

There is one other thing. I have discretionary funds at my disposal. People who give us valuable information, or who help us in a way that leads to the arrest and conviction of major players in this scheme will be rewarded handsomely from these funds. Relocation and new identity cards can be part of this package."

"You are saying, Captain, that if we help, you will give us protection, a reward and new papers, in a new location of our choosing?"

"Basically correct. I cannot guarantee the size of the reward but it could be substantial, and my recommendations are usually accepted."

"Will you put what you just said in writing?" Anna asked.

"Certainly. But I need some indication of your intentions, and of this new information you said you have."

"Speaking for myself, I like it but I can't decide for Geordie, I will be talking to him this morning and will put it to him. One point, and please don't take it personally. How do I know that you are not involved somehow in this diamond racket yourself, and are only out to get my information?"

"Normally that question would anger me, but I accept it as valid here, in view of all that has happened. You're right to be suspicious. What if I have the Chief of Police sign off on my letter to you? I'm not exactly in Chief Ferreira's good books right now but he needs this case to move forward, too. Frankly, it may help me to have him committed on paper."

"That would be fine thank you. I'll tell you briefly what I have and will give to you later, when I'm in possession of your letter. In the confusion at Houghton, Geordie picked up a file which turned out to contain a warning memo about expected police activity and a list of names and numbers of key people in their organization."

The Captain's eyes opened wide.

"I see! That could really blow the lid off the case once and for all. Anybody you recognize on that list?"

"Yes, how about your Sergeant Van de Merwe? I have already verified the number as being his home."

Captain De Klerk was silent for a full minute, as if numbed by this confirmation. His race reddened, his blood was boiling on the inside, and his eyes shifted about in their sockets looking for a place to hide.

Anna spoke again.

"It came as no surprise to me, Captain, in view of the way he acted in Houghton and at my house."

"You were right then about your suspicions of him. I'm still shocked and I apologize to you both again. This of course may explain a lot about our ineffectiveness against our target. Does Mr. Goldstein know about this?"

"No. Any particular reason for your question, Captain?"

"None except curiosity. When can I get this complete list?"

Anna tried to sound calculating in her response.

"We both need to go to work. Can you get the letter I need done this morning?"

"Of course, I'll do it first thing. I have a meeting at ten with the police Chief and will get it signed by him then. Do you want me to come to your office?"

"No. Could you meet me at the Gold City Deli on Jan Smuts at twelve, that's the earliest I can take lunch."

"Sure. I know it well. I often go there myself."

"Let's leave it at that for now, Captain. I need to get ready for work, see you later."

"Goodbye for now Miss Terblanche, and thank you for this important information," he said and smiled.

On the way home Anna stopped at a small breakfast cafe. There was a phone in the corner which was quite private and she was itching to tell Geordie about her progress. She got through quickly, only realizing the time there when a sleepy voice answered and an even sleepier Geordie came on the phone. Small talk was kept to a minimum as Anna hit the details quickly to keep him awake.

"I received the papers and have gone through them many

times. Your translation was quite close actually, our Afrikaans language must be rubbing off on you. Just now, I have come from meeting Captain De Klerk, at the park where he jogs. I decided to catch him off guard and sound him out more. I want to bring this whole affair forward so we can get on with our lives."

"That's fine with me Anna," replied Geordie.

"Anyway, before I give him the documents, I insisted that he draft a letter signed by him and the Chief of Police, stating that we will be rewarded and protected. Then I told him only one snippet of the information, about Van de Merwe. I decided at the last minute not to mention Mervin Goldstein, no need to throw out more bait when the fish is hooked. This is our safest way forward, in my opinion. It's either that or run away and leave it all. What do you think?"

Geordie was wide awake by now.

"I agree completely. It's beginning to bother me being over here so far from the action, that I am thinking of coming back to Jo'burg again. You've covered the angles by asking for a commitment in writing. A reward and protection should allow us to make a fresh start. Excellent, Anna, you're a real star."

"Don't come back yet Geordie. You're much safer there, at least till we get this new deal in place."

"I don't know if I am, after what happened here. A couple of hired English thugs came to Galway on a mission to get me, this past weekend. They asked too many questions and I got wind of it. With the help of some friends I was able to put the police anti-terrorism squad on them and they are now in custody on weapons and other charges."

Anna reacted in shocked disbelief.

"Oh my God! Are you okay?"

"Of course I am. Like I told you I got onto it in time and all is taken care of. The two plebs in question are being tight-lipped, and are being treated as terrorists acting on behalf of a Northern Ireland paramilitary group, hired to commit mayhem in the South. They will lock them up here and throw away the key. That suits me fine and I am totally out of any investigation, but it proves that I'm not as safe here as I thought I would be, and it shows the importance of bringing this thing to a head."

"I'm giving a copy of the list and memo to the Captain at twelve. Is that okay with you Geordie?"

"Sure."

They arranged that he would call her at Liz's house later that evening, chatted a little more and said goodbye.

◆

Captain De Klerk was not long in his office before Chief Ferreira came in. For a man that was usually difficult to get to see, the Chief was now becoming so available that he was close to being a nuisance. After the Captain's suspension of two men the previous day, they had what could only be described as an argument on the telephone, ending with the Chief summoning the Captain to his office for a ten o'clock meeting. It was still only eight-thirty and the chief was already in, being quite conciliatory and friendly.

Seizing on this moment of goodwill, the Captain asked him for his letter of commitment for Anna Terblanche. Wanting to keep the Chief from stealing his thunder, he only told him minimal details of his morning meeting with Anna. Written information that confirmed the fact that the suspended Van de Merwe belonged to the diamond gang, was the only carrot he dangled in front of the Chief and it worked like a charm. The chief complimented him on his good work and wondered out loud if Van could be made to talk. The letter would be no problem.

To compensate for the usual secretarial delays at the Chiefs office, the Captain told him that he was meeting Anna at noon, but avoided the mention of a venue.

When the Chief left, Captain De Klerk had to pinch himself to make sure that he wasn't dreaming. This profound change in attitude by Chief Ferreira amazed him. Maybe they could still patch up their differences and share the limelight when this case was finally cracked, he thought. Then he hurried to complete the details of the letter that he wanted for Anna Terblanche and Geordie McKay, on official police letterhead.

◆

Anna decided at the last minute not to bring the documents to work with her. The deli was only around the corner from her house, and she could pop in and get the envelope after she had the Captain's letter. But she wanted to find a better place to hide it than under the carpet in her room. She paced about, trying to think of a suitable spot. The chiming of the clock gave her the idea. Opening the door at the back of the old grandfather clock in the hall, she placed the envelope in the dark space behind the mechanism.

She was feeling good as she hummed a tune in the shower. Then she decided to wear the new skirt and blouse she had bought recently when shopping with Geordie, a skirt he really liked her in. A final check in the mirror, where she blew a kiss to him as if he were standing behind her and off she skipped to her car.

Traffic was heavy on the main drag so Anna cut across an industrial park. An old car passed her in a reckless manner, causing her to brake pretty hard as it then slowed down in front of her. Unfortunately, it seemed to be going her same route, so she sat on its tail impatiently.

She never saw its brake lights glowing, and was too close to stop in time when she realized the old banger had slowed suddenly. The bump was a solid one as she rear-ended it. Anna got out of her car when the other driver did so. Then she saw the Mercedes behind and its driver beckoning to her. He could be a witness about the brake lights, she thought, and walked towards him. The back door of the Merc opened as she approached it and a young man called her. As she reached the open door, she didn't notice anyone behind her till her arms were grabbed. In an instant she was pushed head first into the laps of two men in the back seat of the Merc. The car began to move immediately as the men pushed her between them. She struggled with them and in the process noticed through the back window that her car was already being driven away from the accident scene.

"What's going on here?" she blurted, in her native Afrikaans.

"For a pretty Boer girl you're causing us too much trouble," replied the big man on her right. "We're taking you out of the picture for a while."

With that, the other man pressed a foul smelling cloth into her face, and in moments her struggles ended. When she came to, they were still in the car. Someone offered her water which she accepted. She tried to calm herself down and figure out how to play this. Obviously she was being kidnapped, she thought. It was a strange, frightening and uncanny coincidence that it was just when she had the chance to blow the case, by giving the list to the Captain. Had she been wrong about him? They had tried to get Geordie and having failed, were they now coming for him through her?

The car stopped at what she figured was a gate. She could hear men outside the car speaking and the sound of rusted gate hinges. Then the car moved on again slowly for a few minutes. When it stopped this time her captors ushered her out. As she exited the car door she glanced about quickly, fighting to focus in the sudden glare of bright sunlight. They began to walk their prisoner to the nearby building. Anna looked about a little more. It appeared to be a small building for a privately guarded estate, probably a guest cottage. A commercial airplane flew low overhead. She figured they must still be in the greater Jo'burg area.

Once inside the building she was hustled down a corridor to a small room with no outside window. The men left immediately, ignoring her questions and her pleas. The door was locked and as the men's footsteps receded Anna took stock of her new abode.

It appeared to be a servants room, small, very basic but at least self contained. In the corner there was a single bed and diagonally across from it, a toilet with a simple partition for a hint of privacy. Near the toilet, a wash-basin with hot and cold taps and a small mirror with wall light. The main light was a single bulb hanging from the ceiling in the middle of the room, under which stood a small table and two cheap wooden chairs. One threadbare rug lay on the tile floor beside the bed. Three hooks on the vacant corner wall served as a wardrobe area, above which hung a small sign which Anna read aloud.

"Home sweet home," she sobbed, sinking into a chair with her head in her hands.

TWELVE

Reluctant Houseguest

The deli was fairly crowded when Captain De Klerk arrived. He walked through and satisfied himself that Anna was not there, so he got a table, a coffee, and a newspaper, to catch up on the world while he waited. By the third coffee his patience was stretched a bit. He asked the waiter for help in case he had missed her somehow.

Ten minutes later he called Mr. Goldstein's office. The receptionist was adamant that Anna had not come in to work at all in the morning, and neither had she called in sick. He paid his bill and drove to her house. There was nobody there except Muti, the maid, who was less than cooperative after her previous experience with the police. With patient coaxing he did manage to establish that Anna had not been there when Muti came to work, which was usual. Neither had there been any visitors to the house all morning. His next call was to the central dispatcher. Captain De Klerk had her check Anna's name against the past six hour's reported incidents. Nothing. Then, against identities of people injured in road accidents. Nothing again.

The dispatcher suggested running a check on her car. After a few minutes she came up with it. The car had been reported as being burglarized and stripped of tires but was not on record as having been reported stolen. It had been removed to a local police compound, while the owner was being traced. He instructed the dispatcher to record a possible abduction but not to put out any details till he did some more checking.

At the compound the Captain met the patrol officer who first found the car. It had been a routine call. Men, usual scavenger type, were seen removing tires from the car in an industrial area. When the police car arrived they ran off. The officer assumed the car was stolen even though it was not on the record as such. He had it moved to the compound to prevent it from being further stripped, until the owner was located.

Captain De Klerk told him that the owner was a lady who was helping them on a big case, and she was now missing, presumed abducted from this car. They went through the officers' actions from the moment the report came in, detail by detail. It seemed that the scavengers had been disturbed early, so that little had been touched by them inside the car, and the patrol officer had not removed anything either. The Captain looked over the car carefully without touching anything that might hamper the fingerprint people later. Nothing but the usual owner's manual in the glove compartment plus a lipstick. He did notice that the floor mats were all misplaced as if someone had searched under them.

Back in his own car Captain De Klerk went through the details he had to date. The scavenger call had come in to the police dispatcher at ten, anonymously. He wished he had a name and could talk with that caller. Local business employees in the industrial estate would be interviewed in case anybody saw anything that may be connected to the abduction. Shortly afterwards, he himself visited the two businesses located closest to the abandoned car, without any success.

At this stage his best assumption was that she was grabbed while on her way to work. Was it pure coincidence that it happened on the same morning of their meeting at the park? Maybe she had been followed and grabbed because she was seen meeting with him. People may be after her, in lieu of McKay, to use as a bargaining weapon against the boy. Unless she had told someone else about the papers she had, which he thought was unlikely, then her possession of them was unknown. Of course, Van de Merwe must have known that McKay had taken them, hence his search of her room. How could he himself have been so stupid not to have already assigned protection to the girl, surveillance at least? The chances were good that Anna had the papers with her in the car, in preparation for their noon meeting, like he had the letter for her. Therefore, her abductors may already have them, even if it was only by a stroke of their good fortune.

The Captain cursed his own bad luck at losing such a great chance to break the case wide open. But if they got what they wanted, why take her? She would either be released immediately or just disposed of. He had messed up and he knew it. For his own and Anna's sake, he had to assume that she had the papers hidden, still leaving at least a few more acts of the drama to be played out. He could just imagine the rage on the Chief's face when he learned that another opportunity to break this case had slipped away.

To save time, he had sent the patrol officer from the compound to Anna's house, with instructions to have the maid close off her room. The officer was to prevent anyone from entering the room. He ordered a list of all the house residents to be compiled, especially the lease holder, complete with phone numbers where they could be reached at work.

By the time Captain De Klerk got back to his office at Jeppe, his secretary had pulled Anna Terblanche's information from the identification card master files. Many of the citizens didn't like the card system, but at a time like this it was invaluable. The Chief had left a message also, and that call was returned first. He was again pleasantly surprised by the Chief's understanding attitude, but grateful for it nonetheless, and was quickly given the authorization for whatever he might need in this critical situation.

The next call was a tough one. Anna's mother was very upset at the news. Captain De Klerk reiterated gently that he was hopeful that she would turn up fine in the next twenty-four hours. He did tell Mrs. Terblanche that Anna had been helping them in an important case, and asked her not to give out any information to anyone, but to contact his office immediately if any calls or demands came in. Anna's mother did not know Geordie or how to contact him. Being as the woman was still very distressed, the Captain gave her his home number too, and told her to feel free to call him at any time.

All was quiet at Anna's house when the police officer checked in from there, with the names of the commune dwellers. A girl named Marie was the lessee. When the Captain called her at work she told him she had already heard from the maid. Marie had decided something serious was wrong and would be leaving work early. He told her of the suspected abduction and in the absence of Anna's permission to search her room, he asked Marie to meet him there. She thanked him for this courtesy and they agreed to meet at the house at three-thirty.

Marie greeted him with questions.

"Is Anna in trouble with the police? What is going on Captain?"

"Far from it. I will tell you, strictly confidentially, that she was helping us with an important case, but that information must not leave this room. I was waiting to meet with her at lunchtime today and she didn't show up. I am hoping there might be some scrap of information in her room that may help us find her."

"Is she in danger?" Marie asked.

"Unfortunately, I would have to say yes. Time is of the essence here, Miss. Can I go ahead and check her room?"

"Yes, please do Captain. I will join you in a moment, after I speak to Muti, our maid."

"Would you please ask her to keep this whole affair quiet?"

"Yes, of course, Captain."

While Marie went off to speak with the maid the captain went along to Anna's room.

He was greeted with a pleasant scent of perfume as he entered. It was a big room on the second floor, well lighted by two windows. It's tidiness struck him immediately. It had a large bed with the usual complement of accompanying bedroom furniture. On the dressing table sat a full array of women's cosmetics. A greeting card caught his eye. Picking it up he saw it was signed by Geordie and was printed in Ireland, no postmark or address on it. He found himself reading Geordie's love lines. At the bottom it read 'when you translate the enclosed I think it will blow your mind'. Up in the corner was written 'say hello and thanks to Liz for me.'

The Captain was still puzzling over the card as Marie entered.

"Do you know Geordie?" he asked.

"Of course. He's in and out of here all the time. He's that crazy Irishman that Anna goes out with."

"Do you know where he is at present?"

"Only that he is overseas, some kind of family illness I think," Anna said.

"Who is Liz?"

"She's a good friend of Anna's. She lives a short distance away, also on Jan Smuts."

"Could you ask the maid to come here to the room, please?"

"Sure. I'll be right back."

While she was gone he slipped the card into his pocket. The waste paper basket was empty. He peeped into some of the drawers. They were full of women's clothes, except one, which was almost empty and contained what appeared to be men's clothes, probably a few of Geordie's things. The magazine pile didn't hide any papers either.

Marie returned with Muti. The Captain smiled and addressed the scared black woman.

"You worked in this room today Muti, right?"

"Yes *Baas*. I cleaned, made the bed and put back clean clothes."

"Did you notice anything different this morning? Think carefully. Anything that indicated she might have had a visitor to the room, either a wanted visitor or unwanted one?"

"No *Baas*, The room was the same as usual. *Baas* Geordie is away, and she has nobody else."

"I didn't mean that kind of visitor. Did you see or tidy away any sheets of typed paper that may have been on the bed or on the dressing table? Was there much in the waste basket?"

"I saw only a magazine on the bed and the basket was almost empty, nothing but a few cotton wool balls in it, Baas."

"That will be all, Muti. Thank you for your help. An officer will be posted here for a few days. He will explain how to deal with phone calls and how we will be monitoring the phone."

◆

It wasn't until Anna cocked her wrist to look at the time that she realized she had lost her watch in the morning's incident. After initial sobbing, she began to focus on the realities of her plight and on what she could do. Above all, she decided that she had to keep a level head. Time was critical. Surely Captain De Klerk would have realized something was wrong when she failed to turn up for the meeting, she thought. Maybe someone saw what happened and gave the police a description of her captors and the car they drove away in? Chances were that she was being held at a property of someone on the file list, but, alas, the Captain didn't have the file. It was reasonable for him to assume that the file had disappeared with her. For once, she hoped the police would search her house and find the envelope. She couldn't even remember if she had told him that she had the file at home or not.

The footsteps in the corridor interrupted her train of thought. They came directly to the door of her room and a key turned in the lock. A young man was shown in, followed by one of the abductors from earlier, who carried a tray on which stood a jar of guava juice, some biscuits and Anna's handbag.

"Good day, Miss Terblanche," the young man said. "You don't mind if I call you Anna do you?"

"Who are you?" Anna asked.

"That's not important. I am the one responsible for getting you this food and your bag. Please sit at the table. We can chat while you enjoy your snack."

"Why have you kidnapped me?" Anna demanded.

"Questions, questions. I thought I was the one to do the asking. Why have you and your boyfriend stuck your noses into our business? He stole our merchandise, set a trap with the police, then took money and important papers belonging to us. Tell me about it, Anna."

"What do you want from me?" she shot back.

"Is this a game of answering every question with another question?" the young man asked, throwing his hands in the air.

"Kidnapping is a serious crime you know."

"So is stealing, Anna. Thank you for breaking the question deadlock. You're a very pretty girl, and I'm told, an intelligent girl too. We simply wish to return to the status quo that existed before Mr. McKay walked off with our property. Now what could be simpler than that?"

"What does all of that have to do with me?"

"Your friend Mr. McKay has been most difficult to meet with, elusive you might say. Perhaps he will change his mind now?"

"We're not that close you know. There's no point in holding me. He has lots of girlfriends."

"Spare the theatrics, Anna. Credit us with some intelligence.

Let's proceed on a positive route. You need to think hard of a way to help us, your life may well depend on it. Do you wish to talk about it further now, or do you need a little time to think about it?"

"I don't honestly know how I can help you." Anna answered.

"Try this to begin with. You have told police that you have a file relating to our business in Kimberley. Your friend, McKay, stole that from us. How about telling us where that file is and we may be able to get you home in time for dinner? All we need is your cooperation. Remember, time is of the essence. I'm a patient man but my colleagues are not. What do you say, Anna?"

"Give me a little time to think it over."

"Fine. There will be someone posted in the corridor. Call them when you are ready to talk more, but don't delay."

With that, the young man walked out. The door was locked again.

Once alone, Anna drank some juice and even ate a little to stop her stomach from rattling. Then she opened her handbag. It had already been searched and rearranged. Geordie's number in Ireland had not been in it, she kept that in a book of W.B. Yeat's poetry, in the page of her favorite poem. She found herself reciting it now at this peculiar time, 'tread softly because you tread on my dreams'. Some dream!

Forcing herself back to reality she washed her neck, rinsed her mouth with water, brushed her hair and touched up her make-up, finished off with lipstick. At least she felt better now. She paced the floor again as she re-focused her options. After a short time she knocked on the door. The man came down the hall and spoke to her through it, without unlocking it, then went away to fetch his boss. What seemed to Anna like another half hour went by before they returned.

This time the young man was accompanied by an older, short, bald and overweight man. He seemed very irritable and uncomfortable.

"So you have decided to cooperate," began the young man, showing off his satisfied grin.

"Yes. What do you want me to do?" Anna asked.

"Why, give us our property back, Anna, of course. Like we talked about earlier." he answered.

"But I don't have it here, Geordie was to call me at work this morning and tell me where it is. Your thugs spoiled that by kidnapping me."

"Come now, Anna, don't play games with us. Our information is that you have the papers at your house."

"Then your informant is wrong. Go search the house if you are so sure."

The other man spoke this time, loud and blunt.

"You need to get McKay back to South Africa with our other property also. He gives it to us, we give you to him."

"What comprises the property, exactly?" Anna asked, in the same tone.

"A briefcase containing money, some diamonds and these documents, which he took from a house in Houghton."

"There were no diamonds in it, and very little money."

"Have you seen it, Anna?" the young man asked.

"Yes. Before Geordie went to Ireland. He may well have taken it to Ireland with him."

The young man continued his questioning.

"And where is this Geordie in Ireland?"

"I don't know. He is moving about there."

"How can you contact him? Do you have a phone number?"

"Not here, as you know from going through my handbag. I have a number back at my house. Loan me a car and I will go fetch it for you.":

"You have been watching too much television, Anna. Could you describe to a third party exactly where the number is?"

"Of course," she replied.

"Excuse us for a moment," the young man answered.

The two men left the room. Anna could hear their subdued voices in the hall before they walked away. Probably ten or twenty minutes went by. The young man returned, on his own this time, carrying a parcel.

"I have brought you some clothes and toiletries. Phoning your house from here is not a good idea. I want you to think hard and remember the number in Ireland. You will find something nice in here to wear. My man will be back for you in an hour to take you to the main house. I want you to join me for dinner. I'm sure as we get better acquainted we will find a way forward. Until later, Anna."

"You're not giving me much choice, are you?" she asked.

He just smiled but said nothing and left.

After a few minutes she opened the parcel. There were a few sun dresses, two pairs of slacks, underwear and shoes. Everything looked new and nice and exactly her size. The toothbrush was welcome and she brushed her teeth first. Then she had a close look around the room for peepholes, finding none. Satisfied, she took off her clothes and had a full stand-up wash at the hand basin and began to try on the clothes.

When the man came for her this time he was very courteous, but silent, as they walked the short distance to the large brick main house. Her questions were ignored with a polite smile. The man showed her into the front hall and left immediately. Her young jailer sauntered out from an adjacent sitting room.

"Anna, you look great. Welcome to my humble abode."

"Thank you for the clothes," she said, blushing.

"You're welcome. Come, let me show you around. My name is Louis, by the way."

THIRTEEN

A Shot in the Dark

Liz answered the phone after the first ring, recognizing Geordie's voice immediately. She had practised what she was going to say and how she was going to remain calm, but fell apart as soon as she heard him speak.

"They've kidnapped, Anna," she blurted, sobbing uncontrollably.

Geordie found himself shouting down the phone at her at first, trying to ask questions. Then he got hold of himself and concentrated on calming her down. Gradually, with his encouraging words Liz quelled the tears, blew her nose loudly and told him the bare details of the incident as she knew them.

She was not able to answer any of Geordie's specific questions and fell into a relapse of snivelling when he pressed her. Eventually he had enough to piece together a vague chain of events.

"Liz, you may get a visit from the police. Don't tell I them we have spoken, or of Anna receiving calls there, please. I can only tell you that we were helping the police with an important case that is undercover and secret. They were supposed to protect us but failed, with the result that I had to come here. Now, with Anna being abducted, I think that someone is double-crossing us. Be nice to them but tell them nothing, okay?"

"I'll be fine now that I've told you and I have an idea what is going on. Do you think you can do anything to help Anna?"

"Sure. I have a plan in mind already. She'll be back visiting you in no time."

"Thanks, Geordie. I feel better already."

They said goodbye and Geordie flopped down into a chair.

The plan he had bragged about did not exist. All he had was a throbbing headache and could think of nothing better than making tea. With the comfort of his steaming mug of tea he sat down by the phone table, thumbing through the directory for inspiration.

◆

When Captain De Klerk drove up the driveway into Anna's house everything looked very quiet, too quiet. Seeing no police car there made him angry and he called dispatch. They told him the officer had left a short time before, on internal orders that the dispatcher thought had emanated from the Captain himself.

"Get two cars here on the double," he roared. "I'm going in to secure the house."

He slipped out of his car and moved quietly to the house. The front door was ajar and a television was blaring in the front living room. Making his way in there he saw a body on the floor and cautiously approached it. He felt the neck and found a pulse. There was nobody else in the darkened room. With his flashlight he examined the person again, recognizing him as Peter, who lived there. He had been hit with something and would be out of it for a while but the wound was not life threatening. The Captain was about to move the man when he heard noises from upstairs, as if furniture was being pushed about. He slipped back into the hall, to the staircase and began to climb. On the second step he heard footsteps coming out of an upstairs room. He just made it to the under stairs area before a person began to descend, obviously in a rush. As soon as the balaclava clad intruder cleared the bottom step, the Captain levelled his gun and shouted.

"Police, stop or I'll shoot."

In the dim light the Captain could identify the figure as a man, now frozen in his tracks. In the same instant the lights of a car came rushing up the driveway towards the open front door, lighting up the hallway. The glare was intense and distracted the Captain's attention momentarily. As he shielded his eyes he saw the intruder turn towards him and bring his hand up. Instantly, the Captain fired, hitting his target in the right shoulder area, spinning the man around. The intruder's gun went off also and a bullet hit the ceiling. The man fell on the floodlit hall floor and the gun fell from his hand. The Captain was over him immediately and kicked it away. From outside, a voice called.

"Captain De Klerk, are you okay, Sir? We are ready to come in, Sir."

"The situation is under control," replied the Captain, "come on in."

With guns drawn, two police officers entered the hallway, to find their Captain standing over a writhing hooded man.

"Turn on that light switch, Kurt," the Captain ordered. "There is another injured man in the living room. One of you call an ambulance."

Two more officers now arrived on the scene.

"Go upstairs and check the rest of the house," the Captain ordered them.

He and Kurt looked down at the wounded man, who was now bleeding heavily and losing consciousness.

"Get that hood off him," the Captain ordered.

Kurt caught the hood by the edges at the neck and pulled it off in one smooth motion.

"Sergeant Van de Merwe!" he gasped.

◆

For the next twenty minutes the Captain was too consumed with securing the scene to dwell on the implications of finding his suspended Sergeant burglarizing the house. Peter had been alone in the house when attacked. Luckily he was not seriously hurt.

Van de Merwe's wound was more severe than at first thought and he was rushed to immediate surgery. The Captain ordered that his room be kept under guard at all times. Nobody was to talk to Van before the Captain himself questioned him. He would personally arrest and charge Van with attempted murder, aggravated assault and other charges, which would send the disgraced policeman to prison for a long time.

Right now he worked to keep this shooting incident as quiet as possible, at least until Anna Terblanche was located and rescued. Peter was taken to the hospital for observation. Apart from a severe bruise and headache he would be fine. Marie and another girl returned from their night out as final clean up was going on. The Captain satisfied their safety concerns eventually, with a promise of a twenty-four hour police presence at the house. In Anna's room things were strewn everywhere, but nothing could be tidied up till the fingerprint people finished.

When all began to quiet down Captain De Klerk went to his car. For a full ten minutes he just sat there in the dark. He had been within a hair's breadth of being shot, but what bothered him more was the revulsion of having his own man betray his trust, and actively work against him. Their wives were good friends and he was godfather to one of Van's children. How were the kids going to understand their father's treason? They even called the Captain 'uncle' and now their uncle had shot their father.

One of the officers on duty interrupted him with some questions. After answering them he gave further instructions and headed home. His wife was upset about Van de Merwe, for his family's sake, but also angry at him. They talked for a long time over a pot of strong coffee.

Chief Ferreira didn't call, which both surprised and pleased the Captain. Sleep was out of the question yet, so he went instead to his office in his basement. He wanted to go through the details of the day while they were still fresh in his mind. Questions flooded his brain, so many that his head throbbed as he wrote them all down in a long list. In his capacity as Captain he was expected to have all the answers. Some of the questions were easy but there were a few critical central ones that he just could not find his way past. He finally went to bed at two o'clock, and eventually caught a few hours of troubled sleep.

◆

Meanwhile in Galway, Geordie McKay had found his inspiration. He had secured a flight, retrieved some working capital from his stash at the train station, and headed for the airport. Rather than carry the Kimberley File with him, he used an express courier service to send it to Mickey Kelly's house. An enclosed note asked Mickey to hold the envelope for him.

Geordie's flight plan was to arrive in Jo'burg by the next afternoon. His mind was now made up. He was going to sort out this whole fucking mess himself, somehow.

FOURTEEN

The Spider and the Fly

Anna was ushered into the main house, like an honored guest. She struggled to make sense of this total change from prisoner status. Louis was like a different person now. He offered her a choice of cocktails and as she sipped her gin and tonic, he insisted on showing her around his house.

It was beautiful. Large spacious rooms that were well furnished and decorated. By the time they got to the dining room the table was laid out with fresh flowers, lead crystal and antique silver-for two.

"Are we eating alone?" Anna asked, with discomfort.

"My colleague had to leave unexpectedly. Don't worry Anna, I'm on best behavior and we have much to talk about. Tonight we have fresh rock lobster from the Cape. I have an excellent chef who comes up with wonderful creations. Just sit back and enjoy the culinary delights he serves up to us."

Dinner was indeed wonderful, Anna had to admit, despite the odd setting. Louis insisted she have seconds when he saw how well she ate. The conversation was polite small talk but mostly directed at her. She did not mention Mr. Goldstein's name in describing her job, instead passing it off that she was a secretary for a small time attorney who mostly did divorces. As they sipped wine after their main course, Anna pressed him for information.

"Louis, if this is not an interrogation then it must be a two-way conversation. Tell me something about you. How did you know my clothes size for instance? Why are you being nice to me now?"

Louis was eager to talk.

"I used to be in the clothes business and I dealt with ladies fashions on a daily basis. Do you like my choices for you? I meant it when I said you look great."

"Yes, all the clothes are very nice, thank you. Why did you leave the clothes business?"

"I didn't really. I just left it on a personal daily basis. There are some very talented managers out there who continue to make money for me. I became, let's say, interested in other lines of business. So much business is inter-related you know. One can hardly be too diversified these days."

"Surely there is a difference between legal and illegal business. You were obviously successful in the clothes trade. Why take the risk of losing everything by getting involved in something like illegal diamonds?"

"What is legality in business, Anna? In small business everything is straightforward, like taxes, employee wages, debt and contracts. However, in big business it is an entirely different game. You know how wealthy this country is in terms of precious metals and gems. Wealthy people love excitement and power. There is no power without risk and risking money is only a small part of it, especially if one has more than can be spent in a few lifetimes. But enough of this talk. I prefer to show you what profitable business can do for people and those who are their friends. I want to hear more about what makes Anna Terblanche tick."

◆

But Louis Trichardt had only told her a very small part of the story. He was indeed involved in the rag trade but his rise to riches was altogether different. It began with a smart kid, too smart to finish school. Instead he made more money per week than most adults were making in a month, except that his income came from running errands for drug dealers. Next on his resume came diversification into money laundering and loan sharking. Clients who didn't pay were given the opportunity, as Louis called it, to lose their businesses instead of their lives. Most chose to let the business go and were then 'persuaded' to show their young partner how the business functioned. He found that he had a flair and a liking for fine clothes, and thus concentrated on accumulating those types of shops. Later he began to put a legitimate face on his growing empire, believing that respectability could be purchased. To that end he even bought some high profile shops, and many well known people in the trade had already accepted Louis' transition to respectable businessman.

The thirst for power is what led him to get involved in an infant illegal diamond operation as diamonds were a perfect match for expensive clothes. The large legitimate diamond companies in South Africa were too arrogant in Louis' mind, and needed to be punished for rebutting him. Returns from his diamond 'business' were very good, but Louis' power in the organization was not at all to his liking. With his arch rival Botha, now out of the way, Louis' hand was strengthened and he saw no reason why he couldn't gain complete control of the group.

Botha was very sloppy on paperwork. Despite criticism at their board meetings, and promises to copy Louis with the relevant documents relating to couriers, payoffs and such, Botha kept it all to himself. He was obviously afraid of Louis' growing power and determined to hold him up at every turn. If there was a copy of the missing Kimberley File, then nobody knew where it was.

Louis decided that McKay's original of the file must be retrieved. It was vital to enable them to assess the damage from the Kimberley area raids, rectify that damage, and get back on track. Louis therefore offered to complete the recovery of the file and punish McKay, as a major step toward his ultimate goal.

Since the convenient 'suicide' of his late wife, Louis had ultimate flexibility to do whatever it took to win. The entrance of a highly desirable woman into the picture was only an added challenge to be overcome, with a bedding bonus waiting to be claimed as an extra.

◆

After dinner Louis resumed the house tour where they left off, on the stairs. Anna noticed the original paintings along the wall as they ascended and asked him about them. He passed them off saying he liked to pick up landscape works from different places on his travels. The rooms upstairs were probably all bedrooms but he only showed her two.

His tour highlight was the master bedroom suite. The bed was enormous, a California king he called it, with satin and silk sheets and covers. In the bathroom there was a sunken tub big enough to hold six, a similar sized jacuzzi, glass encased shower, beautiful wash basins, even a TV-video unit that appeared out of the wall when Louis touched a button on a remote control. There was a large dressing room with wide full-length lighted mirrors and two walk-in closets that were as big as rooms. One was obviously his and the other was empty except for some expensive ladies clothes hanging at one end of the rail. Anna felt it best to comment on how beautiful everything looked, as she emerged from the empty closet into the bedroom.

"You need to buy your wife more clothes to fill those rails," she said, immediately regretting it.

"My wife died two years ago in an accident."

"I'm sorry."

"Thank you. What do you think of all this, Anna?"

"You must love living in this wonderful house."

"Tell me what you really think."

"Well, I'm wondering how one can enjoy this in the knowledge that it is the result of ill-gotten wealth."

"I could have bet money you'd say that. You've got what I call 'the guilt complex.' One certainly cannot enjoy it until the guilt complex is shaken off. Anna, you would be hard pressed to find anyone living in a big estate anywhere in Jo'burg who could prove that all their money came from virgin-pure dealings. I have earned everything I've got."

Louis sat on the side of his luxurious bed and invited her to sit with him. Instead she sat on a chaise lounge by the wall.

"Don't you think it would be much nicer to sleep in here than in the quarters you were in earlier, Anna?"

"Of course. Are you ready to swap with me?"

"I like that. Possibly, but wouldn't you need someone to show you where everything is?"

Anna blushed, but shot back. "Isn't the scale a bit off balance here? I've been propositioned before but never by someone who kidnapped me. You'll have to forgive me if I'm getting confused here. A few hours ago you were suggesting that I'd be lucky if I got out of here alive and now you're trying to woo me into your bed. With your money you can have all the girls you want. What the hell is your game, Louis? Look, I want to go back downstairs now."

He seemed to be caught off balance by Anna's bluntness and meekly stood up and escorted her out of the room. Downstairs he poured coffee for both of them. Anna sipped iced water and bit her tongue in order keep silent.

"Have you gone into a self enforced silence, Anna?"

"No. I thought it was your turn to speak and I was waiting for your response."

"Not many people have the nerve to speak to me like that. You're quite a lady, Anna, I like you. I wish we had met in a less complicated situation. Yes, I do have everything I want, except a meaningful relationship. It's a difficult subject for me to discuss, the past two years since I lost my wife have been tough."

"I have no problem with us being friends but obviously we cannot do so under these captive circumstances. Let's return to the conversation point we were at when you and your friend came to visit me. If I can help you get your file returned, then everything is back to the status quo you asked for, right? You let me go, then we can be friends."

"What about your boyfriend, McKay?"

"Boyfriends come and go, don't they? I have no special ties

to him. But you can't buy my affection either. I'm a woman of the real world, and I'd rather have a good man with money than a good man without money, but note the emphasis on 'good', Louis. I'm sure we could let bygones be bygones once we have achieved the status quo mentioned. But I don't want anything to do with a man who goes around having people kidnapped or hurt."

Louis smiled.

"Like I said earlier, you're quite a lady. My colleague has another plan in motion at present that has to take its course before I proceed. But I note what you said."

"Do you mean he has more power than you?"

"It's called seniority. It occurs right over the business spectrum. But if his plan fails and then mine works, there will be a reversal in that order."

"What is his plan?"

Louis hesitated, but relented when Anna pushed it further.

"He thinks the file is in your room, that's why the police are guarding your house. He is diverting their attention so that someone can go in and search the place thoroughly."

Anna fought hard to retain her demeanor while he finished the sentence.

"Why are you looking so alarmed Anna?"

"I'm, ah, worried that one of my housemates might get hurt. At the very least my room is going to be a shambles and there is nothing in it. Can't you call him off?"

"No. Not at this late stage. Besides, when he comes up

empty handed it will strengthen my position. I hope to have you as my ally, and then I'll be able to wrap this whole business up quickly and go forward like you talked about. Don't worry about your room, I'll cover all your losses. It'll be a good excuse to get a whole new wardrobe."

Just then someone knocked on the door, entering on Louis' instruction.

"Excuse me Sir, you have an important telephone call," the servant said.

"Please excuse me, Anna, I won't be long. Thomas here will keep you company while I'm gone."

Anna tried to make small talk with Thomas, to no avail. He wouldn't answer any questions, despite Anna's telling him that she was now on the same side as Louis. Finally she busied herself walking around the room looking at the furniture, paintings and anything else of interest. She noticed that there was no phone in the room and nothing to indicate where exactly this house was located.

Ten minutes later Louis returned and Thomas left. Anna waited for him to speak. Instead he poured himself another coffee and went to the liquor cabinet.

"Would you like an after dinner drink, Anna?"

"What are you having?"

"Port."

"I'll have the same, please."

He carried the drinks over to where she now sat on a

small sofa, then he paced the room. Anna watched him. When he continued to show no signs of speaking, she broke the silence."

"Is something wrong Louis?"

"Yes and no."

He paused for a full minute before continuing.

"The attempted search at your house was a fiasco. One of our people got himself shot in the process?"

"Is he dead?"

"Details are sketchy but it seems that some police Captain came by to check on his men, who had been diverted, and surprised our man. In the ensuing shootout he was seriously wounded by the policeman. He's in the hospital now, under guard."

"From what you said earlier, this strengthens your position, right?"

"It does, but the price is high?"

"If anything, this incident increases the urgency to get your documents back," Anna pressed. "I—I have remembered Geordie's phone number in Ireland and I'm prepared to go through with the deal we talked about earlier."

"Give me a minute to get this straight here. You will get him to give up the file in return for your freedom. There was money and gems involved too, remember. I need those also."

"I saw the briefcase and there was very little money. The police took the jewels to use in their sting operation, Geordie never saw them again. Money is of little consequence, you said so yourself. Take the file and leave it at that."

"But I saw all of Botha's accounts when I took over, after his death. They showed that there was a lot of money involved."

"Then Botha lied about it."

"Okay, Anna, forget the money. We do know that the police had control of the diamonds although there are some not accounted for. All of that is not as important as getting the file back. You call McKay, according to my instructions and arrange a transfer. I have another condition to add, that he leaves South Africa immediately afterwards, but you stay of course."

"I'll go along with that. Where do we make the exchange? It has to be somewhere public so that Geordie will feel safe. Both he and I must be able to walk away. Once the dust settles I can re-establish contact with you. I suggest somewhere like the Sandton Shopping Complex."

"Fine, let's make the call. Follow me to my office."

They walked down the hall to a wood panelled room which reminded Anna of Mr. Goldstein's, large desk, filing cabinets, phones. Louis sat in his big leather chair and motioned Anna to sit across from him. He wrote a few notes on a pad and handed it to her. It said, "No small talk, get first available flight, meet at specific time at Sandton within the next twenty-four hours."

"I'll be listening on this other phone and I'll cut you off if you get out of line. Here, dial the number."

Anna dialed but it just rang and rang. She then realized how late at night it was in Ireland and indicated that to Louis.

He said to hold on longer. Finally a sleepy voice answered. Anna went straight to the point.

"This is Anna in South Africa. Is Geordie in please?"

"Anna! We thought you had been kidnapped, are you okay? This is Joe. Geordie has already gone to South Africa, arriving there at noon tomorrow."

On Louis's gesture to finish, she spoke.

"Thank you, Joe. I'm fine, but I'm not in a position to speak right now. Sorry for waking you. Goodbye."

Louis spoke as she put down the receiver.

"You did well. It looks like we will all be meeting Mr. McKay earlier than expected, at Jan Smuts Airport. Come, I'll escort you to a guest room upstairs. Thomas will move your things."

He pressed a button which seemed to bring the man instantly, and repeated the same instructions. They walked silently up the stairs, both engrossed in their own thoughts. The guest room was across the hall from Louis' master bedroom. He showed her into her room and switched on the lights.

"Acquaint yourself with everything, Anna. I'll be back in a few minutes."

Thomas arrived with her clothes as she was checking out the bathroom. It was not as luxurious as Louis' room but it was as good as anything one would see in a top class hotel. There were big soft towels and sachets of bubble bath and shampoo. She began to run the water immediately and didn't hear Louis until he was behind her, startling her a little.

"Once you have your bath you will find this nightie comfortable. It belonged to my wife. It is almost new, it's pure silk."

"Thank you very much Louis. It's absolutely beautiful."

"Good night then. If you need anything I'll be across the hall."

Finally Anna was alone with her thoughts, and her tears soon followed. Her great plan to free herself and to help Geordie, had just gone up in smoke. Now, Louis even knew when Geordie was arriving back, and he didn't have to concede a damn thing for that information.

The bath was ready so Anna went ahead with it, but without enthusiasm for her luxurious surroundings. While she soaked, she fought to concentrate on her options. They were very few, she admitted. She thought she had covered up well when her telephone call went sour. That left her with only one ace still in her hand, one she was not keen on playing but it had to be played now.

Louis' door was ajar, as he lay on his bed watching one of his James Bond movies. Suddenly she was there, standing before him in the doorway, dressed in the silk nightie.

"Excuse me Louis, I can't sleep," she said softly, "Do you have any books I can borrow?"

"Anna!" he exclaimed. "You look absolutely stunning. Come in, please. I'm not much of a reader but I like classic movies. Would you like to watch James Bond with me?"

"That would be nice, thank you."

FIFTEEN

―――•―――

A Favor From "Honest Frank"

The Captain slept later than he planned but was still in the office by six. Chief Ferreira came in twenty minutes later just as was leaving, wanting a meeting. Using his need to leave as an excuse to delay it, Captain De Klerk managed to postpone it till ten, at the Chief's office.

On his way from Jeppe to the northern suburbs the Captain grabbed a quick breakfast sandwich. He was knocking on the door of the law office at seven-forty. Finally, the door was opened by an old man, his glasses on the end of his nose.

"Captain De Klerk! Just as the man I need to speak with. Come in please," the old man said, his face lighting up.

"Good morning, Mr. Goldstein. You're looking well this morning."

"I've got fresh coffee, would you like some, Captain?"

The Captain nodded and followed Mr. Goldstein to the kitchen area, filled his own coffee cup and went on to the office where Mr. Goldstein was tidying his desk.

"Congratulations on your victory in Krugersdorp," the Captain began.

"Thank you, Captain. As you can see I'm not so successful in keeping my office tidy. Without Anna here I'm in total disarray. I hope she gets well soon and is back to work."

"That's what I came to talk to you about. She's not sick, Mr. Goldstein. I instructed her housemates to tell any callers that, which is probably your source."

The old man nodded.

"Where is she then, if she's not sick?" Mr. Goldstein asked.

"She was kidnapped yesterday on her way to work. At this time we don't know where she is. No demands have been made to date. I'm pretty certain it is connected with this diamond case. She is probably being held in order to get to Geordie McKay, her boyfriend."

Mr. Goldstein had stopped his tidying. He shook his head in disbelief.

"Oh dear. Poor Anna. But this doesn't fit. The diamonds they lost in the police operation are probably of little consequence to them. I don't understand."

"McKay ran off that night with the wrong briefcase which contained documents that are very important to them. That's what they're trying to recover."

"I see. What are you doing to find Anna?"

"The usual. Monitoring calls to her residence and family. Doing some quiet checking through our contacts in such a way as to not frighten anyone into something rash."

"I wish I could think of a way to help."

"Maybe you can. I would like to have a look through her office in case she has any notes that may help. Are you aware of any strange phone calls she received recently?"

"Personally I am not. With the Krugersdorp trial, I have been out of the office most of the time. We had that brief conversation with you after the police raid in Houghton. Both she and Geordie were very upset with the level of violence that occurred there. They were so worried about his safety that he went back to Ireland. I assume you know that."

"Yes. Events moved too quickly at Houghton. I now know why. Geordie had a legitimate fear although I wish he had stayed. He could have been protected."

"Isn't it a fair question to ask where Anna's protection was? Surely you haven't miscalculated again," Mr. Goldstein asked, pointedly.

"Fair criticism, and one that has not left my own mind since her abduction. We seem to be a step behind the action and that must be corrected. Anna's safety is at stake here."

They searched her office without finding anything useful. Mr. Goldstein sat in Anna's chair.

"Anna is almost fanatical about being organized. You won't find trash in her office."

"I don't suppose you would know a contact number for Geordie McKay in Ireland, would you?" the Captain asked.

"No, Captain, but I do know he is in a city called Galway. Anna and I talked about it, just on a tourist note. It is a lovely old city, in a beautiful part of a wonderful country. It's no wonder that Yeats and Wilde were so moved by the place."

"Are they friends of Miss Terblanche too, Mr. Goldstein?"

"Captain, you are not a student of poetry I see. They were great Irishmen of letters."

The Captain excused his literary ignorance and left, promising to keep Mr. Goldstein informed of progress.

◆

For once Chief Ferreira was ready on time at ten o'clock. He flipped though the Captain's report before addressing him.

"This is depressing reading, Captain De Klerk. You were supposed to have a big day yesterday. Instead of getting the papers from the girl, she is gone now, too. We're not even back to square one, we're another step behind that. Tell me good news, for God's sake."

"As you well know, Sir, luck is a very important factor in our business. We seemed to have the luck running with us but it all changed with her abduction. At this stage we don't know what form her new information was to take. It may well be papers, as you say. Her kidnappers are lacking something, that's for sure. That's why Van de Merwe went in searching the place."

"Whatever. What are the latest developments today? When are you questioning Van?"

"The doctors can't say at this stage, maybe tomorrow or the next day. He's in bad shape. His wife, Robyn won't even talk to me either. Knowing him, I think that unless we have some angle on him he won't cooperate."

Both men fell silent for a moment. Then Chief Ferreira continued.

"I've talked to Robyn a few times, Captain. She is bearing up well, the kids are too young to understand. You are best to keep away just yet while she is at the blame stage. Back on the subject of the report here, do we know yet where McKay is in Ireland?"

"Eh, no, Sir. They don't have an identity card system over there and he hasn't done anything wrong, to justify our taking international proceedings."

"That's a matter of interpretation. Surely you could concoct something that would allow their police to pick him up. Be creative, Captain."

'I'm not in the 'concocting' business, Sir, but I'll work on it today."

"Do, Captain. This incident has not escaped the attention of the Government. I'm expected to have all the answers for them by early next week at the latest. To date I have been covering for you, but l may not be able to prevent them asking for your head if we have no breakthrough soon."

"Thank you, Sir. Your help and guidance will get us through, I know."

"Don't patronize me in that tone, Captain. I'm only doing my job. Now get on with yours, man."

◆

At eleven-thirty two men met in the carpark of Bimbos fast food. Captain De Klerk approached on foot and got into the other man's car. The man looked at him in surprise.

"Don't tell me they took the car off you, Captain. You said this had to be secret but all you're short of is the disguise."

"Keep the wise cracks for your comedy act, Frank," the Captain said. "I'm parked on the other side of the street. How's the 'private eye' business doing?"

"Great, so long as the divorce rate stays high. Don't tell me you want me to follow your wife and take pictures of her and her hairdresser?"

"I'm not in the mood for the smart stuff, okay. This is much more important than that, so listen up."

Frank De Beer, no relation to the De Beer's of diamond fame, sat through the next few minutes with his mouth open, as the Captain explained what he wanted him to do.

"I know I owe you a favor Captain, but this was not the way I had in mind to repay it. Do you realize what you're asking me to do? Why can't you take care of this internally? Hell, you've got all the resources at your disposal, surely you could find an angle."

"Just trust me. It has to be done this say, for reasons that I can't go into. You'll be paid, even if I have to do it out of my own pocket. It shouldn't take any more than a week or two. You must give this your best attention Frank, and I want detailed records kept, complete with times and photographs. Here is my home number, don't use the Jeppe lines. Call me in a day or two to update me, or before then if you see anything very important. You're a true patriot, Frank. Tot siens, goodbye."

"Yeah. Thanks, Captain. Tot siens to you too."

◆

The white Mercedes pulled into the short-term underground parking, the second car alongside it. They had left in good time and made two stops in Sandton, where Louis sent the driver in to pick up some packages while Anna and he waited in the modified plush interior of the Merc.

Two men from the other car came up to the dark windows. Louis opened the door to issue final instructions.

"Let's do a final run through the details," he said. "First, see what gate the British Airways noon flight from London arrives at. Inform me if any delays. Go to the passenger meeting point. Circulate there till you see your man. Do you both know his description so that you will recognize him?"

"Yes, boss. We'll find him."

"Once you locate him, verify that he is Geordie McKay. Then hand him the note you have from Anna. Find a suitable place to do our business and ask to see the brown briefcase and Afrikaans' documents. Then one of you wait with him while the other comes to fetch us. Is that all understood?"

"Yes, Sir."

"Good. Leave your weapons in your car, as Anna asked. Make sure you check and double-check the area for police. He is probably being met by a friend but we cannot take that for granted. If so, then the friend can sit out while we complete our business. Remember my car phone number. Use it to keep me informed. If there is any trouble don't run. Call me immediately or walk out quickly but calmly. Off you go then, it's five minutes to twelve."

Anna smiled nervously at Louis as the men left. She tried to look calm and confident while her stomach was in knots. Hopefully, after last night Louis trusted her enough to go through with her plan to the letter. As a little insurance she now held his hand and didn't resist when he put his arm around her. Within the hour she would be alone with Geordie in the airport. She would then be able to think straight and make the right decision. She looked at Louis at the same instant that he looked at her. They both smiled sweetly. A penny for your thoughts, she mused to herself.

Louis' man called him on the phone almost immediately. The place was crawling with police. Some undesirable 'Kaffir' was coming in on the same flight and the police were there to quell any demonstration against the government.

"Be extremely careful. This Kaffir business could work to your advantage," Louis barked down the phone.

Back in the airport Geordie was alarmed when he saw the commotion, and asked a hostess what was going on. He and the other passengers were processed through immigration quickly, without any questions. That was probably due to the situation, he thought, but it suited him just fine. At least he knew the police were not waiting on him. He finally emerged from the baggage claim and customs area in the company of an Englishman. They stood off to one side watching the thronging mass. Geordie did bag watcher while the Englishman took a leak, then left his stuff with the man while he did the same.

As he came out of the bathroom Geordie knew immediately something was wrong. There was a different white man standing over the bags, not the Englishman.

He rushed over to the luggage.

"What the hell is going on? Where is the man I left with my bags? Where is my briefcase?"

"The other gentleman asked me to keep an eye on this stuff for a minute. Some man grabbed a briefcase, he told me. Two of the policemen saw it and gave chase. He went after them to see what was happening. Is it your briefcase that has been stolen?"

"Yes," Geordie answered.

Geordie looked about uneasily. "Do you mind staying here with these other bags for a few minutes?" he asked the man.

"No problem."

Geordie took his big case with him and hurried off in the direction the man pointed. Once lost in the crowd he made straight for the exit and grabbed a taxi.

It seemed forever before Louis' phone rang again. He listened in silence for a moment.

"What the hell did Andries do that for?" he shouted into the phone.

His man, at the other end of the line was ready with his excuses.

"It seemed like a good opportunity, Boss. You always say never to pass up an opportunity. One of the policemen chasing him shot Andries, it looks real bad. What do you want me to do?"

"What happened to the briefcase?" Louis asked.

"The police have it."

"Where is McKay?"

"No sign of him. I went back to the spot where Andries grabbed the case and someone there said the man just walked off."

"There's probably nothing valuable in the case then. For once, why didn't you keep to instructions? Stay around for a while and see what the police do. Andries will be arrested for theft if he recovers from the wounds, you can't help him now. Follow the case but don't get yourself arrested. Get rid of the note from Anna and the paper with this number, right now.

We're out of here. Call into central with your information and I'll deal with you later."

Louis called his driver who was having a smoke fifty yards away and instructed him to head for home.

"Will you please tell me exactly what happened in there, Louis?" Anna asked.

"My men messed up. One of them has been shot by the police, who now have the briefcase."

"What about Geordie?"

"He just disappeared during the incident. Didn't even bother to wait for his briefcase. It must be empty, or else full of junk. Why do you think he walked off?"

"I don't know. He was probably scared. Are you not going to help your wounded man?"

"There is nothing I can do for him. His stupidity has cost us all dearly today. More importantly, why did your Geordie abandon the case and where did he go? Any ideas, Anna?"

"Possibly my house? That's all I can think of. What are we going to do now?"

"We're not going near your place, that's for sure."

Louis called Thomas, to confirm that all was well at the estate. He made a few more short calls, talking in disjointed conversation which told Anna little. Then he told the driver to change direction, and go instead to Pretoria, to an address with which the driver was obviously familiar. When Anna tried to find out what the plan was, he cut her off rather abruptly, saying he needed to think. They rode towards Pretoria in silence. Anna's confidence in her own security was shattered again. She had to think, and fast too, if she was to regain her momentum.

◆

Geordie told his taxi driver to head for the city. A little while later it occurred to him that it might not be advisable to go direct to Mickey's house in Houghton. They could be followed or someone could bribe the driver later for the address. Instead, Geordie had the taxi driver take him to a hotel in Rosebank. He walked into the lobby, went to the bathroom, and called another cab five minutes later which took him to Houghton. Mickey's maid got a fright when Geordie just walked into the commune, but then recognized him and all was well. None of the lads were home from work yet. He went behind the bar, passed on the hard stuff, settling for some cold Castle beer. As luck would have it, Mickey arrived home early. It didn't faze the Corkman one bit when Geordie asked him from the bar what he was drinking.

"Aren't you surprised to see me?" Geordie asked.

"It's about time you came back to have that drink you refused me at the airport, 'horse'. It's your round, too."

They both laughed and sat on the barstools with their beer. Geordie now told him the whole story, from Kimberley to the present, with the exception of the money in the case.

"That's one hell of a story there, horse. Never mind, 'Paddy maak a plaan'."

Geordie's head was buzzing as he tried to think, talking out loud.

"I don't think I can go near my place, or Anna's, or work even. In fact I don't think I should stay around here, either. I don't trust the police. I've got to free Anna somehow, but I don't have the foggiest idea how to do it."

After some silence they opened more beer and drifted into conversation about football, recent 'craic' while Geordie was away, and mutual friends. Suddenly Mickey's face lit up.

"Bally! He's your man. He'll sort out this mess for you," Mickey said.

"Mickey Kelly, did anyone ever tell you you're a bloody genius, boy?" Geordie shouted. "If they didn't, then I'm telling you now."

◆

Captain De Klerk had made a few other stops after leaving Frank. He had another long look at Anna's car. The kidnappers had been wearing gloves and no prints were found except Anna's, plus some on the outside, which he was sure the scavenger's left. He had contacted the Irish police but only in a routine missing person location request, simply to appease the Chief in case he checked up on him.

His men were still guarding Anna's house and he stopped in there to chat with the officer on duty, as a morale booster.

SIXTEEN

Partners of Convenience

Bally De Bruyne lived in a modest house in Benoni, a working class town that had long been sucked in by the sprawling giant, Johannesburg.

But this was where he had grown up and it suited his lifestyle. Like all white South Africans, Bally was called up to serve his time in the armed forces. He went while very young as he had no desire to go on to further education. Maybe he would learn something useful, his father had said. Indeed he had. Bally was very adept at handling weapons and soon found himself with an opportunity to join an elite command. It was just what he wanted, short on military formalities and long on action.

Over the next seven years his missions took him deep into the neighboring countries to fight the secret war against South Africa's enemy revolutionary guerrilla factions. Mozambique,

South West Africa and Botswana were all very familiar to him. Some missions were in townships at home, which he hated doing, especially Soweto. It was the increase of the latter that made him leave, that and the opportunity to fight elsewhere for big money.

Many of his contemporaries had retired young and went as mercenaries to the Rhodesian bush war. He joined them after a short post-retirement rest. The money to be made was indeed very enticing. As the bush war moved towards its losing climax, greed replaced good judgement. It cost the lives of too many close friends. Bally decided to make one last big killing, literally, which he completed successfully, despite receiving some nasty wounds. He then retired for the second time, but now with enough money to last the rest of his life.

His war wounds healed in due course but he couldn't heal the deepest one, self inflicted, on his family. He knew he had neglected his wife and two children even before the mercenary episode. She had custody of the kids and the divorce by the time he finally hung up his guns. Somehow he believed he would win them all back when he came home. The harsh reality was otherwise, and it took a long time to sink in. The kids were in Durban where she remarried, giving the girls a stepfather who was good to them. Bally was in Benoni, or in the Jo'burg hangouts, playing the playboy, screwing divorcees and college girls, struggling to get back on terms with his life.

Geordie McKay had first run into Bally at one of the bars where they went to play darts. They were both good players, especially when the big winning play was needed. It was a game of singles, winner holds the board and the bets, one Saturday that made them close friends. The game was three hundred and one, and Geordie had beaten three challengers when it came to Bally's turn. Bally doubled off quickly and had already missed one chance of closing on double twenty, while Geordie still had one hundred and fifty-one left. He then teased the Irish champ that he would buy the beer for the rest of the day if he closed out. Geordie hit treble twenty, treble nineteen and double seventeen to win with his next three darts. Bally was flabbergasted. He shook Geordie's hand, hugged him and insisted that a photo of the winning shot be taken, and that Geordie retire to the bar with him to drink his bet. A friendship was born.

Bally was in his early forties, lean, bearded, tanned and full of chatty good humor. He spoke Afrikaans and many of the native tongues of the black African tribes. This so impressed the Zulu waiters at one of their haunts, that they would tell him which girls were hot and kept tables for him. Bally didn't talk about his past very much except basic stuff. Geordie and the other Irish lads knew he had been a soldier of fortune, that he didn't need to work, but so what? Good luck to him, they said. When Geordie and Anna got together, the contact between the two men became less frequent, but they often made a foursome for dinner out or met Saturday afternoons at the Tavern.

◆

Geordie had called ahead and an hour later he and Mickey were at Bally's house. The courier had arrived with Geordie's documents just as they left Houghton. On the way over they had agreed that Mickey would not linger, but just drop Geordie off with Bally. It was best for safety purposes not to open the loop any further. In fact, Mickey suggested, and it was agreed, that he would not even tell the other lads about Geordie's return.

"What's with the suitcase, Irishman?" Bally asked when they arrived. "Has that Orange Free State wench thrown you out for good this time?"

"I wish that's all it was," Geordie answered.

Mickey left as Bally broke out the Amstels.

"I'll have to sip this one, Bally," said Geordie. "I've already had a few with Mickey. I have something very important to discuss with you."

"Fine, go for it," Bally answered. "I'll work this six pack alone while I listen."

Geordie, fresh from his recent summary of the entire story to Mickey earlier, now told his story again, with even more flair than before. Bally listened intently, apart form beer interruptions, as he drank four to Geordie's one. When Geordie finished Bally had two questions.

"One, why didn't you come to me much sooner, my friend? Two, what's your objective from this whole affair?"

"I should have thought of you sooner," agreed Geordie. "I think that I underestimated the original incident as being too simple, and was then sucked into it very quickly. Obviously my primary objective is to free Anna safely, as soon as possible. It would be nice to get some money out of these people for the return of the file. I don't think I'll be able to go back to my job, Anna either, so it would be nice to have enough money to go elsewhere and start fresh. You'll need some compensation too, if you can help me sort this out. How about us squeezing a few hundred thousand rand out of the bastards, after we free Anna?"

Bally sat quietly for many minutes, till Geordie could stand it no longer.

"Don't feel that you have to get involved, Bally. Maybe I'm better trying to cut some deal with the police."

"It's been a while since I did this kind of thing, Geordie. I just got flooded with memories there. Going to the police may lead to a deal but they'll get Anna killed in the process. You and I will take care of this. A proper plan must be formulated which I will have by morning. Let's look over this file of yours."

Geordie broke open the package and handed the contents to Bally. He read through the pages quickly.

"Do any of the names here mean anything to you?" Bally asked.

"Yes. Van Rensburg is the manager at the mine I went to. I think Van de Merwe is the policeman, the one I heard tell his companion that I wasn't to get out of Botha's house alive. Botha is on the list, too, but is now dead, I think.

Goldstein is the son of the attorney Anna works for, he works in the one of the diamond organizations. The rest I have no idea about."

Bally looked again at the names, then spoke quietly, with calm confidence.

"I have the contacts to find out more about this policeman, very easily. He is probably best avoided at first. That leaves only Goldstein and the unknowns, among which are probably at least some of the top dogs in the scheme anyway. It may be worthwhile targeting Goldstein first. If he fails to tell us anything useful we can at least slow down the sales end of their business. Nothing gets people's attention quicker than reduced cash flow, especially a criminal enterprise."

"That sounds good to me," Geordie agreed. "What are we going to do to him? Not major violence, I hope. I don't know if I have the stomach for it."

"You look absolutely knackered, Geordie, as the bloody English say. Take your things into the other bedroom and get yourself freshened up. I'll fire up the braai and throw on some vors."

Within twenty minutes they were eating. Geordie yawned his way through the meal. Now he felt relaxed, in the knowledge that they were going to get things done, and so his body wanted to rest and recharge. Bally told him to forget about shaving for the immediate future, took his identity book and a photo from his wallet. He then sent Geordie to bed with the promise that by the morning "Bally's Plan" would be ready for review and they would begin action.

◆

Louis' mood was changeable during the ride to Pretoria. One minute he was friendly, the next he was distant. Some phone calls he made didn't improve things. Anna remained outwardly calm while inwardly she worried and struggled to be rational. There was no doubt that Louis was smitten by her. However, her guess was that he would be under pressure from his people to treat this very business-like. It would all hinge on whether Anna was to be regarded as an asset or a liability. Anna decided that she must present Louis with sound arguments for the asset theory, for use in any upcoming discussions with his partners. Stir into that mix the sexual attraction ingredient, and she hoped that she should have enough of an angle on him to stay afloat till an opportunity came to escape. She realized she may have to compromise herself at some stage and that worried her as much as staying alive.

"What are you thinking about, Louis?" Anna asked.

"Too many things to make sense of. How about you?"

"I know Geordie won't go to the police. I'm now staying with you by choice Louis, so there are no legal implications to worry about. All we have to do is figure out a way to contact Geordie and do our private deal."

"Sounds good to me, if we can do it. Of course, then you are gone from me again, Anna."

"Let us figure out a way that enables me to stay if I want to, Louis, but you must continue to be sweet to me, so that staying will be an easy choice for me to make."

She squeezed his hand and they rode on, each immersed in their own thoughts, while firmly trapped as it were, in each other's web.

The house in Pretoria was smaller than Anna's first place of confinement, but very comfortable. Louis proudly showed her about and revelled in her praise of the decor. His driver took in the parcels they had collected earlier in Sandton, putting them in the master bedroom. Louis sent the man out to a restaurant to bring back dinner and invited her to open the boxes. Shyly, she began unwrapping them. More beautiful clothes, sheek and expensive. As she giggled, he ushered her into a private dressing room to select what she wanted to wear for dinner. More lovely clothes were hung up there and in drawers, that Anna presumed had belonged to Louis' deceased wife.

She freshened her make-up, changed, and found him downstairs, already dressed for dinner too.

"This is so civilized, Louis. To think that we started out as enemies such a short time ago, and now we are admiring friends."

"You look wonderful, my dear, as indeed I knew you would," he said, smiling.

Dinner was excellent, and the pair talked like old school pals. It wasn't until they were having coffee, that Anna commented on the speed with which Louis had them both eat, then he told her why.

"You'll have to stay upstairs on your own later for a while, my dear. I have business colleagues coming to discuss our crisis, as they call it, namely you, McKay and the missing documents."

"How do you propose to handle things, Louis?"

"I hope to convince them that you are on our side now and that you are helping me find Mr. McKay, so that we can recover our file. Believe me, it will be difficult to win them over but I think I can do it."

"Is there anything I can do to help?" she asked.

"Nothing except wish me luck. Keep out of the way and out of trouble. There, I see some vehicle headlights outside now."

Anna walked over to him and gave him a tender hug.

"You'll win them over Louis, and you won't regret it." Then she walked quickly up the stairs and into the master bedroom.

SEVENTEEN

Showtime

The Irish police were very friendly to Captain De Klerk. Superintendent O'Malley personally called him back. As the Captain already knew, their citizens did not carry identity cards or papers. Furthermore, as part of the European Economic Community citizens could travel between member countries without visas. There was no record of Geordie McKay arriving in the country from Holland. Without an address it was just about impossible to know his whereabouts in Ireland and without an arrest warrant, the Irish Garda could not search for him. Captain De Klerk left it on a friendly lookout basis.

Meanwhile his entire diamond investigation was in shambles. He thought he could have cracked it if the Houghton sting had gone according to plan. He would have had the tapes, the suspects and documents. Either McKay still had the file or Anna Terblanche had it hidden. If he could get it somehow, then the case was his to crack. Van de Merwe was very unlikely to break. Van wasn't smart enough to see the writing on the wall and the Captain was loath to cut any deal with a traitor. Again and again he puzzled over the facts. If only he could get to McKay or find the girl. What he needed was a lucky break and in his mind he surely deserved it at this stage. Frank was also out there on his appointed mission and a success by him could turn the tide in the Captain's favor.

◆

Geordie slept after his meal with Bally, and only awoke at the sound of an almighty crash in the next room. He was confused for a few minutes and just lay there quietly. Then, Bally poked his head into the room.

"I was planning to wake you but the cat did it for me when she knocked over that cooking pot. You had better get moving. We have a lot to do, remember."

"Morning already?" answered Geordie, still tired. "Let me grab a quick shower."

The water felt great and out of habit he reached for the shaving kit. He even went back looking for it in his suitcase before he remembered that it was lost, then Bally's request not to shave. When he walked into the kitchen afterwards, Bally looked up approvingly.

"Don't let my cat get near you or she'll lick that stubble off. Do you think you can turn it into a real beard?"

"It's itching the hell out of me right now. I've had one before and it'll be fine once it gets a hold. I'm starving, what's cooking? Have you got the show on the road?"

"Of course, Irishman! Eat first, then I'll show you my plan."

After breakfast they walked out to the detached garage. Bally unlocked the door and reached for the light switch.

"Jesus, Bally! I don't know a damned thing about guns, but you have enough here to equip a small army. Are you planning to use these?"

"Not necessarily, but they are here if we need them. Handle them with extreme care or leave that end of things up to me, Geordie. I keep this garage under lock and key. The maid doesn't clean in here. Some of the guns have not been fired in years, but my favorites are range fired regularly, and I keep them all in perfect working order. It's my hobby, remember? Your Kimberley file is here, with my notes and maps, where I was working on them last night. Take a seat and I'll brief you."

They sat at a cleared bench where Bally had copied the listed names onto a notepad, one name to each page.

"We don't want to dirty up your typed list, Geordie. It may be needed later, so let's keep it clean. These separate pages will allow us to add in new information as we find it.

I have added notes to some of the people listed already. By the way, Sergeant Van de Merwe is in the hospital, in very serious condition from a gunshot wound. He attempted to burglarize Anna's house, was surprised by his police captain who came checking up on his men, and in the ensuing confrontation, the Captain shot him. He was probably looking for the file copy which Anna had hidden. My information is that nothing was found and Van is to be charged with attempted murder of his commanding officer. He will be out of the picture for a long time whether he co-operates with the investigations or not.

Our first job is to scout some of the other names. We will take everything with us and visit all the addresses I have highlighted in red. That should give us a feel for where each fits into the organization and we'll build from there. Here is your new identity book. You are John Jones, an Englishman! Don't curse me for making you English, with all the trouble in Northern Ireland and such. If the police are looking for you it is best to change nationalities. When the beard comes through we will get your picture updated again. Are you ready to leave?"

"Yes," answered Geordie, with a smile. "So I'm an Englishman, eh! You did that on purpose just to madden me, didn't you, you damn Dutchman?"

Bally didn't rise to the taunt, instead he flashed him his trademark smile. They headed towards Jo'burg downtown area, their first place of call being a plush office suite belonging to Equatorial Trading Company. A phone call got them Mervin Goldstein's office, but they did not manage to see him. Relevant information was written on his page and his assigned number marked on the map. A Mr. Joubert and a Mr. Brauer from the list had downtown phone numbers also. These were checked out and marked on the list. Under the pretence of looking for someone, they took turns going into their suspect's premises.

Joubert was in property development and Brauer in transportation. Both had fancy offices and were obviously executives or owners of their businesses. Bally made appropriate notes and marked the map. Two north suburb addresses on the list were established to be the residences of these men.

"I saw the Brauer fella in the office," Geordie said, on his return to the car. "His secretary spoke to him while I was at reception. He is young, tall, a tough-looking Boer type. I wouldn't like to tackle him."

Bally smiled. "Don't worry, you don't have to. Did you get the impression that he could be a forceful member of this group?"

"Yes, definitely. How about Joubert?"

"He is an older man and not in good health. He is not at work today, probably at home. I'll mark him in as a possible weak link."

"Where do you want to go from here, Bally?"

"Houghton looks the closest. Then on to Hyde Park, Sandton, Randburg and Rhoodepoort."

The morning went by quickly. Geordie showed Botha's house to Bally, where all the action had occurred the previous week. It looked closed up for now but one could still see the scars of that night in the damaged gateway. They pushed on through lunchtime, finally stopping by early afternoon at a 'roadhouse' in Rhoodeport for steak sandwiches and cold drinks.

Bally studied his notebook. "Okay, let's review what we have and what we are going to do next. Have you any suggestions?"

"Only that we hustle at least one of the people on this list today. They know I'm back because of the airport incident and may well be searching for me. You're the military expert, what do you think?"

"They're looking for you, no doubt, and they'll think you're an easy target. We must up the ante. We must show them that we can strike them at will. It's necessary to get a clear message to the leaders that we want Anna released immediately. We must deliver our demands, and we must strike at least one of these listed people today. We don't know which person on the list is the leader, so it doesn't matter who we pick. I see no point in taking extra risk so let's avoid the secured mansions. You draft the letter and I'll pick a few targets."

After a few tries and a little input from Bally, Geordie had his letter ready. He passed it over to him for his review. Bally read it aloud.

THE KIMBERLEY FILE

To whom it concerns—

Let this letter serve as a notice that we are in possession of this file. Your stupid stunt in Ireland backfired. The abduction of Anna Terblanche and now this airport incident has angered me further. My strike team is ready and able to hit back and this Friday's show was only the beginning.

You can have the original file back on the following terms:

1. Release Anna unharmed.
2. Pay me three hundred thousand rand for pain and suffering.

This offer holds for one week. After that, the cost doubles for each week of delay.

Place advert in The Daily Mail, under Personal, in classified, to read—GMK, all is forgiven. Call — at ———o'clock to arrange meeting.

Friday's show was just that. If Anna is harmed or any attempt is made to cheat on the deal then everyone on the list will be treated as fair game, and we hunt very well.

Sample names from your list are Goldstein, Van Els, Van Rooyen, Joubert, Brauer.

We are waiting.

Geordie McKay

When Bally read it back, it felt weird to Geordie.

"Are we criminals now also, Bally?"

"In the narrow eyes of the law, maybe, but these people are not in a position to call the police. Now is the time for action. You can worry about your guilt when you've got Anna back, but I don't think you'll lose much sleep over it. That letter sounds very stiff, and it might be safer not to use the written medium, in case it backfires on us later, for example if the police got their hands on the note. Why don't you telephone them instead, after we give them a wake-up call? I've got three targets in mind."

"You're right, let's do that," Geordie agreed.

Their next stop was Mr. Joubert's house in Randburg. It was located in a quiet street full of established gardens, around medium-sized but nice homes. As they drove slowly past the house, Bally pointed out the partially restored antique car parked in the driveway and the BMW on the street in front. They stopped seventy yards past. Bally let Geordie into the driver's seat, while he took a bag from the back. Geordie was to keep the engine running and wait for him. Bally walked purposefully up to the house driveway and disappeared. A few minutes later he came out of the driveway again, walked back to the car and got into the passenger front seat.

"Geordie, drive on normally. Turn around at the next junction and drive slowly past the house again."

As they passed, Bally looked at the old car and pressed a switch in his bag.

"We have forty-five seconds to clear the area, Geordie. Turn right onto the main road at the end."

They were turning at the junction when they heard the muffled thud behind them and saw a flash of light. Once they were well down the main road, Geordie spoke.

"What did you do back there, Bally?"

"I put on the first act of our show. Mr. Joubert just lost his antique car. Turn at the next robot for Sandton."

Ten minutes drive had them passing Mr. Brauer's house. It looked a lot more formidable, with a security gate. Just past it Bally had Geordie stop beside a black man who was weeding flower beds. Bally spoke to the man in his native Xosa tongue, which Geordie recognized because of all the clicking sounds in the language. The old man laughed at what Bally said, and spoke freely with him. Moments later Bally slipped back into the car and they drove on.

"What's the deal here, general?" Geordie asked.

"Mr. Brauer will be arriving soon and is usually home only for a few hours on a Friday evening. I got the telephone number again, for later."

"Are you putting on a show for Mr. Brauer?"

"Indeed, but not here. Come on, cut across to Hyde Park."

◆

Doctor Van Els's name was displayed on the sign outside his Hyde Park home. To the side was another sign in Afrikaans which Bally translated as a plaque to his prize winning flowers. It was an expensive home in a very elegant neighborhood.

The house didn't have a wall or gates. Bally explained that these were the ways of the culturally elite. They didn't want to be walled in but if any wandering Kaffirs were seen around here, the police picked them up immediately.

"Nobody is home yet, I think. Let me out while you take a drive. Be back for me in five minutes. I need to take something from the trunk."

Geordie didn't waste time with questions. He drove up the road, noticing how clean and white the neighborhood was. Farther on he saw an elderly man and woman patiently tending their flower beds. They never even looked up as he drove past. Then he got delayed by a delivery van which was reversing into a driveway, putting him two minutes late to collect Bally. The moment he stopped, Bally slipped out from the bushes and they pulled away.

"You're in a sweat, Bally. Have you been doing his garden for him?"

"You might say that."

"You're after chopping down his prize winning flowers, aren't you? Man, that will really get this fella's attention. Where to now? It's almost dark, can I switch on the lights?"

"Of course. We don't want any police attention. Head back downtown to Brauer's office and truck yard."

When they got there, someone was still working in a repair shed so they waited. Thirty minutes later Bally was toying with the idea of hitting the place regardless, but Geordie didn't like that plan. Their problem was solved just then, as the lights went out. They waited an extra five minutes after the man closed up and left, as insurance. Dogs were patrolling inside the fence when Bally approached with his flame thrower. *'Whoosh'*, and three trucks inside the fence were engulfed. The dogs were too scared to even bark. At the sound of approaching sirens, Geordie drove quietly away.

Minutes later Geordie called Brauer at home, from a public telephone box. Once it was understood who he was, he got straight through to the man. Reading and ad-libbing from his previously prepared letter, Geordie managed to deliver his ultimatum to the angry man.

Back in the car, Bally laughed loudly at his recounting of the phone call. Then they hit the freeway, headed for Benoni in satisfied silence. Geordie drove while Bally dozed. At the Benoni exit Bally woke up timely, and laughed out loud, into the darkness.

"That was one hell of a show, Bally. I can't believe we did it but I feel great about it."

"Man, it was a blast. Best thrill I've had in years. You know, Irishman, I was supposed to meet that Rhodesian lass tonight. Hot too, but I'm giving it a miss for your mission. She'll be on the bloody phone later, because I didn't call. Remember not to answer it."

"It's terrible to be so popular! Go for it man, I'll be fine on my own. Never let it be said that I came between you and your adoring fans. You know, one of these days your towser will just fall off you in the bed. You'll have kicked it out on the floor before you realize what it was, and if that dog of yours is around it'll be all over for you mate."

"Ya, ya, jealousy is a sin you know. When I'm pumped up on a mission I lose interest in sex. It's always been like that. But when this is all over I'll be like an animal again, you just wait."

"How about some food, Bally? Let's get Chinese on the way home, my treat?"

"Done deal. Then we'll drink some beer and I'm going to whip your Irish backside on that dartboard. Nomination killer, start with twenty, down to thirteen, plus twenty-fives and bulls."

◆

Anna heard the men arriving downstairs. Louis ushered them into the big sitting room where their muted conversation could be heard only as a buzz, punctuated by the occasional louder remark. She ran a perfume bath and put on a nice nightie she found. Then, another quick listen at the door which confirmed that the meeting was still in progress. It was getting late and she was getting sleepy, but she was also uneasy. Uneasy about discussions and decisions concerning her that were being made downstairs by strangers. Uneasy about going to sleep in Louis' bed and the possible consequences.

In some ways she was enjoying the excitement of her predicament. She was no stranger to sex and she was on the pill.

Apart from when she had steady boyfriends she often had one night stands. Louis was very nice but all facade, and she feared what was behind that smile. Still, if she had met him at one of those loose-end times she would probably have had little hesitation in doing it with him at the right moment, and in a cozy pad like this. But her present situation was very different than that. Until she had the freedom to leave and come back as she wished, their relationship was not on an equal footing. Self preservation was more important than the risk of having sex with Louis, so into bed she went.

Her dozing was disturbed by a commotion downstairs and raised voices. She jumped out of the bed and tiptoed to the door, cracking it open quietly. Louis and another man were arguing in Afrikaans.

"You take that statement back Martin, right now," Louis was saying.

"He's right Martin," an intermediary said. "He's holding her simply because that is what we decided. You have no grounds to accuse him of being involved with her. He's just doing his job and has as much to lose as the rest of us. You're upset because of the burning. That's understandable. Now go on, Martin, take it back so we can move forward and decide the important matters. Go on."

"All right, I take it back, for now. But I'll be watching Louis' handling of her very closely," the Martin person agreed.

"The doctor is right," another voice began. "We must take this threat seriously. Look at the damage they've caused. There has to be a number of people involved and they know their weapons. The last thing we want is major publicity in front of the police. What's three hundred thousand rand anyway? Hell, we can make double that in a week. I say we deal now and get the file off the street. If an opportunity comes up to get the boy at the transfer then let's take it. Otherwise let it go. We can hit him later when all the dust settles."

A third voice cut in.

"But we lost a bunch through Botha already, and now you want to give away more. We haven't been able to get anything done lately with all this fuss."

"True Kallie," said Louis, "which is all the more reason to get it over with so we can get back to the business we are good at. What does it matter if we must give away a few drops from the bucket? It is much better than having the bucket taken from us totally. Let's get our priorities right."

The sitting room door was then pushed closed, so Anna couldn't hear anything else clearly. After a few minutes she went back to bed and fell asleep quickly.

Some time later the person entering the darkened bedroom awakened Anna, but she pretended to be asleep. She could sense him standing over the bed and struggled to stifle her growing panic. Finally he went into the bathroom and she sneaked a glance, confirming that it was Louis, taking a pee. She relaxed again and was asleep by the time Louis climbed into the bed. He snuggled close to her, sniffing her perfume.

He reached out a touching hand, but pulled it back as she moved. Laying back, he promptly fell asleep too.

◆

Geordie looked through the classifieds in Saturday's Daily Mail, quickly scanning the list of personal ads. He missed it the first time and almost decided not to look twice. It was the last ad, not in its alphabetical place. Copy was as Geordie had specified and it was signed, Anna, which made him shiver slightly.

"Bally, come see this advert," Geordie called, excitedly.

Bally read it. "There's no mistaking that, with Anna's name. That's a Pretoria phone number, by the way. You've got to call at three o'clock, Geordie. We had better get our shit together."

◆

Captain De Klerk had been in bad humor for days. His wife Margaret knew his form and let him wallow in his misery. But it was Saturday now, their special time, when they talked over a long leisurely breakfast. She had no further tolerance for his bad humor. He was sitting at the table looking at the morning daily when she spoke.

"Okay, let's get it out into the open, R.G.," Margaret said.

"What do you mean?" the Captain asked.

"You've got that hang-dog face on you. We can't go through the weekend with you being so miserable. I know you're upset about Van and about the girl being kidnapped. You're not to blame. Don't be so hard on yourself."

"Margaret, this whole case has turned around from potential glory to a nightmare. I should have known from Van's recent behavior that he was suspect, but I wouldn't allow myself to consider it. The Chief is on my back too, about the whole thing. He has been tipped for new Justice Minister and had told the Government that a big break was imminent in the diamond case. He bragged too soon, to gain favor and will blame me if he falls from grace. I feel like the rock climber who has slipped on the last ascent and is stuck on a ledge."

"You know from experience that cases turn this way and that. I've never seen you down so much, as you are over this one."

"My dear, this entire investigation has had some bizarre and alarming problems. Until the lucky break in Kimberley, everything we did yielded nothing. Then the Houghton debacle. Then the girl's kidnapping and my shooting of Van. I've never shot another policeman before, and not everyone in Jeppe sees it my way. I feel certain that Van has been passing information for quite some time, but proving it is another story. His spying alone does not explain all the problems we've had. I think there has to be more to it than that, and I have someone chasing a few possible angles right now, ones that I'm not in a position to check myself. I'm circling round and round now, waiting for a break, which must happen soon or I'm in danger of getting pulled off the case. It doesn't look good to the top brass when I lose both of my star witnesses and don't know where they are. I need Geordie McKay back here from Ireland, to help me bargain the release of the girl before she is harmed."

"Hold it a second, R.G.! That's where I heard the name Geordie. From you. I saw something in Friday's evening paper that I want to show you."

The Captain sat quietly as she rummaged through the old papers, finally handing him the report. It related an incident at the airport where a man had grabbed a briefcase, was chased and shot dead by two airport police. The briefcase turned out to contain nothing but some magazines and a shaving kit. The airport police established that the owner had walked out of the airport while all this was going on. He didn't report it missing or bother to wait and see if it was recovered, even though he was aware that the police were onto the thief. They were appealing for the man to come forward. An Englishman who had met him briefly at the airport was quoted as saying he was Irish and that his first name was Geordie.

The Captain banged the table with excitement.

"I'll bet you that's my man. He's back here now. Thank you, thank you, my dear. Please excuse me for a while."

Captain De Klerk called headquarters but the duty officer could not pull up the airport details alone, so the captain had him print up the entire incident report for the last forty-eight hours, and headed to his office to pick through it. While he waited for a return call from the airport police he began leafing though the large print-out.

Despite years of police work he still found himself shocked by the horrific things human beings did to each other. He counted ten killings in the forty-eight hour period.

Then his attention fell on some Northside incidents. Destruction of a man's prized flower garden and another's antique car. He recognized the affluent addresses. No suspects. A white man was seen with a flame thrower setting fire to some trucks at Brauer Transport. No suspects again, a case of mistaken identity according to Mr. Brauer. He remembered Mr. Brauer's name coming up at one point in his diamond investigations. When Brauer became aware of police interest he stormed into the Captain's office one day, accusing him of harassment. Influence was brought to bear on the Chief, who ended further investigations, when the Captain couldn't produce any hard evidence.

The airport police called, and Captain De Klerk went there, to examine the briefcase. They had attached little importance to the incident, despite the fatality that occurred. Just a case of a known thug getting his come-uppance, the officer had said.

"Can I go through the briefcase contents?" Captain De Klerk asked.

"Sure, Captain."

The magazines were of UK origin and the shaving kit was typical of the type sold in South Africa.

"Can you get me the passenger lists of flights arriving around that time from the UK and Holland?" the Captain asked, politely.

His suspicions were quickly verified by the British Airways list. Geordie McKay was back! He had completed a landing card on arrival. It even showed his old address, which would be checked although the Captain did not expect him to be there. He had to assume that Geordie knew of Anna's abduction and was back to try and free her.

Again he cursed Van de Merwe's actions at the Houghton sting operation. If Van had not ruined things, then Geordie would still have enough faith in the police to be helping the investigation. Instead, he was out there on the loose and in as much danger as Anna herself. The kidnappers may well have contacted the boy, and then tried in vain to snatch the briefcase, expecting to get their missing papers back without a swap. Andries Meinke, the snatcher was dead. His life was a long tale of violence, prison and thuggery. It would take time to work through his records, but it might yield a clue, as to whom he was working for at the time of his death.

EIGHTEEN

The Exchange

Saturday began as a strange day for Anna Terblanche. When she awoke, Louis, dressed in a brightly colored robe, was wheeling in a trolley of champagne. He parked it in front of the bed while she tried to wipe the sleep from her eyes.

As he popped the cork she asked, "What are we celebrating?"

"Good morning, my dear. You slept like an angel. We are celebrating my success in convincing my colleagues to give me their blessing to go ahead and settle this whole business with Geordie McKay."

"Great! What are you going to do?"

"Contact has already been established with him. He will be calling me on the telephone this afternoon to talk about our deal."

"Can I have a word with him when he calls?"

"Of course you can."

"Wonderful. You're very sweet, Louis. Yes, I think this does call for a celebration."

He poured generous glasses for both of them. They clinked the flutes, drained them and refilled.

"Tell me more, Louis," Anna insisted.

"I'm going to give him some cash in exchange for the file later today."

"What about me?"

"I hope you have begun to like me enough to stay. I have lots to offer you Anna, and I want you to stay."

"Yes I do like you Louis, but I must have the freedom to come and go."

"What do you want me to do, my dear?"

"Let me go with Geordie. I need to talk to him. Then I can return here of my own free will. He won't back off until I settle my relationship with him."

Louis seemed to be in deep thought. A minute passed, which to Anna seemed more like ten.

Finally Louis answered.

"Consider it done. Let's have more champagne."

They were into the second bottle in no time. Anna felt light-headed, both from the euphoria of the moment and the champagne. Soon they were laughing and cuddling. Louis suggested a jacuzzi and went to the bathroom to run it.

"Go on Anna, get in," he said, "I'll get the trolley."

"It's a deal."

When he came back into the bathroom she was already in the swirling, soothing waters. He poured two fresh glasses of bubbly for them and toasted her.

"Any room for me in there?" he asked, confidently.

"It's your tub."

Anna wasn't quite expecting him to be naked under the robe when he dropped it to the floor. His body was tanned and quite muscular and he strutted along the edge of the jacuzzi. She was full of 'Joie-de-vivre' by now too and giggled as he posed. Louis got in. They cuddled some more and he began stroking her breasts, then worked his way down between her legs. She liked it but managed to control herself. The champagne and the steam were making her drowsy, so she got out. He draped a big soft towel over her and helped her to the bed. Anna wanted desperately to lie down. Once she felt the softness of the sheets against her cheeks she quickly drifted into a deep sleep.

◆

By three o'clock Geordie was so nervous he was at the point of hyperventilation. Bally had gone over their plan many times with him and had scouted their chosen meeting location. He knew it was a good plan, yet he worried that he would somehow mess up the phone call.

"It's time to make the call," Bally reminded him.

"Okay, okay. Are you ready to monitor it from the other phone?"

"Yes. Spread your notes out in front of you."

The call went through immediately and a man answered. It was Louis.

"This is Geordie McKay. Let me speak to Anna Terblanche, immediately."

Louis was in no such rush.

"So, I finally speak to the man who has caused us all this trouble. You know what we want, McKay. Have you got the file ready for our swap, originals, of course?"

"Yes. Have you got three hundred thousand rand ready, plus Anna Terblanche?"

"Indeed. Anna has had such a good time visiting me that she's not keen to leave, but she's prepared to go through with it. It's the money you want, more than her. Why don't you just take it and leave her alone? I'll throw in an extra fifty thousand on top. What do you say, McKay?"

"Cut the bullshit, mister. I'll be at the Witt Campus at five today. We'll meet at the park bench seat in front of the Jan Smuts statue, you got that?"

"I had a different place in mind. How about...?"

"It's Witt Campus or Jeppe police station."

"Is this your famed Irish sense of humor? I'll be generous, Witt it is. You must come alone and wear something identifiable, and take our nice brown briefcase along."

"Your monkey at the airport already took the case. A brown envelope will have to do. Five o'clock sharp. Now, I want to speak to Anna."

After a brief pause he heard Anna's voice, weak but unmistakable.

"Hello Geordie, are you there?"

"Yes, yes Anna. Are you okay darling, you sound terrible?"

"I'm fine, just a bit tired, that's all. See you soon."

"That's enough chit-chat for now," Louis interrupted. "Anna and I will find you on your park bench."

"I'll have a straw hat on so you can recognize me from a distance," Geordie said.

"How thoughtful of you, Mr. McKay. I just can't wait."

Geordie put the phone down in response to Bally's signal.

Anna had not been privy to the initial conversation between the men and did not know about the amount of money being offered, especially the bonus to leave her out of the deal. Her few words were spoken from the bedroom when the call was switched through to her. She had been awakened by Louis' man just before three, sporting a terrible headache that was getting worse.

That wasn't the only thing that was troubling her. She remembered the champagne, the jacuzzi and the fondling, but no sex. Yet, she felt sore between her legs. And she had underwear on when she woke up, blue, which she had seen in the drawer and a color that she never wore.

Louis admitted that they had sex, when she challenged him. He told her it had been terrific and couldn't believe that she didn't remember. Right now her head was hurting, so she didn't press the subject, but agreed to take an hour's nap like he suggested, so as to be in better shape for their five o'clock meeting. She would shower and dress at four.

♦

After his phone call, Geordie stood transfixed, savoring the moment.

"How did I do, Bally? I was so nervous, I'm still shaking."

"You did fine, honest. You said everything that needed to be said."

"Thanks. Anna sounded weak and scared. Jesus, it was great to hear her voice."

"We've got to get moving, Geordie. There's a lot to get done to complete our planning."

Geordie was still analysing the call.

"They sounded genuinely keen to deal. Do you really think we need to go through with such an exotic plan, Bally? Why go to all that trouble if it is going to be a simple swap?"

"Nothing is ever simple in these situations, Geordie. Trust me, we cannot afford to take chances. I hope it turns out to be a simple swap. However, if it doesn't, where do we go if we're not prepared for that alternative?"

"Okay Herr General, okay."

Geordie stayed in the car with the engine running while Bally went to the front door of the house. Within a few minutes

Bally was back with another man in tow. He ushered the young man into the back seat ahead of himself.

The man spoke as he sat into the car.

"I hope we can attend to this quickly, as we have guests coming over for dinner later. Is Mr. Brauer nearby?"

Neither of the other two spoke as Geordie drove away on Bally's instruction. After they had gone about a mile the newcomer spoke again.

"I thought you said Mr. Brauer was nearby, but we're heading to the motorway. What's going on here? I think you should pull over and let me out."

Bally had enough.

"Goldstein, I think you should shut up and listen. By the way, the door on your side cannot be opened from the inside, in case you have any brave ideas. Now, firstly, allow me to introduce ourselves. Your driver is Geordie McKay. My name is Bally. Secondly, we have no desire to harm you. We need your cooperation."

"Why should I help people who have just kidnapped me?"

"Because Geordie here is being messed about by your diamond-gang friends. I'm sure you don't want to spend the next twenty years in prison, or have me break your damn neck. We don't have the time to waste on long stories so let's get straight to the point. Your pals kidnapped Geordie's girlfriend. They want their 'Kimberley File' back. No problem. We don't care about your crime deal, it's none of our business. The file is to be swapped for Anna and a small cash bonus, to compensate us for our pain and suffering. We need your help in the swap, it's just that simple."

"What do you want me to do?"

"Don't worry yourself about that for now," Bally assured him. "Just enjoy the ride while we chat. Who is actually holding her?"

"I don't know. I have no involvement with any of this. You're making a big mistake."

Bally was watching the road ahead, also.

"Get off at Braamfontein and go up Yale Road, Geordie. Go in the first gate and do the loop like we talked about. Okay Mervin, have it your way. Take off your shirt and put on this bullet-proof vest. Then replace your shirt."

Mervin looked at the vest in fear.

"I thought you said you weren't going to harm me."

"Correct. That's why we're giving you this vest. You see, I can't vouch for your pals. Here's a nice straw hat for you to keep the sun off that receding hairline."

"But. . . "

"No buts, Mervin. When we stop you'll walk with Geordie to the bench seat in front of the Jan Smuts statue. Carry this sealed brown envelope so that it can easily be seen."

"I won't do it. You're setting me up," Mervin protested.

"Here, have a look into this hold-all, Mervin. Nice guns eh? If you don't do it I'll be forced to change my mind about harming you. Do as I say and you'll still be home in time for your party."

"What do I have to do?"

"Sit on the bench. When your pals show up you just ask them to bring Anna to the bench. Geordie will be nearby with the file, to complete the swap. It'll be a piece of cake. You and your pals and us, in a happy little group."

"Don't keep calling them my pals. What if they have different ideas?"

"Then you'll persuade them to deal straight. I'll be covering the whole proceedings with my trusty rifle. She's a beauty, isn't she? I can bring down a Kudu with it at fifteen hundred feet. You'll only be a few hundred away from me and your vest won't stop this baby, so don't get any clever ideas."

"Thanks a lot."

"It's a small price to pay for all that soft money you've been making on your diamond dealing."

They parked with some other cars and walked round a stand of trees which overlooked the statue area. Bally stayed behind at the top of the slope while Geordie escorted Mervin down to the bench. He sat him down, adjusted the straw hat and envelope. Mervin was trance-like, white with fear. Geordie felt compelled to try and reassure him.

"This should only take a little while. Then you can get on with your life and we can get on with ours. Just keep calm and get them to bring Anna here, okay?"

Mervin nodded and Geordie retreated back up the slope. He could see no sign of Bally till he called out to him in a whisper and was guided into the trees. Bally was perched in a large tree with a commanding view of both the carpark and the bench. He had binoculars around his neck and the rifle laying across his lap.

He flashed a broad smile to Geordie.

"Two minutes to five. You stay down there out of sight. Don't move till I give you the word. If anything goes wrong don't hesitate to use that pistol like I showed you, if you're in any danger, okay?"

"Not okay, Bally. I'm nervous as hell and Mervin is shitting himself down there. I'll have to sit, before I piss myself."

Bally watched a crippled man shuffling along the pathway and sit on the bench with Mervin. His attention was then drawn to the carpark where a white Merc had pulled in, and parked with the engine still running. As he looked back at Mervin he saw the flash from the gun and Mervin fell over.

"The cripple is a fake," Bally hissed. "Stay put, just yet, Geordie."

Bally was giving this commentary while looking at the man through his gun sights.

"The fucking cripple has shot our boy, and now he has the envelope. He's running in the other direction. Go help Mervin. Keep low, I'm going to take the runner down."

As Geordie slid down the slope he heard the rifle crack and heard a man cry out in pain. Despite his jelly legs he pushed on to where Mervin had fallen. As he got to him he saw that he was moving, and appeared not to be badly hurt.

"Mervin, it's me, Geordie. Where have you been hit?"

"Somewhere around the ribs, but I think the vest stopped it. I fell over and played dead while the guy took the envelope."

Geordie helped Mervin to his feet, and as they shuffled up the slope, he glanced over to where the runner had fallen. The man was rolling in agony clutching his right knee. Bally's rifle cracked again now, but the bullet obviously wasn't aimed at the runner this time, for the man was an easy target.

When they got to the top of the slope there was no sign of Bally. Then they saw him driving the car at the edge of the carpark with the doors open for them. Once they were inside, he quickly drove away. He cut through two industrial parks and came out on the city side of Braamfontein, then pulled into a shopping center full of cars and parked among them. Only then did Bally look back at the two in the back seat. He spoke, matter of factly.

"Let me see your wound, Mervin."

He checked it and found the large bruise where the bullet hit the vest.

"You're a lucky man. Your pals tried to double-cross us. What happened on the bench Mervin?"

"This man sat down and said hello. I thought he was just resting during his walk. He then asked if I was there to swap the envelope. When I said yes, he pulled a gun and fired. I—I fell over and he grabbed the envelope and ran. Did you kill him?"

"No, but he'll probably have a limp for the rest of his life."

"Shouldn't we have taken him with us, to get information out of him?" Geordie asked.

Bally shook his head.

"No way. He'll be bleeding all over the place. The police will be there in minutes. He'd be of little use to us and maybe get us caught. Besides, Mervin is going to help us now, I'm sure."

"I also heard another shot, Bally. What was it?" Geordie asked.

"I put a marker hole in the car that was involved," Bally answered. He then turned on the injured man, lifting up his chin with a pinch between thumb and forefinger.

"Mervin, you can see that you're getting into deeper shit here now. Isn't it time you helped us and yourself?"

"But I don't know anything," Mervin replied, feebly.

"We're talking about your father's secretary here, Mervin," Geordie cut in. "Anna has worked for him for a long time and I know he thinks a great deal of her. He won't be pleased with you if I call him and tell him you are involved with her kidnapping, not to mention this whole fucking diamond business."

"The same Anna from The Orange Free State?" Mervin asked.

"Yes, Mervin, Anna Terblanche."

"I—I had no idea. I'm very sorry. Okay, I'll help you, if I can. Let me call my wife so she's not worrying about me."

They let him use a nearby public telephone. Geordie stood

beside him during the call. Bally got some cokes and had his questions ready for Mervin the moment he got back into the car.

"Okay Mervin, who's holding her?"

"I—I think she is being held by Louis Trichardt."

"Come on, Mervin. Nobody is called that. It's like calling a child Jan Smuts."

"Honest. It may not be his real name but that's the way I was introduced."

"Does he have a large white Mercedes with dark windows?"

"Yes, but there are a lot of those about."

"Not with a bullet hole in the trunk, there aren't. Where does he live?"

"He has a large estate in Muldersdrift. She's probably being held there. But it's heavily guarded."

"Let's go," Bally said.

◆

When Anna awoke again it was almost six. Frantically, she jumped out of bed and opened the bedroom door, to find Thomas sitting there. She was half naked but she didn't care.

"Where's Louis?" she asked.

"He had to go alone, Miss. He tried to wake you but he couldn't. McKay called back at four saying he wanted some more money, instead of you. Sorry Miss. Mr. Louis will be able to explain better when he comes back. He left orders for you to stay in your room till then. Is there anything I can get for you?"

Anna went back into the room and slammed the door.

◆

It was dark by the time Bally and his two passengers arrived in Muldersdrift. They drove past the gate one time to look. Everything seemed too quiet.

Bally peered in. "There's a guardhouse inside the gate. I'll go up and ask if he is in."

"Hold on a minute, Bally. What do we do then?" Geordie asked.

"Geordie, if he's there, Anna is there and we're going in after them. We've got to go all the way now, man. Mervin, you will come with me and use your name and influence. Geordie, slip into the driver's seat and drive us to the gate."

Once there, the two men walked up to the gate and rang a bell. After the second ring a man came out of the small building and spoke to them through the gate.

"Good evening *Meneer*," Mervin began in Afrikaans. "I'm Mervin Goldstein, here to see Mr. Trichardt."

"He's not in, Sir. Was he expecting you?" the guard asked.

"Yes, of course. I left a dinner engagement to come here. Where is he, it's important?"

"I'm not supposed to know."

Bally cut in. "But a good man like you would not want

your boss to miss something important. He probably forgot to leave word where he wanted to meet us. Central control got the places mixed up, eh?"

"He's at his house in Pretoria, but you didn't hear it from me," the man replied.

"Thanks a lot. When the time is right I'll put a good word in for you. What's your name?"

"Willie Honnis, Sir."

"Thank you, *Meneer* Willie. Good night."

The pair got back into the car. Geordie pulled away from the gate quickly. "Did everything go okay, Bally?"

"Yes. Mervin did a great job. Trichardt is not in, he's in Pretoria. What's the address there, Mervin?"

"I've never been there myself, but I've sent him some packages."

Bally took the lead again. "Let's top up with fuel Geordie, before we head off. We'll get food too. I'm starving, whatever about the rest of you."

Geordie nodded his agreement and began looking for a convenience store. Bally continued to press Mervin. "Mervin, where does Trichardt fit into the organization."

"He took over from Mr. Botha when he got killed. Louis is one of the big wheels now."

NINETEEN

To Pretoria without Invitation

Hennie Klunstad was barely conscious when the police found him on the Witt campus. He had lost a lot of blood and mumbled unintelligibly. A few people were interviewed at the scene and the incident report contained an outline of a double shooting, but only one victim was found. It was the report of how Hennie had to be forcibly parted from the brown envelope that caught Captain De Klerk's eye later, as he scanned the reported incidents for the day. He had performed this laborious task every day in the hope that something would show up.

The duty officer confirmed that a worthless envelope had to be pried from Hennie's grasp. A chat with the officer who was at the scene further prompted the Captain's suspicions, that something more may have been going on, that the wounded man believed the envelope to contain something valuable. While Hennie was in surgery, minus his envelope, the Captain had it and its newspaper contents dusted for fingerprints. He ordered that nobody was to discuss the envelope with Hennie, and waited impatiently for the doctors to make the patient available to be interviewed. Hennie's record was researched. It was a resume of crime, prison and trouble. On a hunch, he also retrieved the file on Andries Meinke, the hoodlum who had been shot dead by airport police during the briefcase snatch. The similarities of their careers were striking, even to the point of having done prison time together. Captain De Klerk sensed a breakthrough but he lacked the evidence. He needed to rearrange some of his jigsaw pieces into new positions so that he could hit Hennie Klunstad with a broadside the moment he woke up. But what jigsaw arrangement showed the true picture?

◆

Louis Trichardt's trip back to Pretoria was tortuous. He had miscalculated Geordie McKay and that had caused his scheme to backfire. He had watched Hennie shoot McKay and thought they were home and dry, till his own man was taken down. They were about to rescue Hennie when the bullet hit the Merc. Louis then realized he was in trouble and left the scene, empty handed and angry.

It was hard to think after such a debacle, but Louis was good under pressure and he was confident he could find a way forward. After all, he still had Anna, and the envelope was probably a fake if McKay had put on such an elaborate plan. McKay's side still had the file, but they had a wounded leader, at the very least. They stopped the Merc briefly to check on damage from the bullet. A nice clean hole near the model name plate on the trunk but no mechanical damage to the vehicle.

Anna heard the car arrive and peeped out to see it being driven into the garage. She waited anxiously for Louis to come to the house. Thomas had retreated downstairs so she headed that way too. She could tell the moment Louis walked in, that something was terribly wrong. He said something to Thomas, who hurried off to the kitchen, then glanced briefly towards her on the stairs, before entering the sitting room and closing the door behind himself. Thomas followed moments later carrying a glass of water and some pills, then came back out.

Anna intercepted him on his way to the kitchen.

"What's wrong, Thomas?"

"Mr. Louis has a headache."

"I can see that much. Something happened, didn't it?"

"You'll have to ask Mr. Louis, but you must wait a few minutes till he has a chance to clear his head. He cannot be disturbed."

Five minutes passed, then ten. Anna went to the door. She could hear talking inside. Thomas was lurking near her again so she went back to her position, sitting on the stairs.

Inside, Louis had made a series of urgent telephone calls. Despite these, he had been unable to find any solid information about the condition of Hennie Klunstad, except that he was alive, in hospital and under police guard. Nothing indicated that a second person had been hurt. Either it was being hushed up or McKay somehow survived the encounter. He thought about going back to Muldersdrift and called there for messages. Both Mr. Brauer and Mr. Van Els had been looking for him, no doubt wishing to hear that his mission had been completed successfully. He did not return their calls.

Willie had hesitated in his report from Muldersdrift, finally telling his story under pressure. What the hell did Mervin Goldstein want on a Saturday night and who were the people with him? And Willie had as good as sent them to Pretoria. Louis made a mental note to deal with Willie when this was all over.

Thomas jumped to attention and entered the room when Louis shouted his name from inside. On his way out he motioned to Anna to wait where she was as he went out to the garage. Moments later he was back.

"Follow me upstairs, please," Thomas said to Anna.

Anna obeyed and followed him to the master bedroom.

"What's going on, Thomas? For God's sake tell me."

"Here Miss, take this bag. Put some suitable clothes in it for yourself to cover for three to five days. Mr. Louis is taking you on a trip, he'll tell you the details himself in the car. I'll pack some things for him. We must hurry, he wants to leave in ten minutes."

Thomas had obviously done this before and was out of the room with his bag before Anna was half finished. By the time she got downstairs Thomas met her on his way back from the garage. He carried her bag and escorted her to the car.

She sat in the empty back seat of the Merc while Thomas put her bag in the trunk. Louis was not there yet. Two of his men that she recognized, stood beside the car. Finally Louis arrived. He looked into the car and gave her a weak smile.

"Anna, if you haven't been to the bathroom, go now as we will not be stopping for quite a while."

Anna took up the offer and went inside to the downstairs bathroom. On impulse, she took out her lipstick and wrote on the back of the door–Anna left 8 PM Sat. white Merc—.

When she got to the car again Louis was giving instructions to Thomas. The driver and the other man were sitting in the front seats. Thomas showed her into the back seat. Louis got in behind her and Thomas closed the door with a soft "Tot Siens." He was obviously staying behind and opened the garage doors for them.

It was very quiet in the car. The glass partition between the front and back seats was up. They were driving through the wide tree-lined avenues of Pretoria.

"What happened today, Louis?" Anna asked finally.

There was no answer from across the seat.

"Louis, please, you owe me at least that much."

"Your Geordie double-crossed us on the swap and shot one of my men."

"Oh my God! Is he hurt bad?"

"If you're asking about Hennie, yes. He's in the hospital right now. If you're asking about McKay, I don't know how bad he was hit."

Anna gasped again, feebly. Earlier, she had rehearsed her lines for the big show-down with Louis, but now that all seemed unimportant. She wanted to ask more about the Jo'burg shootout but didn't want to break down in front of him. She couldn't handle any more bad news either, so she fell silent, too. They left the city, heading north in the darkness.

"Where are we going now, Louis?"

"We're going game watching, to the Kruger Park."

◆

Geordie was still at the wheel when they eventually found Wessels Boulevard in Pretoria. It was a wide tree-lined street, with upmarket residences on large lots. Thankfully, there were no fences or security gates like the Muldersdrift estate. They drove past number six hundred and twenty, twice, and looked into the driveway. It didn't have a white Merc parked in it.

"Are you sure you have the right address, Mervin?" Bally asked.

"Yes, I'm sure."

"Okay. Park down the street a little, Geordie."

Geordie parked and all three of them walked to the house in the darkness. Bally carried his hold-all, out of which he produced a flashlight when they reached the driveway. There was a small car in the garage, but no sign of the Merc.

Bally halted the trio and gave out new orders.

"Mervin, ring the doorbell. Get whoever answers to come outside on the basis of an accident in the street or something. Go with him Geordie."

Geordie took Mervin with him to the front door. Nothing happened after the first ring, so he rang again and leaned on the buzzer. Eventually a man came to the door and with great irritation asked what they wanted. Mervin answered him without hesitation, in Afrikaans.

"Excuse me, Meneer. There has been an accident out on the street. Can you give us a blanket and a glass of water?"

"What kind of accident?" the man asked.

"A boy has been knocked off his bike by a car. While we are waiting on the ambulance we want to make him more comfortable."

By this stage they had backed halfway out of the driveway and the man was asking which way it way, saying he was ready to get what they needed. Bally slipped from the bushes and pushed a gun into the man's back. The man froze with fear.

"Who's in the house with you?" Bally demanded.

"Nobody. Is this some kind of joke, or robbery?" he asked, uneasily.

"Neither," said Bally. "Now let's step back into the house, nice and easy."

Once inside, Bally frisked him, slipped a pair of handcuffs

on him and pushed the man into an armchair in the sitting room. Geordie had a quick look in the kitchen and other downstairs rooms, finding them empty.

Bally got the man's identity booklet from his wallet.

"Van Ryn, where is your boss, Mr. Trichardt?"

"I don't know what you are talking about. Are you police of some kind?" the man answered, quickly.

Bally called Mervin over. "Mervin, this is Koos Van Ryn. Do you recognize him?"

"No," answered Mervin.

Bally shook his head, then continued.

"Okay Koos, here's the deal. Mr. Trichardt messed us up at the earlier meeting. We need to find him and we don't have any patience left. When did he leave here and where did he go?"

"I don't know any Trichardt. My wife is away for the weekend visiting her sister. There must be some mistake here."

By now, Geordie had returned from upstairs, carrying some framed photos. He motioned to Bally, who told Koos to sit quietly while he and Mervin went into the hallway.

Geordie whispered, "I think we're in the wrong house. Look at these photos of Koos and his wife on their wedding day, and with various family."

Bally turned angrily on Mervin.

"You got us into this mess, Meneer. You had better do some figuring to get us out of it."

"What do you suggest?" Mervin asked meekly.

"Bally pushed Mervin against the wall, then turned to Geordie.

"Geordie, keep an eye on Koos while we sort this out. Say as little as possible and anything you say keep it on the theme that we are part of special security forces."

Geordie went back to the prisoner. Bally turned on Mervin again.

"From your contacts with Trichardt, what do you remember about the house in Pretoria? You had better get it right this time, mate."

"It had a swimming pool," Mervin answered, nodding his head.

"Pools are too common. What else?"

"The master bedroom had a jacuzzi en suite. Louis would have some kind of office room also."

They quickly checked around. No jacuzzi, no office and the pool was tiny, not Louis' style at all.

Bally grabbed Mervin by the shoulders. "So, we're in the wrong house. That's fucking great, you idiot."

"I can't understand it, Bally. I'm sure Louis' house is number seven hundred and twenty."

"But this is six hundred and twenty! That's the number you told us earlier, twice."

Mervin stammered his apology. "I'm very sorry. I must have got mixed up because of all the stress. It's definitely seven hundred and twenty."

Bally was right in Mervin's face. "Now we have to extract ourselves from here without having to take Koos with us or having him call the local police the moment we leave. Have you any ideas how we're going to do that, egghead?"

"No."

Bally motioned to Geordie who joined them again in the hall.

"Mervin here has finally figured out that he got mixed up in his numbers. We should be at seven-twenty instead of six-twenty. Have you said anything much to Koos?"

"No, just general chat to put him at ease. He doesn't speak much English, but I don't think he'll squeal on us."

Bally nodded. "Will you take Mervin out to the car? Be ready to pull off the moment I come out. No lights on, okay. I'll square things away with Koos."

They could hear Bally's opening conversation as they slipped out of the house.

"Meneer Koos, I am Captain Van de Merwe of special forces. Here, let me take these handcuffs off you. I am going to tell you some very confidential information about our mission and ask you to perform some tasks for us. This is of national importance—."

Everything was quiet in the street. Geordie drove the car up and waited in the darkness. Bally slipped into the front seat and had Geordie take the first right turn and pull in out of sight. He then got out and walked back to the corner. In a few moments he was back in the car and they drove around the block to get onto Wessels again.

"What was all that about?" Geordie asked.

"I just wanted to make sure that Koos believed my story. He didn't seem to do anything rash when I left so I think we're okay."

"What did you tell him, Bally?"

"I'll fill you in later. Right now we have work to do. Mervin, are you still sure about your revised number?"

"Yes."

"You had better be, or you'll have serious stress to worry about."

◆

Thomas had not been given any detailed instructions by Louis other than to be on the lookout for Mervin Goldstein. He was to be friendly to him and find out any useful information which could be reported to Louis when he telephoned later. He was told to tidy up, and remove all evidence of Louis' and Anna's stay.

The maid had made up the beds earlier and cleaned the house. Thomas had already finished in the garage where the body patching repairs to the Merc had left a mess. Then he had tidied Louis' office and the kitchen. By now he had a bag of garbage to dispose of, and decided to move one of the two dustbins out of sight behind some bushes.

He had just completed the move when he heard something behind him. Thomas had both instinctive and well rehearsed defensive karate moves, capable of fooling most would-be attackers, but it did him no good this night. A stiff blow to the windpipe had him gasping for air on all fours. He felt a hand remove his holstered gun. A moment later, as he recovered enough to consider retaliation, he heard his attacker's weapon cock, and fear gripped him instead.

A man's voice asked, calmly, "Who is inside, Meneer? You're only allowed one wrong answer."

"I am alone. Is that you, Mr. Goldstein?"

"How did you know I was coming?" Bally asked, pretending to be Mervin. "Don't turn around till I tell you."

"Mr. Louis said you were on your way here. He had some pressing business and asked me to talk with you. Why did you attack me, I—?"

The other man interrupted him. "I'm asking the questions, Meneer. What's your name?"

"Thomas Vorster."

"Walk slowly in front of me towards the house, Thomas."

Mervin and Geordie now came into view. Bally motioned to Geordie and passed him a set of handcuffs.

"Put these cuffs on Thomas."

They went to the back door that Thomas had left open and entered the house quickly. Geordie did some scouting upstairs. Bally wanted his prisoner disabled as much as possible, so he handcuffed him to a ground level metal support for a circular staircase. Thomas was forced to sit on the floor. When Geordie returned, Bally motioned him and Mervin into another room, out of earshot of the prisoner.

Once there, Bally began. "Geordie did you find anything of interest upstairs?"

"Yes. Master suite and jacuzzi. I cannot see any specific clothes of Anna but there are lots of women's clothes in what looks like her size. I just have a gut feeling that she was here."

"How about an office?" Bally asked.

"There's a large pool and a substantial study cum office down the hall. This place has the right feel for what Louis would go for."

"What about Thomas, Mervin?"

"I'm pretty sure I remember that name being mentioned but it is a very common one."

"He was carrying a weapon, and he was expecting you, Mervin. He thinks I'm you. Let's leave it that way. How did he know you were coming?"

"It has to be from the guard in Muldersdrift, I suppose," said Mervin.

"Yeah, I suppose. You two check upstairs thoroughly again for any specific evidence that Louis and Anna were here. I doubt if Thomas will give us any reliable information. I'll check down here."

As the others went upstairs, Bally returned to Thomas.

"What time did they leave here and where are they headed, Meneer Thomas?"

"I'm only the caretaker here and haven't seen anybody since I came on duty."

"Then how did Louis tell you to expect me?"

"A note was left for me."

"Where is the note?"

"In the garbage."

"I'll bet there's a lot of interesting stuff in that garbage you were busy hiding, eh, Thomas?"

"No, Sir."

"Thomas, take a few minutes to ponder what you can tell me that might prevent me from killing you, like I did your pal at the Witt campus earlier this evening."

Bally left the room as Thomas' eyes darted around. First stop was the office. It was quite large with enough comfortable chairs to show that it got used for meetings regularly. One wall was all bookshelves filled with the usual home classics, probably never touched since the decorator put them there. Bally sat in the leather chair behind the desk, with two telephones to his right, and imagined Louis sitting there.

The drawers contained notes and memos about clothes and clothes shops, plus the usual pens, paper clips, letter openers and such. When he turned off the desk light to leave, the small desktop notepad caught his eye. The top page was blank but the outline of some writing could be seen.

Bally flicked on the light again. After a couple of attempts he felt he had something, "R71 Phalaborwa . . . first Rd (Nkomo) north from city limit... dirt 4Km Hunnis Farm beside Park... key under right pot. . . find Richard." Another look in the desk drawers and he found a map of South Africa which he spread out before him. He smiled with satisfaction as his hunch was borne out by the map. Just then the other two came in.

"Well?" Bally inquired.

"Nothing else of consequence upstairs other than Mervin recognizes some clothes he has seen Louis wear."

"How can you do that? What kind of man is this?" Bally asked.

Mervin didn't catch his meaning, and answered matter of factly.

"Louis is also big in the clothes business. It's his front. Anyway he has access to all the best, for free, and dresses very well compared to your average boerkie."

Bally was nodding now.

"That fits with what I saw here. This is definitely his place, but I would like to find something to tie Anna to this place."

"I think they've wiped it clean," Geordie chimed in. "What have you got there, Bally?"

"Just checking some hunches as to where they have gone now. I think I've figured it out. What you just said reminds me, Geordie, go check out what's in that garbage bin Thomas was busy hiding."

"Okay, just as soon as I take a leak."

Bally was in the kitchen when Geordie rushed in.

"Come see what I found, Bally!"

Geordie led the way to a bathroom near the garage. The two of them piled in so that Geordie could close the door. On the back of it he had found Anna's lipstick message.

"What do you make of that, Bally?"

"That's the proof we needed. She was held here all right. This was left by her this evening as they were leaving, Louis having heard that we were on our way here. Go have a quick look in the garbage for anything else useful before we leave."

Thomas was sitting where he had been left. Bally pressed the cold steel of the gun barrel into the back of his neck.

"These are the last questions, and will decide whether you get the winner's prize or the loser's one. Louis and the girl left her earlier this evening. Right?"

"Y–Yes, that's right."

"Good, one out of one. How many others were there and which car did they leave in?"

"They went in the white Merc with two other men."

"You're on a roll here, keep it up. What time did they leave?"

Hesitation on Thomas' part required a little more gun barrel pressure.

"About eight to eight-thirty," Thomas answered.

"Excellent. I found a note in Louis' office that lists an address of a farm in Lydenburg. What's the deal on that?"

"Lydenburg? Oh yes. Some friend of Mr. Louis has a holiday place there that he has the use of. He didn't tell me exactly where he was going, only that he would be in touch. I did see the driver looking at the map and mention Lydenburg."

"What's the owner's name and what is the layout?"

"I've never been there so I only know it is a hunting lodge on a few acres. Owner's name is Hunnis I think, a man who is in the clothes business with Mr. Louis."

"Anything else to add, Thomas?"

"I had nothing to do with taking the girl. My job is taking care of the place at Muldersdrift. I don't even know this area up here. What are you going to do with me, Meneer?"

"Someone will be here in a little while to pick you up. Your fate depends on Louis' handling of Anna."

By now, Geordie and Mervin were back and had heard some of Bally's talk with Thomas. Bally retreated towards the office and asked what they found.

"Just rubbish and some spray paint cans in the garbage bin, Bally. What's the plan now?"

"Bring the car round front. I need to call a taxi for Thomas."

TWENTY

Learning the 'Trade'

Captain De Klerk was used to getting late night telephone calls, and answered quickly.

"Listen very carefully, Captain," the man at the other end of the line said.

"At seven hundred and twenty Wessels Boulevard in Pretoria, you will find a man handcuffed to a metal staircase. He is implicated in the kidnapping of Anna Terblanche. On the back of the downstairs bathroom door she wrote a note in lipstick. Her kidnappers will be hunted down and punished. I'm Buddy. Remember that name, you will be receiving future messages. What is left of the kidnappers will be passed to you. You will also receive the important evidence you need to wind up the Kimberley diamond investigation. We're on your side, this is your lucky break. Good night, Captain."

The line went dead immediately, as the Captain tried to ask a question. He quickly wrote down everything the man had said before picking the telephone up again.

◆

In Pretoria, Bally completed wiping down the doorknobs and other objects before leaving the house. He then cut the telephone lines and joined Geordie and Mervin in the car.

"Head north for Pietersburg, then east to Phalaborwa," Bally ordered.

"But I heard you saying Lydenburg, Bally. Why the change?" Geordie asked.

"Because that was a red herring, my dear Watson," Bally answered, in his best English accent.

The N1 north from Pretoria to Pietersburg was a good road for the most part. Traffic this late at night was usually very light but it was Saturday. That meant the possibility of police checks for drunk drivers and the danger of staggering pedestrians, going home from the 'shebeens'. Geordie had often seen cattle and even game animals on this stretch before. At least he knew the road pretty well.

In fact, he knew the entire countryside better than most people who lived there. In the course of his job he drove something close to one hundred thousand kilometers a year. Late night driving was always dangerous and Geordie avoided it where possible. One of the many times when he drove the nineteen hour trip from Cape Town to Jo'burg he drove off the road three times, when he dozed off, luckily finding flat ground every time. As long as he had someone to talk to he was okay. Bally was napping in the back seat so he told Mervin, seated in the front, to keep him talking.

"What do you want to talk about, Geordie?" Mervin asked, politely.

"Anything. Did you know they grow tea in the Tzaneen area?"

"I didn't. How do you know that?"

"I've been there many times in my job, selling equipment, plus I drink a lot of tea. The Indian tea is the best, though, in my opinion."

A short silence followed, broken by Geordie.

"Mervin, I can't make any sense of this whole diamonds set up that Trichardt, Brauer and the others are involved in. Why are they so ruthless, to kidnap Anna, for example?"

Mervin nodded his head in agreement, stroked his chin, then began.

"You obviously know that the company I work for is called Equatorial Trading?"

"Yes, of course," Geordie answered.

"Do you know that the sale of uncut diamonds is controlled by a cartel, based here in South Africa?" Mervin asked.

"I know that De Beers are the big players in this field. I've sold equipment to their mines. Isn't South Africa the world's biggest producer of diamonds?"

"Correct, Geordie, but there are lots of diamonds mined outside their control. Various countries in southern and western Africa have large diamond deposits; Sierra Leone, Zaire, Angola, and there are quite a few independent small producers here in South Africa. Equatorial Trading was set up to acquire, by purchase or otherwise, as many diamonds as possible from non cartel mines and from I.D.B. sources."

"What's I.D.B.?" Geordie asked.

"Illicit Diamond Buying. Lots of raw diamonds are stolen, especially in the mines of the black countries. De Beers and its cartel can't always find a way to buy control of these mines, especially with the current sanctions against South African business because of apartheid. The cartel finds other ways. If you can control the market of the raw diamonds then you effectively control the industry, and I mean on a global basis."

Geordie was struggling with this.

"Call me stupid if you want, Mervin, but I don't understand. I thought the diamond industry was controlled by the people who cut and polish them, in London, Holland and in Israel, by your fellow Jews."

"You're missing the point. The industry is controlled by the suppliers of raw materials, just like any other. The cartel parcels out raw diamonds in such a way as to keep the price up to what it wants. Their Diamond Trading Company in London holds sales, invitation only, where their clients buy the rough diamonds. These sales, or 'sights' as they are called, happen once a month. The buyer is offered a shoebox full of mixed diamonds to examine, before buying them."

"What about the difference between gems and industrial diamonds?"

"We are only talking gemstones here. The raw diamonds are first sorted into the cuttable gemstones and industrials. I'm not sure what defines the difference, I know that it is tied to demand. What have been picked as gemstones are sorted and valued; based on size, shape, purity and color. Big ones are called 'stones' oddly enough, smaller ones 'macles', smaller again 'melee', and then 'sand'. Anyway, a selection of gems are offered to the buyer in this 'sight'. I'm not sure how much bargaining the buyer can do, but I do know that he must take the whole parcel, he can't pick and choose."

"That seems like strong arm selling. I can't do that in the machinery business."

"True, Geordie. These buyers do very well though. They re-sell them or have them cut and polished, to show off the brilliance and lustre of the diamonds, for mounting in jewelry. After cutting there is another grading and valuation process, with prices going up each time. To make all this work, the cartel must get their hands on all the gems. Equatorial Trading has offices in various countries south of the equator, buying in diamonds."

"And one of your suppliers is Trichardt."

"Yes. His group controls about six to eight small alluvial diamond diggings here in south Africa. They supply us with a lot of good diamonds."

"But there has to be more to this, Mervin. I saw their diamonds at Olantsfontein mine, then I got conned into carrying a bag for them, containing diamonds. I saw these too, and, as little as I know about gems, they were far better than the ones I saw at the mine. How come, Mervin?"

There was no answer from Mervin. Geordie kept driving, glancing at his passenger.

"Well, Mervin? Where are they getting the good ones?"

"You can probably figure it out if you think about it. They are getting their hands on lots of quality I.D.B. stones, from their contacts in Angola and Zaire. Like I said earlier, all we have to do is get the stones into cartel stock, no questions asked."

Geordie was still puzzled. He figured that there was a connection between Trichardt and the recent Southwest Africa robbery of raw gemstones. He decided to push Mervin again.

"That still doesn't explain to me how you seem to be tied in with Trichardt's people. Why don't you fill in the gaps for me, Mervin?"

"There is nothing to fill in, Geordie," Mervin insisted.

Bally had awoken earlier, and heard the latter part of the conversation. He now spoke directly to Mervin.

"I'll fill it in for you, to jog your memory, Mervin. Mercenaries ambush the diamond smugglers in many of these countries, payment being a percentage of the value of the haul taken. I knew some men who went up there on promises of big money. They were dealing with middlemen like your company. When disputes arose over values of some jewels, these mercenaries were themselves ambushed in their camp. I don't know all the facts but the middlemen were the only people who knew the location of the camp. Strange, don't you think, Mervin?"

An awkward silence followed, broken finally by Mervin.

"I don't know any specifics but I did get to know enough about those incidents plus others, to get into a position that put me in line to receive consultant fees from Botha, the man who got killed in Houghton. Once in their grasp, I got trapped by a blackmail scheme that I could not escape from."

Bally was not impressed. "For a guy who claims he is being forced along, you're doing pretty damn good. Why don't you just quit?"

"That's easier said than done. Both Equatorial and Brauer's operation – it goes under the names of Boer Group and Kimberley Group – have a reputation of dealing very harshly with deserters. I'm scared of being shamed on the family side, but I'm more scared of being shot on the other side. Besides, I have another plan."

"What's the plan?" Bally pressed him.

"I've been salting my money away, because I knew the bubble was going to burst sooner or later. Another year or two and I was going to walk away from it all, leaving Jo'burg and South Africa completely."

"Where were you going?"

"My father is retiring to Israel. I would take my family and go, too. The bank could keep my house and my mortgage and Trichardt's operation could go to hell."

"Why are you being so forthcoming, Mervin?" Geordie asked.

"I'm not sure. The pressure inside me has built up to eruption stage, I suppose. I think the Kimberley Group pulled the recent gem robbery in Southwest Africa, on De Beers themselves, in which four employees were killed. I'm expected to buy the gems back at top prices. I can't stomach that, and now this kidnapping. I want out, as soon as possible."

"Does your father know about any of this?" Geordie asked.

"Hell, no. Ironically, he has quite a lot of contacts with the police and criminals, because of his law practice. It'll be a terrible blow to him when this all bursts open."

They stopped for fuel in Pietersburg at 1 a.m. Bally went into the store with Mervin to buy food. The clerk told them about a small hotel nearby that was still open. Bally looked over his map, then decided that they should take a room. They ate quickly and went to bed.

TWENTY-ONE

A Ride in the Park

The late-night car ride held no pleasure for Anna. She sensed a major change in the attitude of Louis towards her, and indeed hers had changed towards him. The fear was back in her stomach and probably in her eyes too. Darkness was her friend for once, giving her the cover to analyse the current situation.

Something had gone terribly wrong in the arranged swap in Jo'burg. Why? She just knew that Geordie would not have tried to double-cross Louis' people, or abandon her. Again and again she went back in her mind over the events of the afternoon. Her partying with Louis deeply troubled and embarrassed her now. Strangely, it was that incident that appeared to be the catalyst for the first change in Louis' behavior. Was it a possessiveness that overcame him because she didn't give herself willingly to him? Would he just not take the chance of letting her go to Geordie in case she would change her mind and not go through with her promise to return?

If Geordie had changed the game for monetary gain then the swap should have gone fine. Louis would have the file and probably didn't give a damn about her, ever. It was pointless to speculate whether or not he would have kept up his end of the bargain then. Instead they were on the run with one man less than at Pretoria. It was only three against one now and she had to presume that whoever was after them was on her side, making the odds very close to even. Louis was deep in some mood that she couldn't fathom. Was he angry or scared or both? Both possibilities frightened her and put her in danger till she could escape or be saved. Her rescuers had to include Geordie, she said, over and over in her head, to convince herself of it and to take strength from it.

The smell of coffee broke her meditation. Louis had just finished pouring a cup from a thermos flask and was sipping it.

"Could I have some, please?" she asked.

"Sure, but you'll have to use this same cup."

"That's fine. I'll wait till you've finished."

Silence returned except for his slurping noises. The car was entering Pietersburg now. Louis touched a button and opened the glass partition behind the driver.

"Pull in at the first suitable place to get coffee. How do you want it, Anna?"

"No sugar, just cream please."

As the car pulled into a roadside shop Louis passed a fifty rand note to the front.

"Get the lady a coffee, with cream, no sugar. Also get milk, bread and fruit for the morning. If you fellows want anything else, get it now, we won't be stopping again."

Anna looked through the car windows into the shop. Louis saw her looking and spoke.

"You don't need to use the bathroom, do you?" he asked.

She shook her head.

"Good, I hate these Portuguese shops. Obrigado this and Obrigado that. Filthy bastards, they're almost as bad as the Kaffirs."

Anna ignored his nasty comments. She had many Portuguese friends, but this was not the time to defend them.

The coffee was old but at least it was hot. Both the driver and his companion had left their doors ajar and with the partition down, some much needed fresh air blew in. It was welcome even though it was warm, sub-tropical air and included a few mosquitoes. Anna stole a glance at Louis. In the light from the shop he looked pale and tired.

Once they got underway again she noticed the Route 71 sign for Phalaborwa as they turned off the main north road. She declined Louis' offer of biscuits. They remained on the little fold-down table, untouched by either of them. In the front she could see the other two men munching on snacks and drinking pop as if they were on a picnic outing.

"Are we going into the Kruger Park, Louis?" Anna asked.

"No, but close. Have you been there much?"

"Only once, a few years ago."

"Maybe I can take you in while we're up there. It depends on some things."

"Do you have a house there?"

"No. A friend of mine owns one, but he is seldom there, so it's as good as mine as far as availability goes."

"Are we still friends, Louis?"

"Of course, my dear. We have had a setback in our quest for the return of our property. I don't like my plans to be upset, but I'm sure the situation will be resolved quickly. My people are working on it as we speak."

Louis' people were indeed on the job, but on the losing end. Hennie was laid up in the hospital under guard, thinking he had managed to get his hands on the elusive file only to lose it again. Louis had not wanted to admit to Mr. Brauer that the file's whereabouts was unknown. So he had contracted some outside hired muscle in the form of Piet Cronje's gang to find out where it went.

Their investigations established that a passing purse snatcher had taken the brown envelope contents from Hennie, as he lay wounded on the grass, prior to the arrival of the police. A search was on to get their hands on the thief before the police did. They had managed only indirect contact with the culprit, even though he was know to them. The thief knew he had something valuable, and was negotiating for a sizeable reward through a third party. Louis had told Cronje to use whatever means necessary to get the papers and promised Piet a big payday on completion.

◆

Captain De Klerk was happy to drive to Pretoria in the middle of the night. Things were finally beginning to turn his way. He had no doubt it was Geordie McKay and whoever "Buddy" was, that caused this surge of good fortune. First there was Van de Merwe getting himself shot committing burglary and exposing the inside link that had undermined his investigations of the diamond smuggling operations from the start. Then Andries Meinke got himself killed at the airport, which yielded the brown briefcase that Geordie McKay had originally taken from Botha, without the 'Kimberley File'. The gang's next botched attempt to get the file back left Hennie Klunstad wounded, all for an envelope containing nothing but newspaper.

The Captain himself would take the credit for inventing the story of the petty thief stealing the envelope. The police had Koppie Schoeman already in custody on larceny charges. In the face of a ten-year sentence Koppie would play any game they wanted if it would help keep him out of prison. A trusted undercover police officer was acting as the negotiator between Koppie and Piet Cronje. The Captain was dragging the negotiations out on purpose, to trap the big fish behind Cronje and to keep Anna Terblanche alive. He had a finesse ready for Hennie too, who was very close to the breaking point.

Now another piece of the jigsaw was put into Captain De Klerk's lap. He had to bite his tongue not to thank the mysterious caller, Buddy. Not only did Buddy provide the Captain with an important clue that could lead to the persons responsible for kidnapping Anna, but he also provided him with the first evidence of any sort to show that she was alive and well. On his way to Pretoria the Captain got confirmation that local police had found the Wessels Boulevard address as described. A man was being held at the house pending his arrival.

Captain De Klerk shook hands warmly with his Pretoria counterpart and friend, Josef Lambert, who had also got out of bed to be there. The two men walked out in the night air while Captain De Klerk summarized the status of the case to date. When they returned to the house an officer at the door handed both men an information printout sheet on their suspect, Thomas Vorster. The officer then showed them the place where Thomas had been handcuffed, and the bathroom with the message. Captain De Klerk had brought a previous letter that Anna had written. He held it up beside her message.

"Do you think that's her writing, Josef?" Captain De Klerk asked.

"There's little doubt," answered his counterpart. "See the way she joins the letters together in her spelling of her name."

"I agree. So, we have her here at eight o'clock this evening but our boy here is pleading that burglars tied him up and wrote any note."

"We've dusted some stuff upstairs for comparison with her prints and also here in the bathroom," Captain Lambert said. "That'll prove conclusively that she was here. Time is still not on our side however. We need to know who took her and where."

"Let's have our boy Thomas fill in these details, eh Josef? Back me up on a pressure squeeze."

In the sitting room they pulled up two chairs, one at the side and one in front of the prisoner. Captain De Klerk began.

"Thomas, you do realize that you are going to be lodging here in the Pretoria Central Prison for twenty years for kidnapping. If the girl dies you will then be up for murder, too. I put a hotel chef in jail here for seven years for smuggling, works in the kitchens. He told me they give you a whole roast chicken to yourself at your last meal, before they hang you. Did you know that Thomas? With a word from me, Geoff will cook you a nice big juicy one."

"You're looking at an innocent man, Sir," Thomas replied, flatly.

"Sure I am. I've seen a lot of men who said that. They were innocent till proven guilty and were hung."

Thomas' eyes were searching for relief.

"Like I told the officer there, before he let me slip and cut my face up like this, I was surprised by three robbers. They took some jewelry and stuff from upstairs. I'll be happy to make a complete list."

"Who owns this place, Thomas?"

"Mr. Louis Trichardt, Sir. He's in the clothes business. I work for him."

"If I had a clothes business I wouldn't have a man working for me that had a police record like yours. Why would a good law abiding gentleman like that hire a punk like you?"

"He's giving me another chance to get my life together, Sir."

"Wow, what a guy. And he's giving chances to Hennie Klunstad, Andries Meinke and others too numerous to mention. Now this might come as a terrible shock to you, Thomas, but your boss, Louis, is a bad boy. He's into illegal diamonds, money laundering, smuggling, kidnapping and murder. You'd be filing a labor grievance against him if you weren't going away for so long."

"Another thing," Captain Lambert joined in. "Even punks like you have mothers. I see here your mother is a sweet old lady of seventy-two. Unless you want her to watch you eat that last chicken you had better start talking and fast."

Thomas looked around, dejected.

"What do you want to know?" he asked.

◆

The jolt of the car woke Anna. She had dozed off after taking a few cautionary malaria tablets. The driver had passed them around to everybody after they got coffee. Anna had asked to keep some extra tablets in her bag, which was okay with Louis.

They were on a narrow dirt road with numerous potholes and washing board turns, which made everything in the Merc shudder. After a few miles they turned into a smaller dirt lane which led to a house. The car pulled up close to the front porch steps, the two front seat men got out and fumbled in the car headlights for keys. The house had a game lodge look to it that Anna had seen before, with lots of lush vegetation around that seemed well cared for. Once inside, Louis skipped the house tour, escorting Anna directly to a guest room.

"You have everything you need here, my dear. For your own safety stay in this room till I call you in the morning. I've got a couple of things to do, then it's lights out, we're all tired. Good night."

He left without waiting for a response. She quickly surveyed the room, hung up her clothes, crawled into bed and was asleep within minutes.

Back in the master bedroom Louis dialed the house in Pretoria. When he could not get through on the third try he called the sleepy operator, and was told that some lines were down in that area. Next call woke up Rissik, his intermediary in Jo'burg with Piet Cronje. The good news was that Piet had established that one Koppie Schoeman had the file and they were close to finalizing a deal. Koppie wanted twenty-five thousand rand, Piet had gone to ten, unauthorized, but didn't want to go higher without permission, Louis was both relieved and annoyed. He told Rissik to go up to fifteen, twenty, even twenty-five if necessary, but Piet must have the file in Rissik's hands within twenty-four hours.

♦

Louis was in much better spirits when he knocked on Anna's door at seven that morning. She was already up and dressed. From her window she looked at the landscaped courtyard and inviting pool. The trees beyond were alive with birds. After he called, she waited ten minutes before joining Louis on the patio. A black man named Joseph was setting out fruit, cereal, toast and tea.

"Did you sleep well, my dear?" inquired Louis with a smile.

"Yes, fine, thank you," Anna replied.

"We're so close to the Park that the animals sometimes keep people awake. Last night was quiet and, of course, we were all tired. After breakfast I'll take you for a visit to the Park. As this property backs up to the main fence we even have our own gate. We'll do a scout around, to see what's moving, then go back in the late afternoon to the best spots."

"Whatever you think best," she answered without enthusiasm.

They both ate very little, in silence for the most part. Anna saw the two men who had driven with them, sitting across the pool drinking coffee and smoking.

Louis excused himself and went inside. Still no phone lines through to Thomas in Pretoria. He talked briefly to the two men at the pool, collected a bag, then he and Anna set off on the dirt road in the Merc. They would bring the open top later when it was checked and fueled. At the gates Louis looked about carefully. He had a rifle slung over his shoulder and a pistol in a hip holster. The correct keys to both locks were found and minutes later they had locked themselves into the Kruger Park.

"We'll head towards Letaba and then north to Mooiplaas," Louis said. "Here are some maps Anna, you can be navigator. There are some good waterholes along the Letaba and Shingwedzi rivers."

At first they didn't see much, probably because of a lack of vegetation near the fence, as Louis explained. A small herd of impala was their first sighting. They watched them for a while with binoculars. Anna recognized their telltale marking around their tails from a skin she had on her bedroom floor in Jo'burg. Her mind drifted there and she wondered about work, her friends and her family back in The Free State. Louis' shout of 'Kudu' brought her back to reality. They watched the large solitary beast in the distant trees while it watched them. Moving on, they briefly stopped when they saw their first elephant. As they got closer to water, game got more plentiful. Giraffe, springbok, a water buffalo with enormous horns and an angry face. Their first two waterholes had little game around them and they continued after brief stops. Louis remarked how people always stop to look at their first sightings but gradually they get blase about these wonderful animals, only wanting to see new and rarer game at every turn.

He drove north to the Mooiplaas area, stopping a few times but for the most part pointing out animals in the same nonchalant fashion which he had just criticized. Other tourist vehicles were now also on the move. Louis drove past one large waterhole because of the presence of tour vehicles. Farther along they found another active hole without a crowd of people and stopped for an extended viewing. There were a lot of hippos moving about in the water, creating great turbulence which attracted many birds. On the far bank they counted six very large crocodiles. As they watched, a steady stream of animals came and drank.

"It's like Noah's Ark here, eh Anna?"

As they watched a huge croc submerged. Moments later there was a great disturbance as it came up from underneath on the birds, with its jaws open. There was a puff of feathers as birds rushed into the air while the crocodile grabbed what he could.

Anna looked away. "Can we please head back now, Louis?" she asked.

He looked at her and sighed. "Of course, my dear."

Even as he drove back, Louis was talking about coming back out in the late afternoon, which he said was the best time to see the big hunters, especially the lions.

Anna wondered whether he had purposefully chosen to

ignore her obvious discomfort with this game tour. She cut into his talking with a question.

"Are those mountains in the Park, too?" she asked.

"I'm not sure. That's Mozambique over there. Those hills could be along the border."

After some silent driving, Anna spoke again.

"When are you going to go through with our deal, Louis?"

He answered without looking at her.

"Very soon, my dear. I expect to have confirmation from my people this evening, that they have possession of our missing file. Once I have that, you'll be free to go."

"So you've changed your mind about wanting me to stay?"

"Yes, Anna. I think it's best that you go your own way, It's what you wanted all along."

Another silence followed, broken again by Anna.

"Why did you rape me yesterday morning when I was zonked out after that champagne you gave me? Why Louis?"

"My dear Anna, that's rubbish. You wanted sex just as much as I did. There is nothing more to discuss about it."

TWENTY-TWO

Kill or Be Killed

In the hotel in Pietersburg that morning, Bally De Bruyne looked at his watch for the second time. The alarm had gone off at five, but he took that fatal five minute lie-in. Now it was six-thirty. He leapt from the bed and roused Geordie and Mervin.

Within minutes they were back in the car, headed for Phalaborwa. Breakfast was seedless oranges and strips of ostrich biltong. Bally sat in the back seat again, with all his hardware, while Geordie drove. Mervin sat up front, too, his unshaven stubble coming through strongly. Another day and they would be a bearded trio.

Bally spoke after a long silence.

"This part of the country brings back a lot of memories. I haven't been over here for a long time but it hasn't changed a bit."

"Good memories, Bally?" Mervin asked.

"Some good, some bad. We lost too many good men up near here. That reminds me, time for our next round of malaria tabs. We don't want to lose anyone to something totally preventable."

"Did the South African forces get involved in that Mozambique civil war with Renamo and all that shit?" Geordie asked.

"Special Forces did," Bally answered quietly. "But that's all in the past now. Let's turn our attention to the task ahead."

As they neared Phalaborwa, Bally spread his maps out in front of him. He had detailed ones at home, even of Mozambique, but for now the standard travel maps of Eastern Transvaal and Kruger Park would have to do, supplemented by his memory. By nine o'clock they had found their road. Bally explained how close they were to the Kruger Park. Geordie posed a question on their strategy, considering it was broad daylight and they were not sure of the numbers opposing them. With Bally's insistence, it was decided that they had to move forward regardless, but they would scout around for a place to observe the house once they found it. A short distance up the dirt road they stopped to let a black man drive some cows past their car. Bally spoke to the man in Fanagalo, a mix of native African dialects, Afrikaans and English, mostly used by mine workers with diverse backgrounds. They talked for quite a few minutes in what Geordie could interpret as a friendly conversation.

"He seemed like an old friend of yours Bally," Geordie commented.

"He wanted to sell me those cows. Time is plentiful out here and for a white man to talk to him in his own language is special. The Hunnis place is about two miles ahead, off the road to the right. Drive slowly past it while I look for a vantage point."

There were a lot of trees around the house entrance. After passing and turning back, they pulled into a stand of thorny trees that largely obscured the car from the road, at a spot about eight hundred yards past the house entrance. They closed the car quietly and made their way on foot, Bally leading the way with his hold-all. He picked an area of thick trees to set up their base camp, less than five hundred feet from the house perimeter fence. Up among the hidden branches Bally armed himself with his binoculars to begin the watch. Mervin sat on a log, unarmed, while Geordie stood over the hold-all of weapons, his pistol protruding from his belt. Bally counted two white men and two blacks, moving about the gardens. Both white men were armed. The blacks appeared to be house servants of sorts. No sign of the Mercedes, Anna or Louis.

Some twenty minutes passed with no change in the count. Geordie was sitting now also and Bally was still up in the branches. They had relaxed and all three were absorbed with their own thoughts.

Bally was planning his best attack route. Mervin was wondering how to explain all this to the police, his wife and not least, his father. Could he plea bargain his testimony for leniency or should he make a run for it? He was definitely finished with Louis and the entire business regardless of the consequences. Geordie wondered what Anna was doing? Did they have her tied up? Was Louis messing about with her? He'd kill the bastard if he was.

The black girl walked right on top of the three white men before she saw them or they saw her. Geordie jumped up at the last second and instinctively pulled out his pistol. She dropped the basket of fruit she was carrying and screamed, fixed to the spot. Geordie was frozen too, gun in hand. In a moment Bally was down from his perch and subdued her. He spoke softly to her in a native tongue while edging her over to where Mervin was now standing up. Her eyes were still wild with fear, but she had calmed down some. She was in her mid to late twenties, quite tall and slim. Bally spoke to her again, more sternly this time, then to Mervin.

"Take her hand and sit down over there with her while I assess the damage."

The damage was indeed done. The men at the house had heard the screams and two of them were already out of their compound and headed in their general direction. Bally quietly took his hold-all and slipped into thick bushes with Geordie in tow. Mervin edged the girl towards the better cover on the other side of the clearing, relaxing his grip on her in the process. She broke away from his hold and ran into the open, in the direction from which she had come, with Mervin in pursuit. The two men from the house were now close enough to spot the running pair and the leading white man fired immediately. Geordie heard cries of pain, followed by Bally's gunburst. The white man who had just fired, dropped in a crumpled heap. His black companion turned immediately for the house. Bally could have dropped him too but did not. Geordie scrambled over to where Mervin lay on the ground while Bally checked on the man he had just shot.

"Are you hit, Mervin?" asked Geordie.

"Yes, somewhere in the side. The girl may have caught one too but she got up again and ran."

"Don't move till we take a look at you," Geordie instructed.

Bally came up to them as Geordie was trying to stem the blood flow from the wound. He took over and Geordie stood back to get some air.

"It's just a flesh wound, Mervin. You're losing some blood but that will stop with a pressure bandage. Geordie, cut as much of that man's shirt as you can with your knife. He's not going to be needing it. Get his shoes for a pillow."

Geordie got the shoes and one clean sleeve of the shirt. Bally put the shoes under Mervin's head and rolled the sleeve into a tight wad.

"Mervin, you must keep this pad pressed against the wound with your hand, here like this. We must go and clear the house, so you'll have to take care of yourself for a little while. Stay awake and keep the pad on. We'll be back shortly and will carry you to the house, where I'll wash the wound properly and bandage it. Okay?"

"Yeah. I'll be fine," answered Mervin, now very pale.

In the trees nearest the house Bally and Geordie watched for signs of movement from inside. They were fairly sure now that neither Anna or Louis were in.

Bally made his visual assessment, looked at his watch and shook his head.

"Geordie, we don't have the time to waste here. If Louis hears this shooting he'll be running ahead of us again, and Anna will be in much more danger. We've got to get into that house immediately."

"Tell me what we have to do, then let's do it."

"Right. Let me check your gun."

Bally checked the gun chamber and mechanism. Then he replaced the full magazine, flicked on the safety switch and offered the gun back to Geordie.

"Here, it's ready to fire. Just remove the safety before you cock it. You have six shots, so count them. Take these two spare ammo clips. This is the plan. I'll be going in the back door and I'll look first for Anna. My guess is that there is only one other armed white guy and the blacks we saw earlier who are more than likely unarmed. Before I move, you get behind that fence over there while I cover you. Move quickly and throw yourself on the ground at the fence. Don't stop if you hear gunfire. Once I'm inside, you cover the front. Shoot anyone who comes out armed but don't leave your cover. If they are unarmed shout stop and then order them to lay face down on the ground. We need to capture at least one of them alive. Off you go. Good luck."

Geordie reached his cover without incident. Then as he kept a watch on the house he saw Bally slip around the back. Time stood still for Geordie now, as he waited for the action to begin. Suddenly a shot rang out from inside the house. Shortly afterwards, another shot. Moments later Geordie heard the burst of gunfire from Bally's gun, which he recognized with relief, then a second burst. Instantly a figure ran out the front door directly towards him. It was a black man, a different one than he had seen earlier. No sign of a gun so Geordie shouted stop but the man kept coming straight for him. Suddenly, Geordie jumped up, as he recognized the man coming towards him. The man was close now and shouted out loudly.

"*Baas* Geordie, *Baas* Geordie."

The man was Richard, the Zulu that Geordie had saved from Vermullen at the Olantsfontein mine. Richard was too close to stop and Geordie was too shocked to move. They collided and sprawled in a confused heap on the dirt.

Before Geordie could regroup, Bally had appeared and pressed a gun into the black man's face. He shouted at Geordie.

"You shouldn't have left your cover. You could have been killed by this Kaffir."

"Sorry Bally, I forgot myself. I know this man, his name is Richard."

Bally turned on the hapless black man at his feet, speaking loudly to him in Zulu. Geordie watched Richard's surprised face but he also saw the fear begin to drain away. Richard answered Bally. They conversed for a few minutes, in what sounded like a friendly interrogation session. The three of them were standing by now.

"I will help you, *Baas* Geordie, I will help," Richard blurted out.

Bally took control again.

"Let's get Mervin down here immediately. You two carry him. I'll cover you both for now till I feel happier that everything is secure."

Mervin had not moved. There was quite a lot of blood around him and he was weak from its loss, but managed a smile when he saw them. At the house Bally had Richard get hot water, and a medical kit was produced from somewhere. Geordie went to get their car. By the time he returned, Bally was finishing his dressing of Mervin's wound. He motioned Geordie over to him.

"Louis took Anna into the Park and they're due back soon. Go check out the house for any useful evidence. Watch out for the two dead men, one in a bedroom and another in a bathroom."

Geordie went down the hallway. The first room he looked into was a bloody mess. The man, the second white gunman, had been flung onto the bed by the power of the bullets and had later fallen over the bed corner onto the floor where he now lay. Both the bed and the floor were covered in blood. Geordie recognized Anna's hairbrush on the dressing table. Further along he found the master bedroom with bathroom en suite. The second body, a black, was crumpled inside the riddled door.

Geordie looked around at the usual stuff, clothes, shaving gear, then moved on to the desk in the corner. The briefcase on the floor beside it was locked and heavy. The desk drawers were open and contained various writing materials. The bottom drawer was larger and locked. Geordie went to the kitchen and found a metal bar and knife with which he was able to pry it open. Inside he found a white canvas bag, took it out and unzipped it on the desk top.

"Wow!" he gasped.

Bally was still up in the sitting room, keeping an eye on Mervin's wound, while talking to Richard at the same time, in Zulu again. Geordie motioned to him. Before Bally came over he spoke again to Richard, who went over beside Mervin, who was by now dozing. He then collected his hold-all of weapons and followed Geordie down the hall. On the desk Geordie opened the white bag for Bally.

"I haven't tried to count it but that's a lot of money, Bally, and all in dollars too. There's a heavy briefcase here but it's locked."

"That's no problem. I'll take care of it. Trichardt has been carrying our reward around with him, eh. Before I start on the briefcase we need to secure this place. Trichardt has Anna with him in the Park, in the Merc, Richard tells me. There's a gate into the place from this property. He expects them back for lunch, which means anytime now. We need to be ready for them. Hell, while we are talking they could come driving up and surprise us, and Louis is definitely armed. It's also possible that they heard the shooting and he has run. Get all this stuff into the trunk of our car and park it, around the blind side from the Park so it cannot be seen if they drive up. Then meet me in the sitting room to prepare our reception party."

◆

Louis had not heard the shots as he and Anna found their way back through the game trails. When they got to the gates he decided to put on just one chain and lock. He would show her the lions at dusk, or drop her off for a private visit with crocodiles. Louis had no intention of setting Anna free. Like so many people in Louis' life, she had served her usefulness and was now expendable.

He eased the Merc through the open gates and went back to lock them, fastening the smaller of the two chains only. Then he got back in the car and drove quietly towards the house.

Geordie had put the case and bag in the trunk and was just getting into the driver's seat when he saw the Merc. In fact they all saw each other at the same time. For a moment everything stopped.

"Geordie!" Anna yelled.

Geordie pulled his gun and moved towards the car. It immediately went into reverse, spun around in an open space and headed back down the trail. After fifty yards Geordie knew it was hopeless on foot and turned back for his car. By now Bally was running out of the house. Geordie shouted to him.

"Bally! I just saw the Merc. It came up the drive as I was getting ready to move our car. Anna was in it, along with a man. He reversed and drove back in the direction of the Kruger again. What are we going to do? Anna is bound to be in danger now that he's seen us."

"We're going after them, of course. Get the car started."

Bally ran back into the house. He woke Mervin and told him to call in three hours for medical help if needed and if they were not back by then. He gave him a phone number in Jo'burg to call, explaining to him that it was Captain De Klerk's home number and to use the code-name Buddy. Then he shook his hand and reminded him that he had never seen Geordie or himself, for the record. He spoke next to Richard and stuffed a hundred rand note into his pocket. Richard thanked him and assured him that he would help Mervin as instructed, then would disappear prior to the arrival of any police. Mervin managed a weak shout of good luck as Bally ran out.

◆

The Mercedes went straight through the gates without slowing down. Pieces of gate and chain and car fender flew everywhere. When Louis got to the north-south main trail, he could see no sign of pursuit and opted for the north, as they had just been there and he knew the road. He shouted in anger at the thought that his money and briefcase were at the house, comforting himself with the hope that his men may have escaped with them or at least hidden them.

Geordie picked his way round the fallen gate to prevent any barbed wire from puncturing his tires. When he arrived at the main trail junction, Bally got out and studied the road in both directions, until he was satisfied that they had taken the north route.

Anna had refastened her seat belt, but sat there in shocked confusion as the Merc sped down the gravel road. The full realization that Geordie was alive and well had not even hit her, as the African savannah flashed by. Louis' face was a mask of fear and adrenaline. With his superior speed he would soon lose them, he figured. He watched the rear view mirror with satisfaction and was still looking in it when the tourist van reversed onto the trail in their path. They would have got round it if he did not brake instinctively. The Merc caught the back of the van, pushing the van into a tree, while Louis fought to pull his car out of the shallow ditch. Anna smacked her head against the door and felt blood trickling down her neck from a cut somewhere near her ear. The car regained the road and on they went.

When Geordie reached the crash site an elderly man waved him down. He stopped only long enough to establish that nobody was seriously hurt and that it was indeed the Merc that had hit them. Bally told the man they were wardens chasing poachers and would try to got help to them, but in the meantime he suggested that the man wave down any other vehicles that pass. They saw where the Merc had gone into a ditch and then came back out, with some of its body parts missing.

The gravel road was straight and level, following a course parallel to the river. Louis had picked up a lot of speed on the straight while fighting with the damaged steering. The sharp left bend was suddenly in front of him and he braked hard, too hard. The car only made forty-five degrees of the turn and careened into the brush. He fought it till the driver's front tire blew. From then on the car made its own intersecting line with the river, finally coming to rest at the water's edge.

Anna was half on the seat and half on the floor, trapped by the seat belt. Louis had been winded when he hit the steering wheel. Both lay there moaning for many minutes before Louis struggled out his open door and then dragged Anna out the same way. He retrieved his pistol from the car, cursing the loss of his rifle. Holding her semi-conscious body in front of him, behind the open driver door, facing the road with their backs to the river, Louis waited. He had his gun and his hostage.

"This is the last hand in the game, my dear. It's just me against him but I'm holding the queen."

Anna was still dazed and unable to answer.

The skid marks were obvious to Geordie as their car approached the bend. He slowed the car to a crawl, then drove on till they saw where the Merc had cut towards the river bank, and stopped.

"There they are, behind the car door!" Geordie shouted.

Bally spoke calmly. "He's holding Anna as a shield, Geordie. You've got to approach him and get him talking. Keep moving side to side but go no closer than a hundred feet. He's so pumped up how he could shoot her any second. Let's be real slow and careful. You get him talking and leave the rest to me."

Geordie took a brown envelope from under the seat and moved forward on foot. He cleared his throat.

"Louis Trichardt, this is Geordie McKay. I've got your file here and I'm willing to trade it for Anna."

"You're lying, McKay," Louis shouted back. "My people already have the file. You and your pal must throw down your weapons. Then it's the car for the girl, and I'll take that copy too, if its real."

"It's real all right. Listen! Page one, Mr. M. Brauer, twelve hundred Myrton Avenue. Mr. Van Els, Mr. Erasmus, Mr. Botha, now deceased, of course, Mr. Joubert, etc. All with home addresses, telephone numbers."

"Okay, okay. Drop the weapons, NOW!" Louis screamed. "You don't want to lose her, McKay. She can do things in bed I never knew about before, especially after spiked champagne."

"You Fucker. I'll kill you for that," Geordie screamed back as he inched forward, ahead of Bally, who was twenty feet off to his right.

Bally just needed another twenty-five feet to have a clear sight of the pair behind the car door. He inched forward during the exchange of insults.

Louis fired at Geordie, missing badly. As he took aim again Anna suddenly came to life and bit into his left arm, with which he was holding her. He let go for an instant and she sagged towards the ground. That was all Bally needed. He fired his modified Magnum, hitting Louis in the upper chest. Louis stayed upright and fired his weapon again.

Geordie felt a jolt of pain in his left leg, but he kept moving forward without taking his eyes off the scene in front of him. Bally's second bullet threw Louis into the river. His partial grip on Anna dragged her in also. Geordie was right up to the riverbank by now and saw them in the bloodied water.

The river was deep, with a slow current. Louis' thrashing to keep afloat was sinking both of them. Geordie jumped into the water's edge and grabbed Anna's foot. He pulled hard, while sliding deeper in himself, but he broke her away from the grip of the floundering Louis. Bally was in at the riverbank now, too, and grabbed Geordie's hand. He pulled both of them out onto the bank in seconds. By this stage Louis had floated out fifteen to twenty feet in his losing battle with his wounds and the current. Anna and Geordie were sitting up on the bank, gasping for air, facing the river.

All three of them saw it happen, One second Louis was feebly attempting to swim to shore, the next second two massive jaws grabbed him around his chest. He got in one last scream before he was dragged under. Anna opened her mouth to scream but no sound came out. She just fell forward in a heap, on Geordie's lap.

Bally was the first to react and lifted her in his arms.

"Can you manage to walk, Geordie? There'll be other crocs out there very soon and they won't hesitate to come up on the bank after us. We've got to get to the car and get away from here."

"I'll be okay. You carry Anna and I'll walk."

Bally placed her in the back seat and went back to help Geordie who was struggling by now, clutching his leg and the brown envelope. The Merc gave Bally an idea and he crawled in to retrieve its first aid kit. Geordie eased into the back seat of the car, where Anna could be propped up against him.

The car had gone a few miles when Bally looked over into the back to see the two wet, crying, hugging bodies.

"Now, Mr. and Mrs. Jones, the next leg of your honeymoon trip will see your trusty guide take you into the mysterious land of Mozambique. You'll have rest and relaxation there with some old mission friends of mine, the religious mission type, that is."

Then Bally laughed in his loud deep voice.

TWENTY-THREE

———•———

A Present for the Captain

When Captain De Klerk called his wife from Pretoria she was eager to relay Frank's urgent call. The Captain returned the call immediately, waking Frank. Once lucid, Frank excitedly related his findings. Even the Captain, seasoned old veteran that he was, allowed a gasp of surprise to escape his lips.

After a few minutes of thought, he was on the telephone again, this time to his most trusted man, Sergeant Coetzer, to whom he issued a number of very specific instructions. Next call was to the hospital where Van de Merwe was recuperating. He spoke directly to the doctor in charge.

Thomas Vorster had been taken away earlier. The Captain felt that between him and Hennie, a fairly strong case could be made, but he still needed some central figures and, of course, the file. After leaving Captain Lambert, he got on the phone again.

It was now eight o'clock and Chief Ferreira answered the call himself.

"Chief, sorry to bother you at home, Sir, but we have a very important breakthrough in the Kimberley investigation."

"Captain, tell me about it, but it had better be good, it's Sunday."

"It is, Sir. During the night Van de Merwe asked the doctor on duty to contact me. I spoke with him just now on the phone. Van wants to make a full disclosure statement to me at twelve o'clock. He said he will finger all the top individuals in the diamond operation, and asks for leniency from the State in return for giving evidence against them all in court. It seemed strange to me, Chief, but he specifically asked that you not be present, Sir. I assume that he just wants to give me all the glory, but I thought you should be present, too, as you have given me such sound guidance during this investigation."

"A good decision on your part, Captain. Well, well, so Van has decided to spill the beans. What sort of security arrangements are you making, Captain?"

"We have no evidence to suggest that the gang knows of his intention to talk. It's Sunday and my men need some family time. The one policeman that's there now should be fine till twelve. After that I'll be there myself and won't leave till we have enough to convict the whole gang. What do you think, Sir?"

"Your judgement has always been good, Captain, and I trust you have it right again. It's a kindly thing to consider your men's family day important. Even criminals rest on Sunday, I suppose. I have a few prearranged matters to take care of and it will probably be a little after twelve when I can join you at the hospital. Go ahead and start without me. Well done, Captain."

By nine-thirty when the Captain's taxi arrived, Sergeant Coetzer had everything secured, per the Captain's instructions.

"Are you absolutely sure that none of our vehicles are in sight, Sergeant?" the Captain asked, looking about.

"Yes, Sir."

"And are our doctors and patient ready?"

"Yes, Sir."

It was ten-fifteen when the three-man group arrived. They went immediately to the fifth floor, to Van de Merwe's room. On the door the note said he had been moved to the third floor in the new wing. A passing nurse told them it was because a bigger room was needed for an important visitor at twelve. Security was lax on the third floor. The lone policeman was plain to be seen in the coffee room at the other end of the corridor. The three men split up and slipped quietly into Van's room, in their disguises and doctor's coats. In the room the patient seemed to be asleep. Two of the men stayed back near the door while the other one approached to within ten feet of the sleeping 'Van de Merwe'.

The man produced a silenced pistol from under his coat and fired five shots into the body. Then, as he approached the bed to check his handiwork the tall man at the door fired his own gun and shot the first attacker once in the back. Before he could squeeze off another shot a siren boomed, freezing him in his step.

Captain De Klerk shouted. "Drop the gun, Mr. Brauer. There are five guns trained on you now."

Within moments the two standing men were in handcuffs and their wounded accomplice was being attended to.

"How bad is he wounded, doctor?" the Captain asked.

"It's just a flesh wound, Captain. He was lucky."

"Indeed he was, doctor, lucky enough to stand trial for attempted murder, and treason. Chief Ferreira, I have here a warrant for your arrest, which I will serve on you with disgust once your wound is treated."

Clean-up operations at the hospital were complete in an hour. Ferreira, Brauer and Van Els were in custody. Van de Merwe watched a video of the shooting of his morgue stand-in, with shock and anger. Yes, a plea bargain deal in return for testimony would be of great interest to him now.

Captain De Klerk was just back home when 'Buddy' called again. By the middle of the afternoon Mervin Goldstein had been removed to the hospital and had conveyed the message that Anna Terblanche had been freed by Buddy's people. Captain De Klerk would be hearing from them again soon, he said. Mervin's story, and the Kruger Park police, led to the crashed Merc being recovered the next day, along with enough of Trichardt's torso for identification purposes.

◆

It was ten days later when the Captain received an early Christmas present, in the form of a large parcel. In the package were the missing pieces of the jigsaw that he needed. His smile broadened as he glanced through the contents. Financial statements, places, overseas bank accounts, courtesy of one deceased Louis Trichardt. On the top of the pile he found the stained but intact, type-written sheets of the memo and the list of names. Someone had written across the top in a black felt-tip pen, 'The Kimberley File.'

He read the enclosed letter from Buddy which confirmed that Anna and Geordie were both safe. Buddy also detailed the assistance which Mervin Goldstein had given and asked for leniency on his behalf.

Finally, he thanked Captain De Klerk and wished him a Merry Christmas. The Captain smiled, and returned the greeting out loud.

"Thank you, Buddy, and a very Merry Christmas to you, too."

◆ ◆ ◆ ◆

ABOUT THE AUTHOR

Michael Gerard was raised on the rugged west coast of Ireland. Like generations of Irishmen before him he left 'The Auld Sod' for foreign shores.

Blessed with the Irish 'gift of the gab', he found his niche in selling. After stints in Europe he moved to South Africa where he sold machinery for several years. His customers included the spectrum of exotic mines for which South Africa is famous – gold, diamonds, etc.

A poet and short-story writer in his spare time, it was logical that he would write a novel. The Kimberley File – his first novel, published in 1997 has now been re-published in 2021.

His two-part historic novel 'Ireland's Final Rebellion and An American Dream' was published in March 2021. Both titles are available in e-book and paperback formats on www.amazon.com plus on other international Amazon outlets, and there is a direct link to Amazon from the author's website.

Michael lives in South Carolina, USA

Readers comments are welcomed and appreciated.
website — www.MichaelGerardAuthor.com
e-mail — michaelgerardcmi@gmail.com

Printed in Great Britain
by Amazon

79342482R00173